Brain Bleed

Jeffrey R Crimmel

A murder mystery

ISBN: 0-9852232-9-4

ISBN-13: 978-0-9852232-9-8

DEDICATION

This is dedicated to the nurses and doctors who helped me through my blood clot trauma in San Diego at Sharp Memorial Hospital in 2012. The events that happened created the idea for the book and fiction detective series that followed.

Also by Jeffrey R Crimmel

Living Beneath the Radar

Learning to Love the Peso

Centavo; A Dog From Mexico

The 60's; If You Remember It You Didn't Live It

Ian's Revenge

Nab Yoga

(available on Amazon)

Brain Bleed

Chapter 1

I held two nines. The dealer's *up* card was a ten. What happened to me next was the same as in my previous twenty-five hands. I made my move.

“Splitting the nines!” Sally, the dealer, announced my intentions to the other four sitting at the table. She was finishing her last hour before taking a break. Her weakened voice no longer carried the same level of support for the players as when she started her shift.

A queen flipped over on my first nine giving me nineteen. “Stay!" I said, with the conviction of a person who couldn’t lose. Another face card landed on the second nine. Two hands of nineteen and five thousand dollars worth of chips rested on top of each set of cards.

The dealer flipped over her down card. It was an eight. The count for her hand was eighteen. Because of house rules, she had to stay, and I’d won both hands.

“Well played, sir." Sally smiled as she cleared the cards from the table.

“Man, are you lucky." The comment came from a seasoned player situated two seats to my left. His sweaty hands, and the

Green Bay Packers sweatshirt covering his 300-pound plus body told me a little about him. The numerous Bud Lights consumed during his tenure at the table probably maintained his bulk weight. He shifted in his seat as he took another drink. “The dealer showed a face card and you won both hands by splitting the nines. Why in the hell did you do that?”

I didn’t want to engage in a lengthy conversation with this behemoth 'cheesehead' from the land of Brett Favre and the Lambeau Leap. “I had a feeling," I answered. "We all get lucky sometimes."

The cards turned over as I'd envisioned. The others at the table made the traditional sounds of ‘oh’ and ‘ah’ as the dealer counted out the chips, and slid them to me across the green felt blackjack table. After gathering my winnings, I tipped the dealer with a $200 chip and walked towards the cashier window. I'd heard a rumor that if a player keeps their winnings below $25,000 no one bothers them. My winnings totaled $22,500 up to that point.

My wife, Leslie, and I had been in Laughlin, Nevada for three days. Two of those afternoons I spent gambling in different casinos to avoid drawing attention. My five foot ten-inch frame, and one hundred eighty-three pound weight, with slight graying of the hair around the ears, kept me beneath the radar. No sports jerseys or anything out of the ordinary. I was the average Joe, but with an edge.

My cash winnings for the three days now totaled $69,000 after paying the income tax. Any winnings over $1,200 needed to be reported to the IRS. I felt it was time to move on.

Three days of consecutive winning is not something the casinos in any gambling town care to support. They'll feed you, rent you a hotel room for a discount rate, and pour drinks on a regular basis. The alcohol assists a player in making those important decisions. One could leave and pay their rent back home, or try to win back lunch money for the next month. The free drinks kept many gamblers at the tables attempting to win it all back.

My ability to know what would happen next at the Black Jack table remained in play. I still felt the pressure at the base of my skull but knew deep down it was time to move on.

Chapter 2

Sixteen days earlier, William and Leslie Ray had planned a trip to Arizona to celebrate her birthday. The reroute to San Diego was not planned. A routine check by William's cardiologists in El Centro, California forced the couple to stay overnight. The town, located in the Imperial Valley, was used for medical purposes. San Felipe in Baja California, where they lived at the time, did not take American health insurance.

A blood test with an empty stomach was scheduled for the next morning. A vascular check, in the lab a few door down, looked for blockages in his veins. Discomfort, swelling and discoloration appeared two weeks before in William's leg. He felt something was not right when the lab tech in the clinic changed his demeanor during the test and hurried out of the room.

William asked, “Is everything ok?” when the tech returned.

He answered, “You need to speak to the doctor before you leave the clinic.”

The doctor was waiting for William in the front office. Her response was direct. “You have a blood clot in your left leg. The E.R. is waiting for you in the hospital. It’s a block away. An ambulance or a helicopter will transport you to San Diego where you'll be admitted. A procedure is planned for your recovery. We need to clear up the clot right away.”

William sensed for the first time this was a serious situation. The announcement by the doctor was upsetting, to say the least. His life would change in ways unknown at the time. He returned to the hotel room and told Leslie everything that had happened.

“Should we eat something before going over? This is nothing to fool around with, William." She tried not to show her fear. Time to fall apart would come later.

The next hour remained a blur to William. All the couple could do was follow the time directive of the medical world and move to the next location. One step at a time was their only option.

“Mr. William Ray, we’re ready to move you to the emergency room," the admission nurse said. "We'll start you on an I.V. and give you a blood thinner called Heparin. This will help ease the clot in your leg.”

William felt like he was floating in some kind of a time warp. The hustle and bustle of ER hospital life swirled on every side. A thin curtain separated him from the other patients, and noises of discomfort could be heard from many directions.

Leslie came back from the cafeteria with something she could eat. “Are you sure you aren’t hungry?” she asked.

“Breakfast was not that long ago. I wish this wouldn't take so long. We’ve been here two hours,” William said.

Another three hours would be added to their wait time before transportation arrived. William was hoping for a helicopter because that option was offered. The ambulance to San Diego arrived at the El Centro hospital around two in the afternoon. It came from Brawley, the next town to the north in the Imperial Valley. Five hours of waiting in the E.R. satisfied any desire to visit this care unit ever again.

“Sweetheart. You need to drive to Ramona and be with Yvonne," William said. "They won’t let you ride with me in the ambulance." Yvonne was Leslie's niece.

“I’ll be fine. Just get better. I've already called, and she's expecting me.”

The two-hour drive to Sharp Memorial Hospital passed quickly. The drug William was on made him feel light-headed and made the ride easier to manage.

“The lab techs are gone and will be back around seven," the head nurse said upon arrival to Sharp Memorial. "You're first on the list. We'll make your stay as comfortable as possible.”

The male nurse spoke with an accent different than anything William ever heard.

“Where are you from?" William asked.

The name C*aesar* was on his nametag. “I'm from the

Philippines. I've been in America since 1988."

"Are many nurses from the Philippines? I hear the same accent being spoken by several people working in the hospital."

"Yes. In the 80's there was a demand for people in the medical profession. Not enough nurses in the States to fill the hospital jobs across the country."

Caesar took pride in what he did. At 5ft. 6in. tall, he looked Hawaiian with his smooth brown skin and good looks.

"Are you Caesar, like the dressing?"

He chuckled. "No, I'm Caesar like the emperor. I rule this floor since I'm here the longest. I see everything that's going on with all the staff." This information was enough for William to realize he needed to get on this man's good side. Caesar was the type of person that would go the extra mile if you were liked. William didn't know what was ahead but felt he could use the extra mile.

William's hadn't eaten since breakfast. "Caesar! I've had no food in ten hours. Anyway, I can get something to eat?"

Ten minutes later Caesar arrived with a sandwich and juice. Dinner, or the closest thing to it, was over in a few minutes. The food would be enough to get William through the night and ready for the day ahead.

At six a.m. William woke. “Do you know what the doctor is going to do?” he asked the nurse on duty.

"A filter will be placed into your vein leading to your lungs," the nurse answered. "This would be completed before the hospital starts you on a stronger blood thinner called Tissue Plasminogen Activators or TPA. The filter will act as a protection device. Any piece of the clot that breaks off and travels through your vein won't be able to reach your lungs or heart area. If this happened your life would end."

William didn't care to0 much for that last statement.

After being wheeled into the operating room, and a thirty-minute procedure of inserting the filter, William was ready to return to his room. He lay in a state of free-floating; mostly due to the painkiller he called the *happy drug.*

“All done." The doctor said. "Any questions?"

“That’s it? Can I get another shot of that painkiller before I go? I haven’t felt this good in years.”

“I’m afraid not Mr. Ray. You’ll be fine for a while. Ask the duty nurse for an aspirin if you start to feel any discomfort. Have a nice day.”

The Sharp Memorial experience became a routine of getting through the day. Every two hours the nurses gave William a variety of pills and checked his blood pressure. Leslie made regular visits from Ramona, starting on day two.

“Are you disappointed, Sweetheart? I’d no idea my leg would change our plans.” William felt guilty because they had to cancel Leslie's birthday party in Arizona.

“Your life is what's important right now, William. I'll celebrate a birthday every year. An emergency like this is not an everyday experience."

A blood clot can change a person’s schedule or even their life. The Rays were about to find out how this emergency would change theirs.

Chapter 3

Ten months earlier, on December 19, The US News, European edition, carried had a third-page story which read, "The body of an American was found in his hotel room in the city of Pisa. The cause of death determined he died of heart failure. The Italian authorities are releasing the body to the surviving wife from Boulder, Colorado. His name hasn't been released at the request of the wife."

A call was made to Robert Woods of Albuquerque, New Mexico, a family friend.

"Robert, it's me, Glenda. I'm still in Pisa. Bryan died in his sleep two nights ago. I'm flying back with his body tomorrow. I'm still in shock so I hope I sound coherent. The funeral's scheduled for next Saturday. I need your help because something's not right. Can I meet you after the funeral and talk about it?"

"Of course, Glenda," Robert answered. "I'll be there. I'm so sorry for your loss. Bryan was a good man. I'll be at the funeral, and we'll set up a time to meet then."

Robert hung up. He'd met Bryan, and others like him, three years before. Through social gatherings, they'd become friends and kept in touch. Working now as a private investigator, Robert had built a successful business, and people found out about him through word of mouth. He was good at what he did. Little did he know, but the call from Glenda would involve him in his most challenging case so far.

Chapter 4

The life-changing event for William happened on day four. He woke up around six a.m. to watch a CBS Sunday Morning News show. Marcos, the duty nurse at the time, arrived.

"Did you sleep well? I've got some more medications for you."

William heard Marcos speak, but when he tried to respond he stumbled with an answer. "I think myyyy taakiing is not soooo clear. I'mmm havvvin trouble."

Marcos knew right away there was a problem. He told William, "Wait here until I return with the head nurse." He then rushed out of the room and headed down the hallway.

William thought, where does he think I'll go?

The head nurse returned with Marcos and asked William a few questions. After the same broken language response from William, both nurses jumped into action. This is where emergency training takes over.

"Remove the IV and I'll call the doctor on duty," the head nurse said. "We've got to get him stabilized right away."

While all this physical movement and conversations around William was taking place, his physical body started going through some rapid changes. His temperature rose, and within minutes sweat covered his body. William stopped talking altogether. Nurses, in blue uniforms, raced around the room preparing him for a move onto a mobile bed. They rushed William down the hall and into the elevator. Final destination, the CAT scan lab. After the twenty-minute scan, William arrived in a different room only one floor above the lab. Several scans were made in the lab before the day ended.

The next day the doctors determined the immediate danger was past. Leslie came into the room and said, "William, the doctor told me the blood thinning medication caused a brain bleed and it affected your speech. It put pressure at the base of your skull."

"I sssstill cannnn't talk weeell. I beeeter just liiiisten," William answered.

Leslie continued. "They removed the IV and stopped the thinner. The clot stopped growing and your condition stabilized."

William breathed a sigh of relief. So did Leslie. It looked like the immediate danger was past.

The next day a new treatment option was presented. The lead doctor said, "You're only the second patient to have this problem with the TPA treatment. The other patient lived so you should be fine."

No shit, they lived. Things are looking up, thought William.

Dr. Goodbar presented his medical advice. “We think you should get physical therapy in the rehab clinic adjacent to the hospital. After a few days, we can see how far you've come and maybe send you home.”

William needed to relearn how to speak, write, and walk. He felt those skills covered the basics necessary to get by in life so he took them up on the offer.

Before being transported to the rehab clinic, William started to notice something unusual. He knew what the nurses or the doctors were going to say before they opened their mouths. At first, it freaked him out but after day two he became used to it.

“How many pillows would you like, Mr. Ray?” the day nurse asked.

Two fingers from William appeared before the question.

William kept his condition to himself. He wanted to experiment to see how far this new ability would take him. The insights happened only when he felt pressure at the base of his neck. According to the doctor, this is where the brain bleed formed.

While watching TV, William was able to envision the weather report before the degrees were posted for the five-day forecast. In sports, he knew the final score before the game ended.

One of the male nurses on the third floor was a Chargers fan, and bet on football each week. William told him how he thought his team would do later that day. He even predicted a final score. The nurse shook his head and said William knew nothing about football. Later that afternoon the game ended and the score posted. The nurse came to William, surprised and angry. His team lost with the exact score William gave him.

“How in the hell did you do that?" He’d been given a tip but didn't place a bet. It really pissed him off.

The move to the neighboring clinic became an opportunity for William to improve his bodily functions. William could walk with the help of a cane at a steady clip. His speech improved, but not his handwriting.

William was released after two weeks at Sharp Memorial. A few more days in San Diego gave him time to exercise his body as well as his new gift. He found a 7-11 store on Main Street in Ramona where he and Leslie were staying. He still had his ability so he decided to continue using it. Six numbers came to him as he filled out the two lottery tickets, but he only used five of the digits. After the drawing the next day, the tickets paid out $800 each.

Damn, William thought. I could really make this thing work. I need to expand my playing field.

A day later William made plans for a side trip to Nevada.

His idea included a visit to the casinos, make some money, and leave before anyone was on to him. Sort of like 'In and Out Burger.'

William showed Leslie the money he'd won with the lottery tickets. He then said, “How about we take this money and have a mini vacation before heading home?" William hadn't told Leslie about his ability yet. He felt he needed to win some real money before he told her everything.

“Really?" She said. "I love side trips. You were damn lucky with those two tickets. How’d you do that?" Leslie was excited about not having to return to Mexico right away. She was doing her best to make a life there, but she looked forward to the return visits to the States every month.

“I just had a feeling,” William answered. His plan was to use his ability in a small casino town and work his way up. Laughlin, Nevada would be a good start.

Chapter 5

Robert Woods had been working on the case of his friend's death for nine months. It was now October and he still didn't have any evidence to go on. The only real facts so far were; Bryan and his wife, Glenda, were staying in Pisa at the Tower Hotel at the time of his death. Bryan was hired to visit a clinic outside the city for research. Glenda did not know who was doing the study because Bryan never told her. Bryan's death came after he was given a clean bill of health before he left to go to Italy.

Six months before Bryan died, another friend from this same group of friends, also passed away in Italy. After a call to the surviving wife, Robert discovered the couple was staying in Pisa at the time of his death. The husband was also visiting some clinic outside the city. Not only that but the hotel where they were staying was the Tower Hotel.

The investigation into the first death did not begin until Bryan's wife brought the case to Robert's attention. The circumstances surrounding the two deaths peaked the interest of Woods. Something was going on in some research center outside of Pisa and the two fatalities were somehow tied together.

Chapter 6

Sixty-nine thousand dollars was now in William and Leslie's bank account and their time in Nevada was nearing an end. During their stay Leslie made walks around the town of Laughlin, shopping in the stores. She had no interest in gambling or anything that went on in the casinos. She would rather practice Yoga in some ashram in India.

After making a bank deposit, William could no longer keep Leslie in the dark regarding his new ability. She needed to see their account balance and clear the air with her. His comment, *he had a feeling*, wouldn't work to explain all the money he had just won.

William returned to the hotel room, handed Leslie the checkbook, and said, " Do you remember when I filled in the lottery tickets in Ramona and won that money?"

"Yes. You were lucky," she said. "Did you buy some more tickets?"

"No. Here's what happened. I've been able to pick numbers and read people's thoughts since the blood clot. I didn't tell anyone, not even you because I needed to try out this ability first. I'm still freaked out about it because it's not going away."

"You have what?" Leslie's voice started to rise. "You can read thoughts, and you didn't tell me? We're married William. We don't keep things from each other."

"I didn't say anything because I'm not sure how much longer I'll have this ability," William answered,

The expression on Leslie's face went through several changes. She was in shock from hearing the news. Then she looked at the deposit amount. A gasp came from her mouth and a rush of blood to her face changed her complexion instantly.

"So you're saying you won $69,000 while we were here in Laughlin? Are you also saying the condition may continue? What the hell, William." Now she was mad.

"Yes, but I don't know for how long." William did his best to justify his actions. "We can't tell anyone about this. If the medical world finds out they may try and put me away until the condition is gone."

"Well, maybe they should lock you up." Leslie didn't like to be out of the loop when it came to events affecting them. She didn't like anything that didn't fit her definition of normal to creep into her life.

"Hear me out first," William answered. "The gambling world does not tolerate people coming up with winning numbers out of the blue. Can you imagine the panic throughout the state of Nevada, and the Native American casinos across the country, if word got out?"

"Yes, it might make me a widow by the end of the week."

Leslie was frantic. She liked the money William won, but the gambling part did not feel good to her at all.

"I'm completely overwhelmed right now, William," Leslie continued. "Do one thing right now. Pay off our credit cards, and make sure we are out of debt. We can figure out what to do later."

"I agree. I'll do that right now." William needed to appease her right away. "U.S. Airways and Citibank would be more than happy to receive the payoff amounts," William said.

He wired the money from their computer while sitting in the hotel living room. $13,000 to one card and $11,000 paid off the second one. This left them with $45,000 and some change.

"We need to make one more purchase before we head back home," Leslie said. "Our RAV 4 is tired out. We need a newer car."

William had never purchased a new car before. He didn't see the need to buy something from the Toyota dealer with 0 miles, drive it off the lot, and depreciate $5,000 before he reached the hotel room. The next day they found a used Prius with 20,000 miles on the odometer for $7,000 less than a new model. He was frugal and had always been that way.

Twenty-five thousand dollars remained in their account after the purchase was completed. William could still envision numbers so instead of returning to Mexico, he came up with another idea. He was not done yet.

“You've always wanted to do a Yoga retreat in the south of France, right?” he asked Leslie.

“Yes, it's a life's dream. Why do you ask?" Her interest perked.

“Your sister, Anne, goes to a yoga center in the city of Arno every year. Living in Paris makes the trip easy for her. Give her a call so she can book you a slot,” William said as he scrolled down the retreat web page. He needed to make up for her missed birthday.

“When's the next one?” Leslie asked.

“The date on the site shows the retreat begins in a week. It would give you time to visit Heather in New York before flying to Paris. This is a way for you to get away and celebrate a belated birthday." Heather was Leslie's younger sister of eight years.

Leslie would be doing something she loved and not worrying about his new ability when doing yoga. She hadn't traveled much so keeping her out of the way, and in a safe place, remained his first concern. He had no idea where this brain pressure gift would take him, and if anything went wrong he wanted Leslie far away from any possible danger.

“Are you kidding me? This would be the best birthday

ever. Are you sure we can do this?" Leslie was ecstatic. She now focused on something other than William's ability.

“I’m more than sure. This money came to us at the perfect moment. We need to use it while we can.” The plan was working.

Leslie spent the rest of the afternoon calling her sisters and arranging the travel schedule. William laid out a trip for himself. His plan; Take a leap into the unknown, and explore the biggest casino of all, the New York Stock Exchange.

Chapter 7

Leslie booked a flight from Phoenix to New York, leaving in the afternoon. She and William returned to Arizona that day and stayed with Leslie's brother who lived in New River. Peter was a retired builder remodeling a home for himself.

"All packed? I can tell you're excited. Did you sleep much?" William asked.

"I can always sleep on the flight," Leslie answered.

The couple planned the next afternoon with a movie and a pizza lunch at Picassos'. After lunch, they made the drive to the airport where Leslie would catch her flight east. A day in the Big Apple then Leslie was on to Paris and a twelve-day Yoga retreat with her sister, Anne. William hoped this would be enough time to make some stock investments before his condition stopped.

"Have a wonderful time, Sweetheart. Don't worry about me. I won't do anything dangerous. Hopefully, we'll have a few more dollars to add to our retirement portfolio."

Leslie seemed concerned. She had no idea what William planned to do while she was gone. Planning the trip had occupied her mind for the past two days. She liked to be around when William made financial decisions.

"I'll miss you, and at the same time, I'm really looking

forward to this trip. I'll give your love to Anne and Heather. They wish you were coming as well because you're their favorite brother-in-law."

"Funny, Leslie. Anne uses that same phrase on me all the time. I'm their favorite because I'm their only brother-in-law. It's like winning by default."

Leslie boarded the four p.m. flight and was soon in the air. William needed to do more research regarding the NYSE. His options included an open invitation from an old college buddy who knew something about the subject.

William left the airport and drove on the 101 heading towards Scottsdale. His friends, Herbert and Melinda Moody, had moved to Arizona a few years before, because of the year-round golf weather. Herbie's college degrees in math and economics led him to the world of investment and finance. He'd reached a level of success with his *online* trading and real estate ventures. William needed a basic lesson with stocks and Herbie could provide it.

"Melinda, is that you? It's William. William Ray, Herbie's college roommate."

"Hi, William. How are you? Herbie did say you were planning to spend a few days with us. I heard you spent some time at a hospital in San Diego?"

"Yea, about two weeks. I'm coming to your place to get a

lesson with *stock trading.* Are you up for this?"

"I don't mess with the exchange, William. That's Herbie's domain. Cooking, playing golf, and doing things with the women in my church, keeps me busy. When are you coming?"

"I dropped Leslie off at the airport ten minutes ago. I'm coming up the 101 now and should be in Carefree by six this evening. I've got an errand to make before I get there." William planned a visit to the *Talking Stick Casino* to play a few hands of Black Jack to help pay for his extended vacation in Phoenix.

"We'll see you when you get here," Melinda answered. "If the garage door is open just come through to the kitchen. You know the way."

*****

William arrived at the Moody house as the sun was setting over the surrounding hills to the east. The 3500 ft. elevation kept the area ten degrees cooler than the desert floor. After settling in at their home William came into the kitchen. Herbie was pouring a glass of wine for him.

“Try this Cabernet, William. It sure beats the Red Mountain we drank in college at $1.49 a gallon." Herbie's early years after college, while living in the Bay Area of Northern California, were spent cultivating his pallet for wine with weekends in the Napa and Sonoma winery regions. He learned what he could about this grape and how it's processed.

William's visit and stay with Herbie wasn't about grapes. His intent was to learn as much as he needed regarding stocks.

While drinking his glass of wine, Herbie laid out the ground rules. "William, here's my schedule. I get up at five and prepare for the day. By the time I make coffee and eat something, the market is starting."

"I wake up early as well," William answered. "This doesn't sound too difficult so far."

"This is my life from Monday to Friday, and I take the afternoons off. If Melinda and I need to run errands, we complete them after the market closes. We usually get in nine holes of golf at the course just down the road. On Saturdays, we play the whole eighteen. I've been doing this for over fifteen years, so you'll need to put up with our lifestyle while you're here."

"No problem, Herbie. I'll watch you, and ask questions while you're at the computer. I'd like to see how online trading is done in case I decide to buy a few stocks."

William kept his interest in check. He wanted Herbie to think his attraction towards 'online trading' was a passing fluke.

"The only advice I have for you is to make sure you want this lifestyle. I'll be the first to tell you, 'online trading' is not for everyone."

"I'm only here for the basics," William said. "After that, I may take off and do a little traveling."

Later that night William was in his room. Leslie called right before William went to bed. "I arrived in New Youk and took a cab to Heather's apartment," she said. "The weather here is fantastic. You remember her place, right next to Central Park?"

"I do remember," William said. "Take some pictures. I'll put them on your Facebook page when you get back."

"All the trees are starting to change. Colors are everywhere. It's a little cool in the evenings, but not too bad," she said.

Before hanging up, William laid out his itinerary. They wouldn't be able to talk after a few more days. Her Yoga retreat started the day after she reached France, and no cell phones were allowed.

"I'll call you when I get to Paris, Sweetheart." Leslie was excited. "This is the best birthday present ever."

The next morning William was seated in the chair right behind Herbie. Different market channels gave Herbie everything he needed to know. This was a different world and even the language was foreign to William.

The morning ended with a list of notes for William's

homework assignment.

"How about the talking head, Cramer," William said. "Is he always so excited when he raves about stocks? He certainly entertained me with his comments."

"Pretty much. He makes the morning interesting with his predictions." Herbie shut down his computer and went to the kitchen for a late lunch.

After a bite, William headed off to run errands, while Herbie and Melinda packed their golf clubs for their afternoon game. They planned to be home before six.

William needed to buy another laptop for trading so the Apple Store, located in the Scottsdale mall, was his first stop. When he arrived the story was crowded with assistants helping the many customers desperate to be on the cutting edge of technology.

"Can I help you?" a cute Apple tech asked William. She was a computer geek and beautiful at the same time.

"I'm looking for a computer fast enough to do 'online trading'. What do you suggest?" William kept his conversation to a minimum. He eventually chose the 17-inch model in the Pro series because it was in stock. The smaller screen models were on order. Along with the apps suggested by Herbie, William felt he had the necessary tools to make online trading a reality. After a few more errands he headed back north to Cave Creek.

William arrived in Tonto Hills above Cave Creek, half an hour before the Moodys. Dinner arrived with Herbie and Melinda in the form of takeout from the Olive Garden. After the meal, William joined his friends in another glass of wine. Being college roommates in the late '70s, many of their evenings were spent recalling events they shared during their years in Santa Barbara.

After testing their memories regarding old classmates, William decided to call it a night.

"One glass of wine is enough for me," William said as he stood up and headed to the bedroom. "Five o'clock comes early. Goodnight." He felt one more day of 'online trading' should do it.

The next morning found William once again sitting behind Herbie and his computers. After the morning session, William said, "I think I've got the basics, Herbie. I'm heading back to New River for a few days. Peter is on a remodeling job in San Diego, so I'll have the house to myself."

"So, you're really going? Good luck with the market. To make money you have to pay attention 24/7, William. I've done all right, but the market is like a wild animal and moves unexpectedly. Let me know if you get any hot tips."

"No problem, Herbie. Say goodbye to Melinda. She went hiking with her women's group, right?"

"Yea, she has all the fun, while I stay here and do the heavy lifting." Herbie's trading skills had purchased a beautiful home high in the hills above Phoenix and he was proud of his accomplishment.

Both men hugged before William got into his car headed down the hill to Cave Creek. Herbie was one of those hugger types. He loaded his van with golf clubs, preparing for his nine holes on the nearby course.

Another side trip to the *Talking Stick Resort* was part of William's afternoon agenda. A little seed money was necessary to play the market. The tribe, who owned the casino, would provide the start up fees. When you win almost every hand, your chip stack can grow rather quickly.

Three separate blackjack tables, and $18,000 later, told William his time on the reservation was over. He didn't want to take any more than needed. His retirement portfolio was growing and he was now ready to play the bigger game online.

Enough time in the day remained to pick up some food at the organic food store. Bulk nuts and dried fruits would keep William sustained while mounting his attack on Wall Street. He wanted to avoid distractions and food shopping was one of them.

The next day began with William and the computers set up in the living room in New River. His attention focused on certain stocks he observed while doing his internship with Herbie. When a number came to him, showing a change in the stock of $3.00 or more, he bought it. Everything available went towards a purchase. When the stock reached the closing high, it was sold.

The closing numbers were reached with every trade. By the next morning the earnings in William's trading account, minus costs, equaled $53,000. The first day of trading saw the $18,000 from the casino earnings triple.

William needed to wait until Monday because the pressure on his brain hadn't returned. For him, investing in stocks without his ability remained a blind gamble at best.

Chapter 8

A call from Leslie came early Monday morning. She was in Arno with Anne, about to start the retreat. She'd flown to Paris the day before, and met her sister at the train station. The two women would be out of touch for 12 days.

“When does the retreat end and when will you be back in the States?" William asked. He needed to plan his schedule and accomplish any goals he'd set for himself before Leslie returned.

“The retreat lasts until November fifth. Afterward Anne and I want to visit Cinque Terra and spend a couple of days in the town of Vernazza.”

“Do you have enough money for the trip? I can wire more cash to you." William didn’t want Leslie to skimp.

“I can always use more money," Leslie said. "Wire it to Vernazza.”

“Okay. I'll send the money to you after the retreat is finished. Call me when you get to Cinque Terra. Maybe then you'll have your return flight date? I need a few days notice to make sure I'm in Arizona when you arrive.”

"Where else would you be?" she asked.

"I may take off and head east. I've never been to Texas or any southern states."

“Good for you, but take it easy. You only checked out of the hospital a few weeks ago."

"Okay, Sweetheart. I love you." William missed her already.

"I love you too. This is so much fun being here with Anne. I never thought I'd be able to visit Europe again. I'll call when we get to Italy. Anne says hi. All our love.”

William hung up and returned his focus to the TV as the day on Wall Street opened. His concentration on the present stock on his screen gave him the trade value. There was little movement so far. It was a large drug company, and the rumors, according to the spin-doctors, said they might have a new drug coming out in the treatment for cancer. No one made a move to buy the stock because investors wanted more information regarding the outcome of the tests being conducted. The results were due sometime later in the morning.

Forty-five dollars a share at the opening bell seemed to hold steady. The number that came to William was fifty-five. "That's a substantial jump," William said out loud. He placed a purchase. Five hundred shares at the present price put $23,000 in the hands of the market. Twenty minutes passed in which a couple of pieces of toast and some oatmeal were consumed before William returned to the computer screen.

The numbers were changing. Forty-five, forty-six, and forty-seven came next. News must have reached the airwaves because the buyers were active. Forty-eight and forty-nine came quickly. Traders walked around with their usual frantic movements. The drug results came in. The first tests were positive. The stock numbers continued to climb. The price of fifty-five was reached within thirty minutes. William sold everything.

$5000 in an hour of trading was not much in the world of big finance, thought William. The amount would go unnoticed. I could have made millions if I had a larger amount of cash to invest. Oh well, I can only work with what I have.

The other three stocks had modest gains of two and three dollars. William's account totaled $60,000 to use the following day. He got in, invested and sold. A clean getaway, or so he thought.

Some physical activity after a morning of watching a computer screen remained high on William's list. He drove to a public indoor pool near Phoenix promoting lap swimming. The five o'clock lap swimming time allowed him an hour to do a little shopping. Big-Five sporting goods provided the Speedo swimsuit and goggles. Fifty laps in the 85-degree water gave William what he needed to shake out the kinks in his half-century old body.

Back to New River and an evening of TV shows and relaxation. *Survivor*, one of William's favorites, had just started.

He missed his evenings with Leslie. At the same time, he knew this opportunity could provide them with more choices to travel and live the retirement years comfortably. Early to bed, because he needed sleep. When *The Market Bell Tolls* it waits for no one.

Chapter 9

The next morning brought a quieter day on Wall Street. Of the three stocks William focused on, only one showed any real change. The stock traded at twenty-two at the opening bell. Twenty-three appeared as the closing number. Two thousand shares cost $46,000. A $2000 gain at the end of the day was a poor showing for William.

William decided to change his plans. The ability to trade online could be accomplished anywhere. All he needed was a computer and his trading account.

Peter, William's brother-in-law, left a message on the home phone saying he'd back to New River tomorrow. William decided that sharing his new ability with anyone, especially family, could not happen. If you want to keep a secret, the last person you tell is a relative.

William left a note for Peter, telling him he'd be gone for a while, destination unknown. His suitcase was packed and the cooler filled with food he'd need for the road trip. Albuquerque, New Mexico would be his target city for tomorrow, and Santa Fe the following day.

William pulled out of the driveway onto New River Road. The old Route 66 had been changed into Highway 40 passing through Flagstaff, AZ. A two-hour drive up the hill on the 17 took him to this mountain town, famous for its temperate summers.

Lunch in *Old Town*, plus a short walk around the plaza, brought back the past of his ten years living here. Shoveling snow in the winter, and ducking into buildings when the monsoon rains drenched the streets in the summer, were fond memories. William loved Flagstaff.

The drive to New Mexico on Highway 40 took him past the community of Winslow, Arizona, made famous by Credence Clearwater Revival. For the traveler passing through, there is a statue of a person *Standing on the Corner*. This, plus a small shop selling music from the 60's era of 'Rock and Roll', completed the tourist trade.

Just down the street is where the La Posada Hotel was located. The building and restaurant were now renovated. The black bean soup made the 50-mile drive from Flagstaff worth the trip. William ordered a bowl to go.

I need to make Albuquerque by dark, he thought. I hate night driving. It can be dangerous.

This was especially true in the desert when most of the wildlife, including chickens, crossed the road. William's destination was reached before dark. The Hotel Albuquerque, located in the Old Town, provided everything William needed. A good Wi-Fi connection for trading, and some of the best Mexican restaurants nearby worked for William. Chili Relleno remained his personal 'test meal' to judge how well a restaurant did .

Morning with coffee made with Starbucks instant packets provided the best caffeine brew available for the road traveler. An English muffin with a banana, purchased in Flagstaff, allowed William time to set up the computer, make a trade, and be on the road before noon.

The time spent with the stock market gave him another $4000 dollars in two small financial exchanges closing with small gains. So far his condition remained intact.

Santa Fe was only a short drive on I-25 from Albuquerque. William reserved a room at the Georgia Inn. A late summer visit to this art community, tucked away in the Sangre de Cristo Mountains, suited him perfectly. He was traveling and making money at the same time.

"I might stay a few days," William said to the hotel manager booking him in. A late lunch and a nap rounded out his first day in the coolness of this high elevation community. His cell phone woke him. Little did William know but the call would change his life.

“Hello, is this Mr. Ray?"

“Yes, it is. Who is this?" No name came up on William's phone screen so this person didn't exist in his contact list.

“I’m sorry to bother you at this time. My name is Jason Burns. I'm calling from New York City. I would like to set up a meeting with you to discuss a business matter.”

“What’s this about?” The hairs on the back of William's neck started to rise in unison.

“I'm sorry but I can't discuss the topic over the phone. I'd be happy to travel and meet you at your convenience where ever you are.”

Nervousness set in. Had the casinos caught up with him? Did he do something illegal in his daily trading with the *Brass Bull Gang* of New York? William felt a chill going down his spine. He thought, am I in trouble?

"Is something the matter?" William asked nervously.

“Mr. Ray, I'm sorry if I caused you to be upset. I can detect the tone of concern in your voice. I assure you this meeting will be of a positive nature.”

“Really, and you can't tell me what it's about over the phone?"

“The meeting is connected to what happened in San Diego a few weeks ago. You understand a face-to-face meeting, without the intrusions of the telephone system, is always the best way for people to meet, and get to know each other."

Crap, William thought. He knows about San Diego.

"You want to meet me face to face?" William answered.

"Yes. The reason is obvious for both of our privacy. I'd be the person to fly out to where ever you are. At the moment Santa Fe seems to be your present location. I'm free to meet you anywhere you want."

"How do you know I'm in Santa Fe?" William asked. This was getting out of hand.

"Operating a phone system with the ability to find a location is necessary for my business. In my line of work I find this information to be essential," Mr. Burns confessed.

"You're kidding me. You can do that?" William's inquisitive mind took over. He needed to find out more.

"Please, don't feel like I'm intruding on your privacy. The world of electronics today allows certain people, with technological knowledge, to pinpoint where anyone is while making a phone call."

Knowing a phone call could be traced to reveal a location in a matter of seconds caught William off guard.

"I see," William answered. He didn't really, but nothing else came up for a response. "I'd be willing to meet with you if you can assure me I've done nothing wrong, and I'm not in any kind of trouble.”

“You’re not in any trouble, Mr. Ray. All I need to do is present a business proposition to you, and that's it. Take all the time you need to think it over and get back to me when you've made your decision. You are under no obligation to take part in the proposal, and can walk away at any time.”

A long pause before William answered. “Okay. How soon can you fly out to New Mexico? I am staying in Santa Fe for a few days. I'm willing to listen, so where should we meet?”

“I can be there by tomorrow afternoon. I'll fly into Albuquerque and rent a car. How about noon?"

"Twelve sounds perfect. Where?"

"Have you heard of the Tia Sophia restaurant? I visited once before and really liked it. I'll buy lunch and present the business proposal to you there.”

“I noticed it on San Francisco Street on my drive thru town," William said.

“Good. You're under no obligation to do anything you don't want to be involved with. I'll see you at noon for lunch.”

“Okay, Mr. Burns. I'll be waiting.” William hung up. The more he thought about the meeting he realized he needed to listen to the man. Maybe something big would come out of his condition.

He needed to at least find out.

Sleep for William came around midnight after watching a DVD of the latest *James Bond* flick. The world surrounding his present situation had taken a 007 turn. William remembered Mr. Burns' promise that he could walk away at any time.

William stayed in bed until eight the next morning. Trading today was not possible. If Burns knew where he was from a phone call, he probably could follow William's market activity as well. This stranger from New York had entered the privacy of his mind and scrambled it like the breakfast he was about to order downstairs.

An omelet, and the morning paper kept William's thoughts off the approaching meeting. The time was now ten o'clock. He walked around the town plaza visiting different shops. A visit to the Georgia O'Keeffe Museum was included. Only an hour left before lunch.

At 11:45 William drove to the restaurant located near his hotel. A table was secured as the lunch crowd started to fill the remaining seats. William had no idea what Burns looked like. He thought if Mr. Burns knew where he was with a simple phone call, he probably owned an eight by ten glossy picture of his face as well. He didn't wait long.

A little after twelve a man, about 5'10", entered the dining room wearing a tailored sports jacket, pressed pants, and an open collar with no tie. Even though the person did his best to fit into the relaxed lifestyle of the Santa Fe art community, he looked like an outsider. The name Burns seemed to be stamped on his forehead. He looked around the room, searching for a face he recognized. His gaze fell on William and he raised his hand as he approached.

“Mr. Ray, my name is Jason Burns." He shook hands with William. "I talked to you on the phone yesterday. I’m pleased to meet you. The opportunity to get out of New York for a few days is a welcome trip for me, especially coming here to Santa Fe." He seemed relaxed.

“Glad to meet you, Mr. Burns." William felt the tight grip of a man who probably spent much of his work duties meeting people and presenting businesses plans. He appeared to be in his late forties. Gray streaks spread thinly through his jet-black hair. His good looks told William that Jason was accustomed to getting his way. He could have been a poster boy for the New York lifestyle.

“I haven't looked at the menu yet. My curiosity about what you want to talk about has thrown me for a loop. A person flying all the way from New York to talk to me is a first.”

“Maybe we should order before getting into the reason for our meeting, Mr. Ray. The food on the plane looked good, but I ate before the flight. I only snacked on the nuts. In other words, I'm starving."

Jason motioned for a waiter to come over.

“The elevation seems to contribute to the need of food as well as oxygen. It’s been a while since I visited this part of the world. Every time I come, the same question arises for me. Why do I still live in New York? This town is a real change from my Manhattan life.”

“Why do you still live in New York?" William asked.

“I believe life in a city like New York gets into your blood. Not all cities are the same and don't offer the same amenities. Paris, London and Rome, are a few other centers that match the pace of New York. In those cities I find the French are rude, Londoners speak funny, and Italian food puts on the pounds quickly. Visiting those places is a cultural experience for sure, but the Big Apple is what I know, and the money is fantastic.”

Burns had worked up an appetite and ordered the special offered by the restaurant. Smoked trout, a baked potato, and homemade apple pie for desert. The simple Greek salad William ordered did not match the calories Burns was about to consume. The order was placed.

“I'm sure you have many questions for me, Mr. Ray, but first I want to ask you something. Can I call you by your first name?”

“Sure." William had no problem with an informal approach to the conversation. "And I'll call you Jason."

“William, I represent a group of investors interested in your approach to the market. We're able to track investments coming in from on-line traders, and have a system telling us who's doing extremely well.”

“You know my investment record?” William said. Concern for his privacy was evident in his voice. William was on the defensive already.

“I cannot indulge how we know this information. At the same time, nothing is recorded in any meetings. In my pocket, there is a device telling me if you're wearing anything used to record this conversation. You're clean. If you weren't, a beeper would go off, and our meeting would be over. That's the way we do things. Everything is off the record.”

The look of shock on William's face let Jason knew that he needed to calm him. “Please don't worry," he continued. "None of the information we have on you, or others like you, will ever go public. It's private and extremely important for us to keep it that way.”

“What do you mean, others like me?” William could not believe what he just heard.

The drinks started to arrive. The conversation ceased while the waiter placed the coffee and juice on the table. The table was isolated, but William still made a sweep of the patio with his eyes. No one else could hear the conversation.

“Let me get right to the point, William. You're not the only person who has experienced a condition like yours. We started noticing you last week when you made the medical stock trade. When you sold at the peak you were one of only a handful of investors who made such a move.”

William said nothing.

“We've kept an eye on you this past week. We researched your history and found out about the medical procedure and blood clot. Your treatment, plus a large deposit in your bank account after a visit to Lockland, Nevada led us to believe you were the benefiter of a condition the medical world wants to keep quiet.”

William's jaw dropped. He was now officially overwhelmed by the conversation.

Jason continued. “The medical world knows about the condition. They monitor patients who say they have this ability. Hospitals make the person wait until the ability is gone before they release them. In your case, you were able to take advantage of your situation and make a few bucks. Your silence paid off.”

William couldn't believe what he was hearing.

“This is where we come in. We have an offer for you and your wife. We are also able to track where she is at the moment. I assure you, we only monitor the family of possible clients to make sure they are not in harm's way.”

“You know where my wife is?” William asked in disbelief.

“Yes, we do. She is safe and enjoying her Yoga retreat with her sister in France.”

Not knowing how to respond restricted William's comments. His head was spinning. It might take more than a James Bond movie to help him sleep tonight.

“What do you want?" William finally asked. He felt powerless, and could only trust Jason's statement from the day before. He could walk away at any time.

“Our group knows the condition is temporary. We have worked with others experiencing the same phenomena. It's not always due to a blood clot and a blood thinner causing a brain bleed. Some simply received blows to the head. These clients eventually recover, and go back to living normal lives without the ability to predict the future.”

William continued to listen.

"I'm here to offer you a chance to make a large monetary gain. Our resources are unlimited due to the financial levels of the group I represent. My company is prepared to help you make a substantial improvement in your finances by using your ability to predict the future.”

“How much is substantial?” William had to ask.

“A lot more than the amount you're making right now. Also, you don't have to invest on your own. The monies you earn would be deposited into an account away from the scrutiny of taxes or government watchdogs. In other words, this opportunity is like a free ride. All we want from you is information, based on your ability, to see things before they happen.”

The food started to arrive. By now William had lost his appetite completely. He needed time to think about the proposal. Time is what Jason needed to eat some of his lunch. He'd been doing all the talking. Both men sat in silence.

A few bites of fish and potato were devoured. Jason remained calm during his monolog. This was not the first time he revealed a life-changing opportunity to someone. Right now it happened to be with William.

“How do I get in touch with you later?” William finally asked. "My head's spinning and I need to clear it."

Jason reached into his coat pocket, brought out a black cell phone, and handed it to William. “I'll get in touch with you. We're like a ghost in your life, and others like you. We appear, make this presentation, and disappear. If anything happens, and certain authorities discover you, there's no way of contacting us. We leave no paper trail, and you were never connected to our group. The financial gains made by our clients are untraceable. You're safe with your secret."

William took the phone and glanced at the front. No brand name.

“The phone I'm giving you is solely for me to call you. You can't call anyone else. When we're finished with our business venture, we'll destroy the phone from our communication center. It will heat up and become completely useless. Throw it away. It can't be traced to us. Any tampering with the phone will set off a code, and the phone will self-destruct as well.”

“Jason. I can pretend to be calm and give you a decision right now, but that'd be a lie. This is like a time warp, and I've been shot into the future. I'm completely unprepared to deal with this. I've got so many questions. How much time is needed for me to make a decision? Also, how will you know if I'm ready to give you my answer?”

“How much time do you think you'll need?” Jason asked.

“A couple of days. I'll be able to make a decision by Sunday or Monday. A few things are influencing me. Figuring them out is a priority right now.”

“All right, William. There's no pressure," he paused, "except for the one on your brain. Not everyone decides to go through with our proposal, and they simply back away. They're left alone to live out their lives, and never hear from us again. Push the pound key on the phone, and I'll call you back.”

“Jason, it's been a pleasure to meet you. I'll let you know when I'm ready to talk. As you can see my appetite has disappeared. I need to leave you and your lunch alone, while I go and clear my head. Are you staying overnight?”

“No. My return flight is tonight. I don't get to be away from work for long. Another client has surfaced in another town, and my services are needed. I'm paid well, but time to enjoy the benefits comes later. I plan on having enough saved to retire soon."

Enough is a funny word, thought William. The word is not the same for everyone. *Enough* for Jason must be a large number.

“Thank you again, Jason. You've given me a lot to think about. Enjoy your lunch and please excuse me for leaving.”

Jason and William stood up, shook hands, and parted ways. William proceeded to his car parked in front of the hotel. Driving always helped him clear his head, so he headed north out of town.

Outside Santa Fe, William noticed a sign for a Spa. *10,000 Waves*. He'd seen a brochure in his hotel room. He could try and get an appointment for the afternoon. He dialed the number on his cell phone.

“Is this the 10,000 Waves Spa?”

“Yes, it is. Can I help you?” the woman asked with a French accent.

“I'm only in the area for one more day and I wondered if you had any openings.”

“Let me see. I think we had some cancellations. I'll check." After a few minutes, the woman returned and gave William a time for the afternoon. An opening at two p.m. was available with the sauna, hot tub and hot rocks treatment.

“I can be there in twenty minutes. It's 1:30 now. Will that be enough time?” William asked.

“That's fine. Thank you for thinking of us. I know your experience will be satisfying. We'll see you then."

William gave her his credit card number to hold the slot. It was exactly what he needed at the moment.

Chapter 10

Robert was busy with his investigation into the deaths of two men in his social circle when another lead popped up. The man Robert used to work for six years ago was flying into Albuquerque. His name was Jason Burns. The two men, who died in Italy, also worked for Jason. Robert traced Jason's movements through credit card usage and discovered which flight he was arriving on. Burns only left New York when he met potential clients.

Waiting for Burns at the airport, and following him to Santa Fe, was a piece of cake for a private investigator. Woods followed Burns into the restaurant in Santa Fe in order to identify the other man he was meeting. After seeing him, Robert waited outside and followed the gentleman to his car, which was parked on the street. He now could now find out who he was. He sent the Arizona plate number to his assistant, Alan. He soon had a name and phone number.

Burns had all the information he needed at the moment and returned to Albuquerque and his office. Robert could now put his plan into action. He needed someone on the inside of his investigation, and this new player might be able to help.

Chapter 11

The spa check in desk was situated in the middle of the diversified gift shop selling hundreds of items. A white cotton bathrobe, like the ones William saw other clients wearing, or a cat sitting in a meditative pose, were just a few of the many purchases available.

The cat was added to his bill. "I getting this for my sister-in-law," William told the cashier. "She's a major cat lover in all respects. You know world domination is the objective of the cat family don't you."

The cashier looked at him with a funny grin on her face. "No, but I know about people in the past who tried to accomplish that feat." She obviously knew a little about world history.

A sauna and hot tub were followed by a 90-minute massage. William didn't remember much after lying down on the table. A touch on his back by his therapist woke him. “Take your time getting up. I'll be waiting for you in the gift shop after you're dressed. Your clothes are hanging on the door.” William had gone to sleep ten minutes into the session.

William made his decision regarding what to say to Jason Burns, during his *10,000 Waves* visit. He was not exactly sure how working for Burns would work, but he knew he had to give it a try.

Evening approached and Santa Fe remained a twenty-minute drive down the road. An Italian dinner completed his afternoon of relaxation. William's body needed to be close to the hotel and his bed. Even a movie couldn't keep him awake tonight.

*****

The fall weather prevailed during the trip south to Albuquerque. The colors surrounding the drive towards the lower elevations dominated the countryside landscape until the 6000 ft. mark. The high desert plants took over below the tree line, waiting until spring to put on a show.

William returned to the Hotel Albuquerque because he liked the view from the eleventh floor. The Wi-Fi had a strong reception and Starbucks was right across the street. He would make a call request to Jason and talk to him in the morning.

William woke early and sipped his first cup of coffee when his personal phone rang. Again, no name came up from his contact list, and area code for the call was local.

“Hello.”

“Hello. I’m sorry to bother you so early, Mr. Ray. Are you awake?”

“Yes, I am. Who's this?”

“My name is Robert Woods. I live in Albuquerque and wanted to talk to you about something you're going through right now. The topic has something to do with Jason Burns and the people he represents. Please don't hang up. I realize how overwhelming the condition can be. I know because I experienced the same one, six years ago."

William almost dropped the phone. What else could happen on this trip? He didn't want to complicate his life anymore, and now he received a call from some stranger who used to be like him. He didn't see this coming.

"What do you want, Mr. Woods?" William's inquisitive mind took over, but caution still dominated his thinking.

"Nothing at the moment. I do have one question for you. Did you accept the offer of Jason Burns? If the answer is yes, then I would like to meet with you later today."

"I haven't given him an answer yet." William decided not to hide anything at the moment. Strangers seemed to know everything about his life so he decided to play along for now.

"Good. I only wanted to warn you to watch your back. The reason for that comment could be answered with a meeting. Most important is the silence you and I need to maintain regarding this conversation. Give me an hour of your time, and I can fill you in."

Robert Woods included in his conversation with William that he knew about the separate phone used to call Burns. He also explained his call to William could not be bugged by anyone, but he still preferred a personal meeting.

“All I need to do is talk to you. I wanted to let you know what I've discovered so far with my investigation."

"You're conducting an investigation?" William asked.

"Yes, and it may or may not pertain to Jason. I'll tell you more in private if we meet."

“Burns is going to call me today. I plan to accept the offer. Could I meet you tonight for dinner? I'd like to hear what you have to say. At the same time, I need to keep my situation as simple as possible.”

“Thank you, Mr. Ray. I'll tell you what I know so far. Burns and his group will reward you fairly and can change your financial picture for the rest of your life. They did so for me. Meet me at the Church Street Café. It is located on Church St at 2111 in Old Town. There's a patio where we can talk without being overheard. Jason cannot know about our meeting or this phone call."

Overwhelm was again setting in for William. “Fine with me. I'll see you then." As the two men hung up, William couldn't believe he'd agreed to a meeting with another stranger. He was alone, and couldn't discuss the situation with anyone?"

William had an alternative motive regarding his dinner

with Woods. He wanted to meet someone else who experienced this ability he had. Talking to Robert Woods might help him get through this challenging period. A request was made by William to have Jason call him. He pushed the pound key. The return call came twenty minutes later.

“Hello, William? It’s me, Jason."

“Hi, Jason.” They were still using first names.

“I bet you've had a lot to think about in the last few days. I see you're in Albuquerque. Did the slower pace of Santa Fe finally get to you?”

“No. I needed a change of scenery. I plan on doing some traveling before my wife returns from France. Albuquerque is right on the 40 and I-25 to the south."

"Travel? Where do you think you might go?" Jason asked.

"I might head southeast and see some of this country. I realize my condition is temporary, but it's with me no matter where I go. I've decided to have a mini vacation during this alone time.”

“That's a great idea, William. I'm envious. If you get as far east as New York, let me know. I can meet you and we can share a meal together. Maybe, this time, you'll be able to eat something, and not have to rush off?”

“Thanks for the invitation. There are a few places I want to see first." There was no mention of the conversation with Woods. William's new situation was now surrounded in mystery. He needed to practice when to keep his mouth shut, and this was one of those moments.

“Have you made any decisions yet? If you need more time let me know, and I'll call you later.”

“No, I think I'm going to give your offer a try. I really don't see myself sitting in front of a computer each morning watching numbers fly by on a screen. I can accomplish what you have in mind without doing that, right?”

“Yes you can, William. I'm glad I'll be working with you. Without making this a drawn out conversation can we get right to the nuts and bolts? We'll work out the minor details like bank accounts, and how to access them later.”

“That sounds fine to me.”

“I need to talk you through the process as to how this works,” Jason continued.

“Perfect. Give me the basics. I'm ready.”

"Here goes. We have one other person working with us at the moment who has this ability. No names are exchanged, and no one knows who anyone else is. I'll make contact each week and give you several company names with the potential for gains. All we ask is for you to observe them and see what comes up."

"You mean closing numbers?"

"Yes. From what I've learned from others like you, a number appears representing the stock high. We just need to know what that number is. Push the # button when you want a call back from me. We'll do all the rest."

"I don't do any online trading at all, right?"

"No. You really need to close your account now. That'll keep you out of the stock market and protect you. A percentage of the gains will be deposited to a bank account in your name. Only you'll be able to access it. The amount deposited depends on how well the stocks do. There are a set number of investing members in our organization. No one on the outside knows any names. The organization I work for is paid from the profit of these investors. We, in turn, pay our employees. In this case, that'd be you."

William was going over all the information in his head. If he made no trades, his part in this operation was not illegal. No one ever went to jail for seeing future numbers. What Jason and his partners did was another matter. Insider trading is illegal. Still, the information coming from a person who could predict the future would be laughed out of court. They're probably safe as well.

"What should I do right now?" William needed to stay in the moment. That's the only way he'd get through this, and keep his head on straight.

“I'll send you the names of three companies we feel have the potential for gains in the near future," Jason said. "We have a team researching the NYSE constantly. Focus on each one and retrieve the peak numbers. When the stocks reach those highs and are sold, it should take a day for the profits to be processed, and your earnings deposited into your account."

“Really, only a day? I thought it took several days for profits to be paid out.”

“Yes, but the members have funds supporting their earnings. They don't want the people, working for them, to wait for their paycheck.”

“How thoughtful." William started to wonder how much he'd make working with these investors. It could be substantial.

“I'll give you your account number when we finish our first transaction. After that, I'll call you when we're ready with more companies. Any questions so far?”

“Yes, I want to be sure of one thing."

"What's that?" Jason asked.

"You said I could back out of our business arrangement at anytime without hard feelings or repercussions. Is that right?”

“There's no problem if you decide to call it quits, William.

We've got others working for us. The last thing we want is any backlash. So far we've got an excellent track record."

"OK, let's get this ball rolling. I'm ready to start with the first companies. It may take a day but I should be able to receive some information soon."

"What do you mean a day?"

"I forgot to tell you. I don't have this ability all the time. The pressure at the base of my head only happens for two or three days in a week. Nothing is happening right now, but I expect the pressure to return. I'll know tomorrow if I can do this."

Jason's voice changed pitch, but he still responded in an upbeat manner. "We've had employees like you before. Some retain the ability for a short time while others can access this gift for several weeks. Almost all of our clients stay with us until their ability is gone. Each individual has to make their own decision regarding employment with us."

"You're right," William said. "I'm sure there're many different approaches. To me, my privacy is important."

William needed to make this opportunity work. He also decided to donate some of his earnings to organizations in need. *Doctors Without Borders* and a few animal rescue groups topped his list of companies to help. How much he sent to each group depended upon how financially successful he was.

“Three companies will be sent to you through an untraceable email. No messages, just the names, so write them down. The email will delete five minutes after you've opened it. We can't have anything traced. Remember to push the # button on the phone when you're ready. After I've received the information from you I'll give you your account number and temporary access code. You'll change the code after you've gained access. That way only you'll have the ability to view the account.”

“Where is this account located?"

William really didn't need to know and was shocked when Jason answered.

“The Cayman Islands.”

“The Cayman Islands? Really? I've always wanted to go there for a vacation. I now have a reason. I'll call it a 'visit my money' vacation,”

"You're a funny man, William. I'll have to get used to you."

"It's how I survived teaching for twenty-five years," he answered.

“Anyway, that's all the information you'll need for now. I'll expect your call request soon.”

“I think I've got everything," William answered. "I'll beep you soon. If anything else comes up I'll ask you then. Thanks again for this opportunity."

William hung up and fell back into his chair. He landed so hard that the legs rolled two feet across the floor. All this secret stuff had him tensing up in his neck and upper back. The need to relax became a priority.

The closest spa was a block from his hotel. The deep tissue session for 90 minutes broke down most of the knots that developed in the last hour. Lunch came next and then a return to the room to read the email from Jason. William wanted to get all the business out of the way so he could give his full attention to Mr. Woods at dinner.

William checked his email and found the one sent by Jason. He wrote down the three company names and waited. He wanted to see what happened to the message after five minutes. Exactly 300 seconds after opening the email it disappeared, just as Jason said it would. It didn't go into the *computer trash* or appear in the *message-received* folder. It never existed. Crap! These guys are serious, William thought. I need to be careful or I might disappear like the email.

Chapter 12

It was time for William to drive to Church Street, only a few blocks from his hotel. William had no idea what Mr. Woods looked like. William told the hostess at the restaurant he'd need a table for two in a corner of the patio area. The table was set and he was seated right away.

The wait was not long. A blond haired man, in his late forties or early fifties, approached William's table and held out his hand.

“Mr. Ray?" he said. "I'm glad you decided to meet me. I'm Robert Woods.”

William shook his hand and sized him up as best he could. Robert took a seat and ordered one of the Mexican beers with the XX on the label, while William ordered lemonade.

“Mr. Ray. Can I call you William? I hate formal conversations and like to talk to others on a first name basis.”

“Sure. I do too. Just don't call me Bill. I've always gone by William."

"I'm not Bob so now we're even," Robert said.

The drinks arrived a few minutes later and Robert told the waiter they were in no hurry to order. He wanted to enjoy the evening on the patio before the dinner crowd arrived. They'd get another drink in twenty minutes and order then.

"Very good, sir. I'll be back in twenty minutes with more drinks." The waiter acknowledged their need for privacy.

William was impressed with the relaxed mood of Robert. He must be living well. His tan face and trim physique demonstrated that he made time for his body. How healthy his mind was, became a topic of focus for William. He had a few questions lined up to uncover any areas of weakness.

“Why'd you want to meet me? More than that, how'd you find me?” William asked.

“William, I’m sure all of this is pretty overwhelming. It was the same with me six years ago. I found you because I've been keeping an eye on Jason for a while now. He was my manager when I worked for The Company. I was surprised when I found out about his flight to Albuquerque last week.”

“Really? You can do that?” William asked. He continued to be surprised by the technical abilities Jason and Robert demonstrated.

“Sure. In this day and age, information comes with a price. After Jason landed in Albuquerque, all I did was follow him to Santa Fe. I knew it was another potential client for The Company because that's his job. I found out who you were by following you back to your car from the restaurant and writing down your license plate. Your name and phone number were easy to trace. Knowing Jason only meets people with this ability placed you as a potential employee of The Company. By the way, that's the name they use for themselves.”

"The Company? Really? That explains how you found me. What's the meeting?”

“First of all let me tell you a little about myself. Knowing my story may help."

"I'm listening." William took a sip of his drink and focused on Robert's face during the monolog. Meeting someone who used to have the 'sight' was the main reason William wanted to meet Robert.

"I used to be a carpenter in Utah. I lived in Salt Lake City at the time, and my main job was remodeling. The building boom was over and not many houses were going up.”

“Arizona got hit hard as well. I was affected too." William always had to get a comment in, no matter who was talking.

“Anyway, most people made improvements on their homes instead of selling. Older people or families having demanding jobs employed outside carpenters to come in and do the work, so they hired people like me.”

“How did you develop the condition I've got now?"

William asked.

The waiter returned with more drinks. The two men placed their food orders and Robert continued.

“One day, while on a job, I had an accident. I took a fall from a ladder and hit my head right at the base of my skull. I was taken to the hospital and given tests to make sure I was okay. By then a blood clot formed and put pressure on a part of my brain. The doctors said I'd recover but it would take time for the brain to absorb the clot. I needed rest. I couldn't return to work until my balance returned and the doctors cleared me. I had no means of earning a living.”

“What'd you do? This sounds like one of those 'Up a creek without a paddle' stories.”

“Well, it was," Robert answered. I was trapped and didn't know what to do. Before I was released from the hospital I discovered something I'd never experienced before.”

The story was getting good. William guessed what happened next because it started to sound like his story.

“I knew what people were going to say before they talked. I knew the answer, in the form of a question, on Jeopardy before Alex could give it. Crap, I didn’t have any idea what the categories were about, and still, I knew the answers. I was a blue collar worker, not a pen pushing geek.”

“What'd you do then?" William hung on every word.

“I left the hospital without telling anyone. I found out later I might've been stopped from leaving if they knew about my condition. Silence saved me from a lot of bureaucracy hassle.”

“Wow, I did the same damn thing.” William felt drawn to Robert.

“Eventually I met Jason. Before meeting him I first went to one of the elders in the church."

"Church, what church?"

"The Mormon Church. I needed to talk to someone because this ability started to drive me loony. To make a long story short, I was told I might be going crazy. The church would hold special prayer sessions to help me gain a level of normality. In other words, they had no answers. They thought anyone with such an ability had to be nuts.”

“What happened next?" William didn't want Robert to leave anything out.

Before Robert continued the food arrived. The waiter asked if the men wanted more drinks. William hadn't touched his second lemonade because he was enthralled with Robert's tale. Robert ordered another beer. William thought that this is one Mormon who seems to like his alcohol.

“I received a phone call like you did. It was Jason. He said he heard of my condition through a friend who lived in Salt Lake City. This friend was an employee of The Company and worked for them as an informant. He was also a Mormon.”

“But they were going to have a prayer session,” William said.

“Yes, but this guy knew what was happening. My story filtered through the gossip channels in the church. He took note and called Jason. He didn't share the same beliefs about me being crazy. He was an elder, but acted as an informant.”

"Holy crap," William said. "This story's mindboggling. There's a spy within the sacred walls of the Mormon Church." He took a bite of his burrito and a sip of his drink.

“Jason probably made the same arrangement with me as he as he did with you. He flew to Salt Lake and presented the business plan. He told me I wasn't crazy. He explained the pressure at the base of my brain created this condition.”

“Same with me." William was bonding with Robert.

“He also said the ability wouldn't last long. If I agreed to work for The Company I'd never have to work again. I'd have enough money to do whatever I wanted, and not worry about my next job. He was giving me a retirement package, and I was only forty-two. I'm no dummy so I said yes.”

Another bite of William's burrito disappeared.

“After that, I never attended the Mormon Church again. No answers or help came from the elders, and I was not about to give 10% of my income to a church organization that basically said I was crazy. They really pissed me off."

"I would've been mad too," William said. He really liked Robert now.

"I moved from Salt Lake City to Albuquerque the following week without giving a forwarding address. No way was the church going to find me. I changed my name to Robert Woods and I've been living here ever since.”

“And I thought I had an interesting story, but it's nothing compared to yours. That's one outrageous adventure. Have you told anyone?”

"Those with the ability shouldn't tell friends or family members, other than a spouse because people will try and take advantage of you. They'll want you to give them the winning lottery numbers, or which horse finished first in the fifth race. I've talked to others in the past six years and some wild stories came from those conversations.”

“Really. What have you heard?”

“Every time the so-called friends used the person with the

condition for his or her own gain. Relationships were lost. Some of the stories are even more drama packed than mine. I'm telling you this because I'm only trying to protect you."

"Protect me from what?"

"We humans have a condition. It's called greed and it takes over our being. When a situation arises, and we see an opportunity to take advantage of someone, we do so. Only a saint like Mother Theresa might not act in this manner."

William asked Robert one more question. "How many others have you spoken to who have the sight? I'd like to talk to others as well, but have no idea how to contact them."

Robert studied William's face before he answered the question.

"The problem with that request is most of these people don't want to be bothered with anyone asking about their past. They're well off and benefited from their contact with Jason and The Company. Living out their lives in peace and quiet is what they want. The best expression I can think of is they want to 'live beneath the radar'."

"But they didn't do anything illegal,"

"I know but it makes no difference. I'm the only one who's tried to make contact with others with this ability. Right now I'm trying to protect those with the sight."

"You keep saying protect. What do you mean by that? Am I in any danger?"

"No, I don't believe you're in any danger. That subject leads me to why I wanted to talk to you."

William could sense, by the change in Robert's tone, this meeting would reveal more about his new job with The Company.

"I've been following Jason for a few years." Robert's voice became a loud whisper. "My ability to forecast numbers for his group ended six years ago. My earnings set me up financially for life. When I told The Company I'd lost the ability they understood and terminated my contact with them. My Company phone melted internally, leaving no trace of any connection with them. I still have the phone as a reminder of my time spent with Jason."

"Why are you giving me all this information?" William asked.

"I'm telling you because I'm working on a theory concerning The Company and what they're really doing. I've got no hard facts at the moment and you're the only one I know right now who's employed by them. I'd like to remain in contact with you while my research continues."

"That's a possibility. I have another question for you,"

William said. "How do you keep tabs on Jason? Do you have access to the same technology he does?"

“There are people in the tech world who make more money working for private industries than for the government. All I did was find such a person and tell him what I needed. I can now trace Jason either through his credit card or calls. I can't hear the conversations. Only the phone number appears. It takes money to do this and I've got that."

The waiter arrived with the check and Robert paid the bill with cash. No paper trail with a credit card. He waited for the waiter to leave and then continued.

“That's all I can tell you right now. The only advice I have is for you to continue with the business deal, and put money away. Remember this. When the ability to forecast the future disappears, The Company will cut you off, and contact with Jason will be over.”

“You mean my phone will melt and that’s it?” William asked.

“Pretty much. It's like you never did anything with them at all. There's nothing to connect them to your overseas accounts. Nada. They disappear unless you do what I'm doing. I don't suggest that.”

“Don’t worry. No way am I going to spy on these guys.”

“All I'm asking is for you is to hang in there with me while I do my research. I'll contact you, and let you know if I need anything in the future. I've discovered something recently, but I'm not ready to move on it yet. I don't know what I'll find, but my gut tells me there's more to this than just a bunch of greedy bastards trying to make more money than they could ever use in ten lifetimes."

William got the feeling Robert had no love for The Company. Something big must've happened that pissed him off. To William, Robert sounded totally sane and didn't talk like a raving madman.

“Thanks for the information and dinner, Robert. I appreciate you telling me all this." William still had a worried look on his face.

"It's a lot to digest, my friend. I wouldn't be surprised if you wrote me off. I've no hard evidence yet. Remember, this dinner never happened. Secrecy can be the difference between life and death, especially when investigating rich and powerful men." Robert's eyes glanced out at the crowd sitting on the patio. His focus returned to the table.

"Wait a second. Life and death! Are you shitting me?" The worried look on Williams face changed to anger.

Robert leaned forward and lowered his voice. "No, you're

not in any danger. Trust me on this. They only want you for your ability, and that's all."

"I trust you, but the life and death comment is a little over the top."

Again, Robert continued in a soft voice. "We're brothers of the 'sight'. We have a common bond. I'm not messing with you. I'll keep you informed about everything I find out." Robert still had a calm look and appeared undaunted by the information he'd given William.

The meal ended and the two men shook hands before parting ways. William returned to his hotel room to unwind. Robert was parked down the street. He drove around the block, making sure he wasn't followed and headed east to his home outside Albuquerque. He made this maneuver as a part of his routine before returning to his house every day. Secrecy as to where he lived was part of his lifestyle.

Robert hoped he'd won William over. William might play a part in his scheme to take down The Company. Robert needed help and his new friend had now reached the top of his list of possible recruits. There was more to come and he had to take advantage of the situation.

William went to bed early. The wake-up call at the hotel rang around five a.m. Some coffee and a bagel took forty-five minutes. He now sat at the computer, ready for the market, and the opening bell. The pressure at the base of his head let him know he was plugged in. Watch out Wall Street, he thought. There's a new investor in town.

Docette Construction was the first company on Jason's list. They built nuclear plants. The news on the stock market station talked about China and other countries without oil needing the energy to carry on their worldwide manufacturing.

The number coming up for William indicated a substantial jump in their stock. He wrote it down. The remaining two companies, in medical research, showed much smaller gains.

William pushed the # button on the Jason phone. Breakfast, after completing his morning job, was a priority. Before leaving the room The Company phone rang.

“Hello, William. It's me, Jason. How'd you sleep?”

“Fine. I going to breakfast right now, but I've got a few numbers for you.”

William relayed the information and in return, Jason gave him the access code for the Cayman account. He also reminded William, for the third time, to change the password as soon as he gained access.

"Remember, the deposits can't be traced. I'll call in a few

days," Jason said.

Jason's tone became deeper and serious like someone making a business deal. The friendly voice, interested in William's life, no longer was in play. The conversation ended and they both hung up.

After breakfast, William decided to take a walk around *Old Town* one more time before getting into his car. He'd never been to any southern states and thought he might have time to visit one or two before Leslie returned from Italy. A nephew lived in Atlanta, Georgia, and Texas was somewhere in between. *Remember the Alamo,* and *Eastward Ho* became his new travel mantra.

William's plan was to make the drive to Las Cruces, New Mexico before dark. The Prius ate up the miles on the I-25. He even had time to soak in a hot pool spa located in the community of Truth or Consequences overlooking the Rio Grande. The coolness of fall forced William to pull out a sweater he'd purchased in Santa Fe and put it on after the hot water experience.

The dinner with Robert and the business deal with Jason added tightness to his shoulders. The soak helped but he needed more. He found a spa down the street from his hotel with an opening at eight o'clock. Deep tissue work was the specialty of the house.

The attendant's name was Janet. She looked to be in her

late 50's or early 60's. William thought age would inhibit her from bringing too much pressure to his sore areas. The phrase, *never judge a book by its' cover*, came to mind after ten minutes of bodywork. Her steel grip kept William on the edge of pain for the whole hour.

"Thanks, Janet. It's been a long day. I need to eat and don't know the town. Can you recommend a restaurant?"

"Habanero's Fresh Mex, a few blocks away, has a great menu. They're open late. They're on Solano Dr."

William thanked her again and left a large tip. He found the restaurant and spent an hour relaxing over a meal. He was done for the day. He decided to wait till morning to check his overseas account. He knew Jason's group made money, but how much he earned was still an unknown.

Morning arrived and the clear crisp chill of the fall season in Las Cruces was evident. William decided he'd need a light jacket for the coming weeks. The southern states cooled down in the fall and sometimes a snowstorm rolled through. He wanted to be prepared.

The overseas account page came up on the computer. William changed his personal code as soon as he was in. Now only he could tap into his pot of gold at the other end.

After the spreadsheet loaded, William realized Jason and

The Company were no small potatoes. Four hundred and seventy-three thousand dollars had been deposited into the account. All he did was focus on a few stocks and write down the numbers. William thought, if I'm paid this much, I wonder how much the investors made? It had to be millions.

One hundred thousand dollars was sent to each of the three companies William supported. That left him with $173,000. Never in his wildest dreams could he imagine this amount of cash in an account with his name on it.

Three other companies need to be found before the next transaction with Jason happened. William made a list after a little research and found a group working with abused women. They would get a check the following week. Other groups in need would follow.

Texas was next on his trip east. Oil created most of the wealth in this state. The TV show, Dallas, showed what happens to people whose lives are consumed with money. They never got enough. J.R. getting shot became a highlight for William. That Ewing character was an asshole, William thought.

The Prius headed south on the I-10 towards Davy Crockett's last stand. The Alamo was a place William wanted to see ever since he was a boy and found his first TV hero.

While driving through this vast state, William thought a lot about the dinner with Robert. The flat countryside held few distractions. Straight roads and wide-open scenery allowed him to drive in cruise control while his mind raced. Robert Woods was onto something, and somehow William knew he'd be involved.

Chapter 13

San Antonio was further south than William expected. Six hundred miles of driving, with a few rest stops in order to stretch, broke up the trip. He found a hotel in Old Town with the rich heritage of the Mexican southwest.

The walking distance to the Alamo, the next morning, gave William some exercise. After arriving at the fort, the size of the building caused William to reflect on how small it was. Wealthy people have houses bigger than this place, he thought. How in the hell did a handful of men hold off a Mexican army for ten minutes, let alone a few days? The tour and detailed account of the famous battle lasted about 90 minutes.

While walking back to his hotel the Jason phone rang.

"William, how are you? I see you're in Texas. How'd you like the Alamo?" he asked.

"So far it's been great. I saw where my first American hero died and I also ate a Tex-Mex lunch for the first time. This vacation is exactly what I needed."

"Did everything work out with the Cayman account? I hope you've done all the necessary changes and set yourself up independently." Jason's business voice kicked in.

'Yes, Jason, I fixed everything. Thanks for the fourth

reminder. I was surprised at the amount so I assume the trades went well." William was ecstatic but kept his emotions in check.

"They went fine," Jason said. "Even though this is a secure line I'm making a request.

"And what's that?" William asked.

"I'd like to use a few code words for our business arrangements. How about food items?"

"Fine with me. What'd you have in mind?"

"How does 'salsa' sound for the word trade? 'Chilies' could refer to money and 'tortilla' for the company we're looking at."

"Give me an example," William said.

"Ok, here goes. We've got two 'tortillas' we're observing. Each has the potential to make a lot of 'chilies'. Knowing which number the 'tortillas' reach could make a good 'salsa'. Is this too confusing?"

"No, I get it," William replied. "This whole experience might make it as a TV show. Either as a mystery series on CBS or some reality cooking show on NBC." William's funny bone was kicking in.

"We're doing this to cover our bases, William. Sounds a little mysterious I know, but it's necessary."

Jason paused for a moment, waiting for a William comment. When none came he continued. “The new 'tortillas' are in your email now. Remember, the names disappear soon after you open it.”

"Got it," William answered. He was starting to feel like one of his old students.

Jason cut the conversation short without going into any attempt at small talk. Their relationship remained neat and clean with no leftovers.

After Jason hung up, William had the rest of the day to himself. The email could wait. The warm afternoon presented the weather conditions to shop for some warmer clothing. Another sweater completed the outing. Back at the hotel he opened his email and wrote down the business names he'd be working with in the morning.

*****

A wake-up call from the front desk along with room service coffee helped prepare William before the market bell rang. He showered and began sipping the cup of Joe from some Free Trade country in Africa. It was as black as the population from where it came and tasted almost as strong.

William found the two 'tortillas' and wrote down the opening stock prices at the bell. Not much was happening. The spin-doctors were giving their outlook on what investors might expect to see happen as the day continued.

After ten minutes of looking at a company having something to do with technological research, a figure came to William much larger number than the opening price. He wrote it down.

The second company took longer for a number to appear. After ten more minutes William had what he needed. The second 'tortilla' had its investments in global mining such as copper and silver. These areas of the world market were expected to rise due to the demand for metals used in all sorts of technical equipment.

William placed a call request through to Jason, and the return call came almost immediately.

“Hello, Jason. I've got the 'chili' amounts you wanted for the 'tortillas'.”

“Fantastic. It sounds like you're really adjusting to Mexican cooking. Making a good 'salsa' is not as hard as one would think, especially when one has the right ingredients.”

“I find some of the meals here in Texas a little different than the dishes served in San Felipe. A lot more meat seems to go into the food."

“Yes, I believe the cattle industry has a lot of pull in that part of the world," Jason said. "Beef and Texas Tea are the top exports. These industries don't want anything or anyone getting in the way of their product." Jason paused for a moment before continuing. "I don't eat the stuff anymore and haven't for five years. 'Eat more chicken' is my motto now."

As Jason rambled on about his eating habits, William held back and listened. He thought this was the most personalized telephone conversation he'd had with Jason so far. Eating healthy was a hot topic for sure.

Jason began to wind down realizing he'd gone off on a tangent and brought himself back to the subject at hand.

"Anyway, if you could give me the 'chili' count for the 'tortillas', I'll let you go. Good talking to you, William. Sorry, I rambled on. Healthy eating is important to me as I get older."

William gave Jason the 'chili' figures and thanked him for his food tips. Jason sounded embarrassed because he'd put aside his mask of *business only* and showed another side of himself.

"Today is Friday. I'll call next week and come up with some more 'tortillas'. It'll be interesting to see where you are when I call."

"Thanks for sharing, Jason." William felt he'd made a breakthrough with the man on a personal level.

*****

Dallas lay to the north. It was the city where the life of President Kennedy ended. One more night in San Antonio and another stroll along the River Walk. So far William was pleasantly surprised by the state he knew so little about.

On the Road Again played in William's head as he drove north to the city of suits, cowboy boots, and big hats. Austin provided a lunch break and a chance to stretch his legs. Driving a Prius in a state that might not even allow hybrids to be sold was living on the edge as far as William was concerned.

The remaining drive to Dallas took the rest of the day. There was heavy Saturday traffic on the I-35 so William didn't arrive until after dark. He checked into the Regalton Hotel located in the heart of downtown. By now he wanted the big city experience, and the chance to sleep in luxury accommodations normally available to high rollers. Having money made all the difference.

A valet attendant gave William a claim ticket before driving the Prius to the garage. A bellman rolled William's bag to the front desk, but the computer remained in William's hand.

“My name is William Ray." He waited as the desk clerk typed in his name on her hotel computer.

“Yes, Mr. Ray, we have a suite for you on the fifth floor

facing the downtown civic center." The hotel in San Antonio made the reservations for William and booked a room with a view.

“Thank you, Judy." William read her nametag.

"The dining room is still open and serving until nine," Judy added. "We also offer a complimentary gourmet breakfast. Juan will accompany you with your suitcase. I hope your stay will be pleasant and enjoyable.”

“Thank you, Judy. It's a pleasure meeting you. You're doing a great job helping a traveler like myself feel comfortable." William liked to compliment those working in the service areas.

William entered the elevator and arrived at the fifth floor accompanied by Juan. They arrived at room 528 and Juan opened the door. A slight gasp came from William as he entered the suite. He scanned the room. Two double beds were situated in two separate chambers with a living area between them. An office area with a walnut desk stood in one corner. A 50-inch screen TV located on the wall over the gas fireplace completed the finishing touches. "So this is how the wealthy travel," William said out loud.

A quick shower, along with a clean shirt and new jeans, prepared William for the dining room with time to spare. He took the elevator to the dining room and was seated in a large booth area facing the bar. William decided to try the local catch of the day. Rainbow trout from a local stream and a draft on tap helped him unwind. With beer in hand, William sat back and took in his surroundings.

Five big-screen TV's surrounded the solid oak bar with a marble top. Most of the chairs surrounding the circular drink entertainment center were done in red leather. The evening crowd had arrived and filled most of the seats.

From the looks of the clothing and cleavage of some of the single women drinking at the bar, William drew a conclusion. This could be where the high rollers of Dallas connected with the women who supported the expensive boutiques. The Regalton Hotel did not appear to be a family oriented establishment and seemed to be geared to a fast-paced lifestyle.

The trout dinner arrived along with asparagus tips and potatoes cooked in some western style unknown to William's limited fine dining experience. After the meal, he asked the waiter to pass on his approval to the chef.

“They're called cactus apple potatoes," the waiter explained. "The chef leaves bits of the skin in the mashed section. The secret is in the added spices, and only the woman in the kitchen has the recipe.”

“These are the best I've ever tasted. If she ever goes national with her side dish, what name would I look for?”

“Her name is Sera Leigh." The waiter did his best to not

laugh.

"Really? This is a joke, right?" William was sure he was part of a prank by the waiter.

"No, that's her name. She's teased a lot about it."

Not wanting to keep the waiter from doing his job, William stopped asking any more questions. He thanked him for his conversation and left him a big tip. A fifty-dollar bill for a forty-dollar meal made William feel he was living the high-life.

William returned to his spacious suite and went to the window to take in the lights of the Dallas cityscape. The lifestyle of travel and new experiences remained exciting for the moment. William also realized he needed to get back to a simpler way of living. It was fun to visit this lifestyle but it was not really who he was.

The overseas account showed a deposit of $550,000 connected to the latest company observations. Overwhelm was the best description for how William felt at the moment.

Three organizations, chosen as recipients for donations, were each wired $100,000. The remaining $250,000 was added to the $175,000. His new balance was now $425,000. No way I could do this well on my own, William thought.

A phone call to Judy at the front desk booked William a

sixty-minute massage the next morning.

"I can make sure you get the hot rocks treatment as well, Mr. Ray."

“That'll work. Thanks, Judy, for all your help. It’s been a long day and I'm looking forward to the session. Tomorrow is Sunday, right?”

“Yes, it is,” she answered.

“Are the Cowboys playing at home?”

“Yes, I think they are. It's a sellout so the game's televised. Actually, I think all the games are sold out. You do realize football is a big deal in Texas don’t you?”

"I sure do. I've heard it's the number one religion in this state."

She laughed. " It might be." She said she'd be watching.

Saturday Night Live was turned on the T.V. After half an hour of watching the introduction and first two skits, William turned off the television. To him, humor, like music, is a generational thing. What SNL called funny today didn't connect with him at all. John Belushi, where are you when I want a good laugh, thought William. Oh yeah, he remembered. Belushi was dead.

Chapter 14

Breakfast in the dining room was not a simple continental spread. At $450 to $700 a night, this high-end hotel laid out a buffet appropriate for the price of a room. The nightlife had taken its toll on many of the guests so the dining room remained mostly empty. As William sat down with his plate of individually cooked food, his personal phone rang.

“Hello,” William said.

“Hello, this is Robert. Remember me?"

“Robert Woods. It's only been a few days. My memory's not that bad. How are you?”

“Fine. How's your visit to Dallas?”

The ability of Robert and Jason to know where he was, no longer surprised William.

“If I ever wanted to disappear from you and Jason and still have a telephone, how could I?”

“I believe you'd need to block our calls. This would stop the tracker in our system from locating you. I hope you're not ready to hide from me yet.”

“Not yet." William said. Who knew what the future would bring.

“What can I do for you on this Sunday morning?”

“How would you like to go to a football game today? I'm in Dallas and obtained a couple of box seats, courtesy of a businessman I know.”

“Are you kidding? The game is completely sold out and you call out of the blue with a couple of seats in the rich guy’s section?" Suddenly it hit William. "You've got some information for me don't you?”

“Yes, I do,” answered Robert.

“Bribing me with a chance to visit the most modern football stadium in the country might work. Of course, I'll go.” William did his best to disguise the pleasure in his voice.

“Fine. I came into town yesterday. I'll pick you up at your hotel at noon. That'll give us time to park and find our seats. You're at the Regalton, right?”

“Your phone can even tell which hotel I'm staying at? William asked.

“No, I went into the database of the hotels in town and typed in your name. It's another service I pay for. I couldn't have found you if you used a false ID." Robert had an answer for everything.

“I'll be in front of my hotel at noon. I'll talk to you then,

Robert."

"Okay. Thanks for not bailing on me." Robert hung up. He had a plan for William and he was counting on the home of the Dallas Cowboys to help make it happen.

The massage at ten would give William enough time to relax, change clothes, and be in front of the hotel on time. William wondered how people live like this? Woods seemed to thrive on this fast pace lifestyle. William wanted to get out as soon as possible, but instead he seemed to be getting deeper into the drama.

The hot rock therapy and work on his neck helped tremendously. He made his way back to the room, changed clothes, and walked out the front door of the hotel at twelve. Woods drove up at the same moment in a blue Lexus with Texas license plates. Perfect timing.

"Hi, Robert. Good to see you again."

"William, I'm glad you're willing to meet with me, even though I had to bribe you with a Dallas football game."

"I figured the meeting must be important enough for you to come all the way from New Mexico. I assume you flew and rented this car unless you have a vehicle stashed in different states?"

"It's a rental. I like riding in style. Money can really change your life. I think you're finding this out right now."

"I've made some changes," William replied.

"Can I assume you're making money with The Company? This hotel earns a few stars more than the one in Albuquerque where you stayed. I think you're starting to understand what I mean about money and trying the finer things in life?"

Robert knew what he was talking about. Having the cash to try out a few high-end items became a temptation William wanted to experience.

"Do you want to start with the information, or wait until we get to the game?" William asked. He didn't want Robert distracted in the heavy traffic.

"I can talk and drive. Since our last meeting I've found out more about Jason and The Company." Robert's tone of voice became serious. "Here's what I've learned. Over the past few years, I've made contact with several Company clients. I placed a trace on Jason's phone so I could find out who had this condition. I contacted them after they finished working for him. By then all contact was cut off from The Company."

"You didn't wait with me," William said.

"Your case is different. A lot has happened in the past year."

"No shit," William said.

"In the Southwest, I've contacted six families over the years. We get together in social situations, like birthdays, and talked about our time working for Jason. We've all kept quiet about our past, and only mentioned The Company when we're together."

"Were you concerned about your safety?" William asked.

"If you mean keeping safe from people who might manipulate us and our ability, then yes. Let me finish the story." Robert's expression told William to stop asking questions.

"About a year ago I received news about a friend from this group who died while on vacation to Italy. His wife found him in his hotel room. He had a massive stroke caused by a blood clot. The Italian coroner found nothing suspicious." Robert gave William another look in order to keep him quiet.

"I gave his death little thought, given the health history of the man. Six months later, another friend from this same group said he and his wife planned to go to Italy for a two-month trip and would be back before Christmas."

William glanced out the window and saw that Robert was taking the exit to the stadium.

After turning off, Robert continued. "This happened last December. I knew Bryan well. His wife, Glenda, called me from

Italy after they were there for a month. She was in shock and told me her husband died in his sleep. They'd been staying at the Tower Hotel in the city of Pisa. The cause of death on the certificate said his heart stopped. She said she'd fly back with her husband's body, and would like to talk to me after the funeral." Robert was piecing the puzzle together so William could come to the same conclusions he had.

"Two deaths from the same group within six months of each other while touring Italy? Bad water?" William couldn't help himself and had to make a terrible joke.

"Here's where the story gets interesting. I agreed to meet with her. I had a weird feeling about the deaths. Something seemed a little off. I called the wife of the first person who died six months before. I didn't know them as well, and she never called me regarding her husband's death. I found out from her that they also stayed in Pisa. That's where he had the stroke."

"No. You're kidding? The same town?" William could barely contain himself. Shock was setting in.

Robert nodded. "Listen to this. The first couple also stayed at the Tower Hotel for three weeks. Nobody touring Italy stays in Pisa for three weeks! After seeing the Leaning Tower, and a few different sights, most tourists move on."

Roberts story came to a halt as the car approached the

parking gate for the VIP box seat ticket holders. Robert showed their passes to the attendant and parked near the elevator. "Our seats are a gift," Robert said. "Business executives use them to attract clients. I did some work for this gentleman last year and this is the way he's thanking me."

William and Robert arrived at their destination right when the two teams began lining up for the kick-off. By now the excitement of being at the stadium had peaked for William. Every cell in his body was tingling with excitement. At the same time, he was overwhelmed with the news of two deaths and their possible connection. Both men worked for the same company he was now working with, and that was a concern to William.

Both men sat in the back of the VIP box so they could continue their conversation. They also didn’t want to bother the two couples in the front row. Some people come to watch the game and others come to party. These people were here for the latter.

The kick-off ended and the visiting Giants had the ball on the 20-yard line after a non-attempted run back. One of the top rivalries in football was underway.

Robert continued his story where he left off. "I went to my friend's funeral and met with his wife the next day. The main question for me was; why were they in Pisa? I asked her if anything seemed strange about her husband’s death?"

"And?" William hung on every word in this wild story, and he was not able to give the game his attention.

"My last question made her cry," Robert said. "Her husband had been given a clean bill of health just before they left for Italy. He wanted to be sure the flying and the stress of travel wouldn't affect his heart."

Something happened on the field and a roar went up from the crowd. When the noise died down Robert started again. "The wife didn't know the whole story as to why they had to stay in Pisa. All her husband told her was he'd been hired to attend some kind of clinical study outside of town. A driver picked him up from the hotel on the days they needed him. When the study was over they planned to travel to the south of Italy and take in more sights."

"What did the wife do when her husband visited the clinic? Stay in her room?" William started to slip back into questioning mode.

"She did short day trips to places near Pisa. She spoke fluent Italian and felt comfortable traveling alone in Italy," Robert said.

"Did she ever find out the name of the group conducting the study?"

"No, she never did. Her husband never told her and she wasn't interested. She also didn't do much follow up after his death because of her emotional condition at the time."

William became so wrapped up in the story he didn't even notice how the game was going until another roar came from the crowd. The Giants fumbled on the thirty-yard line after they'd marched down the field for fifty yards. The Dallas fans went wild. The thrill of being at the stadium had lessened for William and Robert's story became the reason for being there.

"Someone paid for their hotel room, but the wife didn't know who footed the bill," Robert said. "That's why she wanted to see me after the funeral. There were too many unanswered questions."

“Where was the husband found?"

“He died in his sleep at the hotel. He complained of being tired in the evening and went to bed early. His wife said he hadn't been to the clinic in several days. They'd just returned from a side trip to the coast of Italy. A place called Cinque Terra. She gave me a detailed account of their stay and said her husband showed no physical problems at all.”

“Holly crap," said William. "That's where my wife's going after she finishes her yoga retreat. She's with her sister. Oh, you already know that don't you?”

“William, I've got an idea who runs this clinic but no proof. I've been trying for six months to find out. I'm a suspicious person and can't let this go. This is one of the reasons I wanted to talk to you."

By now William could see where this story was headed. He sat quietly and finally said, "Let's hear the pitch, Robert."

"Okay," Robert said. "You mentioned your wife doing yoga in France during our meeting in New Mexico. I have a huge favor to ask and it involves travel."

"You think it's The Company behind all this don't you?" William said. "Isn't this investigation stuff meant for the police? Any questions about a death should be handled by the proper authorities, right?"

William's whining tone alerted Robert. He needed to tell a convincing story to get William on his side. Robert leaned forward and whispered, "William, I believe there's a cover-up by the local authorities in Italy. Here's what I'm asking. I need a past Company employee to go to Italy. At the same time, the trip can't appear out of the ordinary. If any old client suddenly shows up in Italy, and The Company is tracking their movements, their cover could be blown."

"Did you ask any of your friends from that group you know?" asked William.

"No, and here's why. Jason knows your wife's in France and she plans to go to Italy. Your traveling to meet her is not out of the ordinary. I need someone to stop in at the Tower Hotel and ask a few questions. After that the job's done. I'll pay for the flight and travel expenses for you and your wife."

"If I decide to do this, how do I continue my work with Jason?" William asked.

"You can continue giving them the numbers no matter where you are. There are only one or two days in the week when they need you. It takes time for Jason's group to research the market trends."

William paused for a moment. He thought of Yogi Berra and one of his famous expressions. *When you come to a fork in the road, take it.* What the hell did Yogi know? This adventurer was in a whole different league other than baseball.

"You're right. It does take time for The Company to get the information together." William was warming to Robert's plan.

Robert reached out and gave William's arm a squeeze. "You'll have enough time to fly to Italy, meet your wife, and still give The Company what they want. The only way Jason will know you're in Pisa is if you make a phone call request to him, or he calls you."

"Oh yeah. My location will come up on his phone."

"If you decide to do this, and you're in Pisa when he calls, don't answer. Better yet leave the phone with your wife in Cinque Terra. You can always call back and make up some reason why you couldn't answer."

"You don't think Jason will get suspicious?"

"No. I already told you Jason knows your wife is in France and is scheduled to visit Cinque Terra. You'd be going to meet her. Pisa is a short train ride from any of those five villages. Nothing unusual about you spending some vacation time with your wife in Italy." Robert had an answer for everything. "Are you in?"

"This is not the retirement package I thought I'd signed up for. Damn it, Robert, you're persuasive. All right, let's do this." The wild side of William started to take over. "I've got my passport with me, but I also have my car. Where do I park the Prius?"

"How does this idea sound?" Robert answered. "I'll take your car back to Albuquerque. When you fly back to the States, come to my house, get your car, and then drive home."

"That should work," William added. "Travel to Europe sounds exciting. I finished a transaction with Jason two days ago. What I should do is call and let him know I'm going to meet Leslie in Italy. That way he won't get suspicious of me suddenly showing up in Europe."

"Great idea. I should've thought of that. Telling Jason your plans should keep him in the dark. I can book a flight for you out of Dallas for tomorrow morning, and leave the return fare open. Ten thousand dollars should cover any travel expenses." Robert felt William had crossed over to his side. Now, all he needed to do was keep him safe.

“That's more than generous. Let's kiss this game goodbye. I'm too excited to watch it and the first quarter is almost over." William felt the adrenaline flowing through his body. He was pumped and ready to go.

The two men left the VIP booth to the four people in the front row. By halftime, they'd be drunk enough to complete the real goal for their Sunday afternoon. Getting laid.

On the way back to the hotel the new partners made plans to transfer William's car to Robert and arrange for the tickets. Robert reserved the airfare from his phone. He planned on picking up the Prius after he took William to the airport.

They arrived back at the Regalton around three p.m. and William got out. Robert was staying in another hotel a mile away.

"See you in the morning, William. Try and get some sleep."

Back in his room, William made a call to his nephew to cancel his trip to Atlanta. He explained his vacation plans to Jon and promised to visit on the way back. Jon said he understood, and would look forward to seeing him and Aunt Leslie on their return flight from Europe.

"Since you're going to be in Italy, I have a request."

"Sure, Jon, what's that?"

"Bobola. It's a certain type of olive oil sold only in Italy. They make enough for the Italians and don't export it. Can you buy me a bottle?"

“It'd be my pleasure. How do you spell it?"

"B-o-b-o-l-a. Thanks, Uncle William. See you in a few weeks."

Another call to Mexico told the landlord he would be gone for a few more weeks. Any clothes William needed, he'd buy in Italy. He sent an email to Leslie, but she couldn't read it until the retreat ended on Monday. He planned to fly into Milan and take a train to Cinque Terra via Pisa. William wanted to take care of business first without Leslie around.

William pushed the # key on the Jason phone.

When Jason returned the call and heard his travel plans, all he said was, “Enjoy your vacation, William. Cinque Terra is another place I'd love to visit when I retire from this rat race.”

Jason sounded sincere. This was the second time he'd mentioned retirement to William.

William replied, "I'll be ready to view the market on Wednesday. I'll be in Vernazza by then."

Jason told William to expect a call on Tuesday. Currently, the market remained flat. “Maybe, while you're in Italy, you could see what they put into their dishes. Our business conversations in Italian cuisine terms might spice things up." The attempt by Jason to make a joke went flat.

William played along. “Ok, Jason, I’ll do that. My sister-in-law knows the region in Italy where we're going. She'll introduce us to some Italian dishes."

“Live it up, William. You've got the money to enjoy the finer things in life now."

“You’re right. We can stay anywhere we want."

“Are you going to visit the Leaning Tower of Pisa? It's a must see in Europe, and not too far from where you'll be in Cinque Terra,” Jason said.

“I think we might get to Pisa while we're in the area. Why do you ask?" William's suspicious mind peaked, following Jason’s question.

“I know a five-star hotel right on the river flowing through the city. I believe the location is a short taxi ride from the Leaning Tower. I know a few people who stayed there, and they recommend it.”

“Thanks for the travel tip, Jason. What's the name of this

place?”

“The Tower Hotel. A good name for a city specializing in towers with a tilt.”

“I'll look into it after I've completed my travel schedule. Leslie may already have an itinerary made up. I'll check in with her first.” William tried to sound calm by showing only a minor interest in Pisa. Jason's comment moved William closer to Robert's theory about The Company and their involvement with the two deaths.

"I'll talk to you on Thursday," Jason said, and he hung up.

William immediately made another call from the hotel phone. “Robert! You're not going to believe what happened. I'm so hyper right now I may not be able to sleep tonight.”

"Take a few breaths, William. Did Jason get you riled up?"

"Yes." William quickly relayed his conversation with Jason. "He even recommended I stay at the Tower Hotel." He waited tensely for Robert to respond.

“Nothing's changed," Robert said calmly. Go to Europe as we planned. If you're being monitored, and do things differently, The Company will know. Jason may be testing you to see how you'd react after mentioning the Tower Hotel. Being nervous might tell him something's wrong.”

"I think I sounded calm." At least William thought he had.

"Remain that way, William. I'll see you in the morning with travel money, and a new plan of action. Things have changed a little, but we'll adjust."

"Ok, Robert. As long as I don't end up with a stroke or heart attack. Death wouldn't be my way to end a vacation."

"You'll be fine, William. I didn't know for sure if The Company was involved before but now I am." Robert fell silent for a moment. "You don't need to stay at the Tower Hotel if you don't feel safe. You decide. This may be an opportunity for us to find out more about the clinic.

"Really. How's that?"

"Finding the clinic's location would be a start. I'd pay someone if any dangerous work is involved."

"Shit, Robert. How much money did you end up with before your condition stopped?"

"Enough. I made some investments on my own, and I'm part owner in two successful companies. My finances are virtually unlimited."

"Why are you so bent on getting back at The Company? Didn't they help you achieve your financial success?"

Robert hesitated before answering. "William, here's my

short answer: Supplying some rich bastards with numbers is not illegal. We only reaped the benefits. When the death of two friends occurred at the same location in Italy, I needed to find out the truth. Sure, we were paid lots of money, but if we're supporting murder in any way I want no part of it. Simple as that."

"You're right, Robert. I'll continue as if nothing's happened and fly to Europe. I can't tell Leslie about this right now. Maybe when it's over I can." William gave a heavy sigh.

Robert nodded. "I'll see you in the morning, William. Sleep well. We'll get through this, and figure out some way to stop these murders."

As soon as Robert hung up he made a call to his assistant. "Alan, get a hold of Karl. I've already got him working on this case. Now we need him to return to Europe."

Alan made the call while Robert did the paperwork to get William ready for the flight the next day. The wheels of the investigation had now shifted into second gear. William needed backup.

*****

Robert arrived at the hotel just before eight in the morning. He'd been up for several hours getting William's travel arrangements together. He booked a night for him at the Reme Hotel near the Milan airport, a train ticket to Pisa leaving at nine a.m., and a room at the Tower Hotel. William came out of the Regalton with his suitcase and got into the car.

"Here is a Visa credit card and your passport to go with it," Robert said as he handed William the documents.

"I've got my passport, Robert. I always travel with one because I live in Mexico."

"Now you have two. This one is for James Paul. Use it when getting cash from the card. Every good spy travels with two or more documents."

It was a Canadian passport. William opened it and saw a duplicate picture from his American passport.

"How'd you get my picture? Also, how'd you get a passport made overnight?" William was amazed at what Robert did in such a short amount of time.

"I've got my connections," Robert said with a grin.

The passport showed James Paul's occupation as an insurance adjustor from Canada. "Use it only when getting cash," Robert said.

"I don't speak Canadian," William said trying to be funny.

"Cute, William. James Paul is your alias and he's from Vancouver so you don't need to fake a French-Canadian accent. You would if he came from Quebec. The age and birth date are the same so you don't have to memorize anything."

"If I asked how you got this together in one night your answer would be what? Money can get you things not available to the normal citizen?"

"You're starting to catch on. I actually had that passport made before I came to Texas."

"You what?" William didn't know whether to be mad or afraid of his new friend.

"I realized after our first meeting you were the type of guy who'd do the right thing. Doing this is the right thing."

"Man, you're too much, Robert. You read me pretty well."

"Here's what I want you to do in Pisa. I've hired a man who'll be accompanying you to Italy. He'll do the real spy work. All you need to do is distract the front desk at the hotel while he does his job."

"What's the other guy going to do?"

"At this point the less you know the better just in case he runs into trouble."

"Where is he? How'll I know him?" William asked.

"When you take your seat on the airplane, look to your left. He'll be sitting right next to you."

William rolled his eyes. Knowing what came next out of many people's mouths, due to his condition, was not unusual. With Robert, William seemed to be one, two, or even three steps behind.

"Is there anything else I should be aware of before taking off?"

"No, at the moment we're taking things as they come. All this spy work is designed to force The Company to show their hand. I need them to do something so I can connect the dots to these deaths. Knowing where the clinic is located would be a start." Robert remained calm and in control while talking to William. "This is where you get off."

Robert pulled up in front of Delta next to U.S. Airways. He didn't want his face on a surveillance camera at the same airlines William used. Robert was cautious and had reason to be. This was how spies stayed alive.

William got out, while Robert stayed in the car. He drove away as soon as William grabbed his bag and closed the trunk. It was a 100-foot walk to U.S. Airways for the new *spy-in-training.*

William thought about Leslie and wondered how she was doing at that moment. She should've received his email by now, and he could hardly wait to read what she thought about him joining her in Europe.

The security check took the usual hour. Long lines and

magic wands passed over bodies took time. Travel was so much easier before 9/11. Thirty minutes before boarding gave William time to read the email response from Leslie.

Most of her message contained surprise about his plans. She and Anne would be arriving in Cinque Terra that evening. They'd have a few days together before William appeared.

"I'm about to board the plane," William wrote. "Saw part of a football game yesterday in Dallas and now I'm heading your way. I'll book a room for us in Pisa, and check out a certain hotel someone suggested we visit. See you soon. Love, William."

If the Company could monitor phones, hacking information from a computer would be a piece of cake. There was no mention of Jason or Robert. Caution took over William's thinking process.

No answer came back right away. Leslie and Anne probably had boarded the train to Italy by now.

*****

William's smiled and thanked the flight attendant after she seating him in his 1st class seat. He stretched out and chose a movie to watch for the flight. Five minutes passed. Another traveler sat down next to him. Robert's hired troubleshooter had arrived.

"Hello. My name is William." He held out his hand.

“Karl." Both men shook hands. "I believe you've met Robert?" he said.

William realized, from Karl's heavy German accent, that he wasn't from the States. “*Sind sie ein Deutscher*?" William's college German kicked in. He wanted to show Karl how international he was.

“Ja, ich bin ein Deutscher. Sind sie auch ein Deutscher?” Karl asked.

“Ja aber ich kann nur ein bisschin Deutch sprechen. We'd better stay with English if we want to communicate at any level other than the basic German,” William said. He thought that was enough showing off for one day.

“Ok, English it is. Robert has told you a little about me and what I'm hired to do, ja?”

“Not everything. He wanted me to meet you. What you're doing is on a 'need to know' basis. I don't need to know, according to Robert. Anything you want me to do should be discussed before reaching Italy.”

“This isn't complicated," Karl said. "All I need you to do is distract the front desk attendant. If you are facing the counter he is the one on the left. The phone used to call the manager, is on the wall next to that location. I checked out everything when I visited last month.”

“I'd ask what you'll be doing but I won't. Just tell me what to do.”

"I'll arrive in Pisa before you," Karl continued. "We can't be seen together. If you see me don't say hello, or acknowledge me in any way."

William studied Karl. He now realized the man was a professional spy. His short answers and business-like approach told William to stay on topic.

“Distracting the desk attendant is important, so get him to place something in the hotel safe," Karl continued. "If you can do that, I can do my job. After I'm done, check into your room, stay for the night, and leave the next day.”

"Anything else?" William needed this conversation to be over. There was no room for small talk.

"No, that's it. Have a good flight," Karl said.

William now understood how serious this mission was. What if someone on the plane observed them right now? He swung around in his chair, faced forward, and cut off all conversation with Karl.

After takeoff, William made one more check of his email. Damn, he thought. No answer from Leslie. She'll probably write me later before going to sleep.

The movie William chose ended ninety minutes later. Lunch was served. A beer with Karl's meal, and several more during the flight, demonstrated his German heritage. William slept for an hour after lunch. After waking up he checked his email. Karl was sitting next to him still drinking beer.

“We're now in our room and going to bed," Leslie wrote. "We've had a full day and the trip has tired us out. You'll love this place. I'll write tomorrow. Love, Leslie." William gave a sigh of relief, knowing the girls had reached their destination.

The plane landed in Milan and the passengers filtered through customs. William observed Karl walking to the car rental window near the baggage claim. He wouldn't see him again until the next day.

William took a taxi to his hotel near the airport and checked in. A room service meal of pasta and wine helped him unwind. Bed, after a hot bath, brought the day to a close.

*****

The train ride to Pisa occupied most of the next day and gave William plenty of time to think. During the trip, he came up with the idea of purchasing a ceramic piece of art in a store somewhere between the train station and the Tower Hotel, as a part of his diversion plan.

William arrived in Pisa sometime after three. He was able

to purchase a two thousand euro vase with the help of the storeowner's daughter who spoke English. William's first spy prop was now in play.

Twenty minutes later the taxi arrived at the hotel. The driver carried his suitcase, while William walked in with the vase and his computer. A fifty-euro tip for his help was well received by the driver.

As William got in line to check in, he spotted Karl sitting in a chair. He sat near the front desk reading a German newspaper and didn't look up.

“Welcome to the Tower Hotel. How may I help you?”

“Buena sera, Luca." William read the clerk's nametag. "My name's William Ray. I've made a reservation for one night.” Luca focused on his computer screen and scrolled down to the R's.

“Yes, Mr. Ray. Your room's ready. It's overlooking the Arno River on the fourth floor.”

“This hotel was recommended to me by a Mr. Jason Burns from the States. Do you know him?” William studied the face of Luca hoping to catch any reaction after mentioning Jason's name.

“No, I don't, but I'm glad he directed you to our hotel. I hope your stay will be pleasant.”

William didn't notice any change in Luca's face, but he did

hear a shift in his tone. It went up an octave. "I've one more request. I've purchased an expensive vase, and wondered if you'd place it in the hotel safe for the evening? I'd feel much better knowing it's with you for the night."

"Absolutely, Mr. Ray."

Luca came around the counter through a side door to receive the wrapped item. After he took the vase from William, he turned towards the hotel vault. Karl made his move. He stood up, walked to the spot where William was standing, and reached under the counter. William could not tell what he did. Karl then turned and continued down the hall towards the hotel offices.

Whatever Karl did, he accomplished the mission without being noticed. Damn, he's good, thought William.

When Luca returned from the safe he motioned for a porter to carry William's bag to his room. William's second evening in an Italian city, famous for a tower with poor foundation work, had begun.

In his room, William sat on the bed and took a breath. I'm glad that's over, he thought. He emailed Leslie. "Meet me at the station around one. That's when I'm scheduled to arrive. Miss you. Love, William."

Keeping the appearance of his trip as normal as possible was William's main concern. Robert and Karl were doing the *heavy lifting* regarding any spy work. Acting like a tourist, making money with Jason, and returning to the States seemed easy enough, or so he thought.

Chapter 15

The first step of the mission was completed. Karl placed the listening device under the counter and walked down the hallway towards the offices on the ground floor. Five minutes later Luca made a call to the manager. By then Karl had already placed another device, the size of a quarter, in the gap under the door of the manager's office, and walked to the end of the hall. Karl spoke fluent Italian, and with his earphones, he overheard every word of the conversation.

"Mr. Ray checked into his room a few minutes ago."

"Thank you, Luca. That's all I need to know," the manager said.

After Luca hung up the manager placed a call to New York.

"Hello, Mr. Burns?"

"Yes, this is Jason Burns."

Karl was in luck because the hotel manager had the call on speakerphone, and he could hear Burns on the other end.

"This is Marcos at the Tower Hotel. I'm calling to inform you that Mr. Ray has checked into our hotel. Is that all you want me to do?"

"Yes, I have someone else who'll keep an eye on him.

Thank you for your help."

"If you need me just call," Marcos said.

After the call ended, Karl returned to the manager's door and flicked the listening device out from under it with his pen. He then proceeding down the hall to the front desk and sat down again to read his newspaper. After five minutes the lobby cleared out and Luca went on a break. Karl got up, reached under the counter, removed the first listening device, and walked out of the hotel. Mission accomplished.

Karl then called Robert while walking to his own hotel a few blocks away. "Hello, Robert. Karl here. You were right. Jason Burns is tracking William. The hotel manager phoned Burns to inform him William had arrived. The manager asked if there was anything else he could do. Jason then said he had someone else keeping an eye one him. I think someone in Pisa is following William."

"Good work, Karl. Where are you staying now?"

"I'm in a small hotel a few blocks away."

"Stay in Pisa," Robert said. "I believe William's returning with his wife and sister-in-law after a few days. Maybe we can find out more then. There's no need for you to go to Cinque Terra. We have to focus on Pisa and find the clinic."

"Fine with me," Karl answered. "The beer's pretty good in Italy, and I can watch soccer from my room. I'll hang around the Tower Hotel and keep my eyes open. Something might pop up."

Robert hung up and turned to Alan, his computer assistant. "William is being followed by someone working for Jason. I'm not sure what this means but Karl will try and find out."

"If you can get me a photo of the person I can run it through the face recognition program," Alan answered. "If we find who they are we can see if William is in danger."

"Karl will do that. I still don't think William's in any danger. I believe Jason is keeping his asset is safe. William is making a lot of money for The Company right now, and Jason wants that to continue."

"You're probably right," Alan said. "I guess we have to wait and see how this plays out."

*****

Leslie and Anne waited at the train station, located on the main road leading back into the town. The summer tourists no longer filled the streets of Vernazza and the warmer clothing, worn by the locals, indicated winter was headed their way. Long pants and light jackets replaced the string attire called bathing suits.

William got off the train and gave Leslie a kiss and a hug.

"Hi, Sweetheart."

Leslie returned the hug. “You totally surprised us with that email two days ago. I missed you. We really enjoyed our yoga retreat and want to go back again.”

“Good to see you, Anne. It's been a few years." William gave his sister-in-law the standard cheek-to-cheek European kiss she taught him on her previous visit to the States. Her last trip to Arizona was three years ago.

“Can we help you with anything?” Anne asked.

“Yes, if someone can carry this vase, and the other one takes my computer, I can handle the suitcase.”

“How about I wheel the suitcase and you carry the computer?" Leslie knew how attached William was to his laptop. After twenty-one years of marriage, she knew him well.

“Ok, but can we eat before going to the hotel?” William asked. "I'm starving."

“We found a cute café right on the waterfront last night," Leslie suggested. "Do you want to try eating there?”

“Is the food good? Cute may work for you but the quality of food is still important to me.” Travel made William hungry and cranky.

“Of course the food's good," Anne replied. "This is Italy.

Bad tasting food in a restaurant can kill a business. Italian cuisine is much better than the French food I'm surrounded with in Paris."

The walk through town took about ten minutes. The cool breeze off the Ligurian Sea forced them to sit inside the restaurant.

"Are you feeling up to par, William?" Anne asked. "Leslie told me you came close to checking out on us. She also said you needed to relearn how to walk, speak and write. That must've been a little scary." Leslie told Anne about William's blood clot, but not about his ability to see future numbers.

"I seem to be recovering. I need daily naps, but other than that I'm progressing. The doctor wants me to wear this elastic stocking to help the blood go back up my left leg when I sit a lot. Makes for an interesting tan line when I wear shorts," William said with a grin.

William didn't share anything with Anne about the San Diego visit or what happened afterwards. A whole new chapter had been written in the past few weeks, which even Leslie knew nothing about. He knew he would have to catch Leslie up with what had happened but now was not the time.

After lunch, they headed back to the Hotel Gianni Franzi. The only difficulty was maneuvering the staircase to the third floor where the rooms were located. The access was more like a circular fire escape. There was only enough room for one person and one suitcase at a time.

Leslie and Anne planned a walk around the town, while a nap remained on William's schedule. He crashed out and did not resurface until the return of the sisters sometime after three.

During the time Anne and Leslie rested, William tried out the Internet connection and discovered a strong signal. The computer age had reached Vernazza so he practiced his ability on a couple of companies just to make sure everything was working.

Leslie woke up around five. She went next door to wake up Anne. “Dinner in an hour," she said, knocking on the door. She now had time to change her clothes and talk to William.

“What happened in Dallas?" she asked. "I thought you might head back to Mexico and do some traveling there. I never expected to find you in Texas.”

William chose his words wisely. "Texas was a side trip. Sweetheart, I've got a lot to tell you, but I can't right now. You need to trust me. Soon as Anne goes back to Paris, I'll fill you in on the details. Let's focus on having fun. Please, wait until Sunday.”

Leslie was caught off guard with William's response. "This sounds a bit mysterious. Are the casino's after you?" she asked.

"No, they aren't. After Anne is gone I'll give you the whole story."

"All right, but I want to hear it all. Anne purchased a ticket leaving from Pisa. She booked it when you said you wanted to visit that city. We can take the train to Pisa on Saturday and we'll get two more days in Cinque Terra."

"As soon as Anne leaves we'll sit down and cover what's happened to me since you left for France. All I can say is I'm not visiting casinos."

"I figured as much," Leslie said sharply. "You'd probably be in jail by now if you'd continued."

"I visited Herbie and Melinda to find out about day-trading. Success in the market led me to work for a company, but I'll explain more on Sunday. First, I'll need an hour tomorrow to complete a transaction. I'm getting a phone call from my manager soon. I'll be free to do what we want after tomorrow's transaction is completed."

"Do you still use your ability to predict stuff? I mean can you use the gift to invest in stocks?"

"To a large extent, yes. I'm no longer connected to the market. Also my ability seems to be lessening because I only feel the pressure for three days each week. All I can say is we are financially much better off than when you left for France."

"Really? How much would that be?" Her interest perked and she wanted to hear more.

“I'll tell you on Sunday. What I need from you is the name of a business or company you would support financially. I've already helped the animal group you like and a few others of my own.”

“What do mean? You sent money to them?

"Yes. It's the only way I can rationalize what I'm doing." William also knew it was the only way Leslie would put up with his working for The Company.

"Ok, I'll wait until Anne is gone before I grill you. I'll want to know everything but right now let’s get ready for dinner.” She loved William but she feared his decision making, without her help, could be reckless.

“Oh, another thing. I'm also Canadian.”

Leslie stepped back from William and glared at him. “We've been married for over twenty years and you're now telling me this? William, are you sure you're not in any trouble?”

“No, I'm not. But in case you see me getting Euros and using a Canadian passport, don't worry. Another partner is paying for this whole trip. He wants to be sure there's no connection between him and us. My Canadian name is James Paul.”

“James Paul. I like the name. Should we move to Canada so you can keep the new identity?" Leslie never held back when it came to sarcasm.

“Enough," William said. "I still want to enjoy our dinner."

Leslie added, "As long as you don't get hauled away by the Italian police in the middle of our meal, I'll be fine. After that, you've got a lot of explaining to do. Better give me some Euros in case they take you away. I'll need to pay for the meal and the hotel.”

“Here's a thousand Euros. That should cover everything. Tomorrow you and Anne can walk to the town north of Vernazza. I'll take the train, meet you two for dinner, and we can ride the ferryboat back."

"How'd you know about the ferryboat?"

"Says it right here in this information packet. I picked one up at the front desk after lunch. Like I said, I need to make a business transaction, and I'll probably take the afternoon.”

“Fine with me. Anne and I'll enjoy the walk. Tomorrow I'll give you the name of a company I support.”

“No hurry. We can transfer money at any time.”

The three travelers were now ready to climb the back streets of Vernazza to the Camere Elisabetta restaurant overlooking the plaza and the waters of the Ligurian Sea. Light sweaters were necessary for the evenings. The lack of customers allowed the trio to have their pick of window seats and enjoy the sun as it disappeared in the west.

“How'd you find this place?" William asked. "The ocean looks magnificent."

“The manager at the hotel," Leslie said. "We thought you'd appreciate dinner with a view.”

William ordered a stuffed pepper mostly filled with rice and vegetables. Leslie and Anne split one of the many pasta dishes available. They all tried a glass of the house wine.

"How bout the plan for you two walking to Monterosso al Mare tomorrow?" William asked after taking a few sips of wine. "Does that sound good? I can meet you for dinner around six."

“That'd be wonderful," Leslie agreed. "Let’s get a name of a restaurant from the hotel manager. Probably one near the waterfront will make it easy to find each other." Leslie always thought ahead.

After dinner, the three headed to their room and bed. Before reaching the stairs the Jason phone rang.

“Hello, William? Are you still awake? I realize it's getting late in Italy but I wanted to email some tortilla names so you could prepare for tomorrow." William motioned for Leslie and Anne to go up to the rooms. He needed to take this call.

“Hi, Jason. Yes, we're just finishing dinner and heading to our rooms. I'll get the names tonight or tomorrow morning.”

“There's only two this time. Not much is happening in the market, but a couple of strong possibilities are in the mix. My phone tells me you're in Vernazza on the Italian coast. I've seen Cinque Terre on a map, but never visited the place. Worth a trip or not?"

Jason was becoming more personal with every phone call to William.

“The town is beautiful and even more so without the crowds. You should come after you let go of the New York rat race.”

“Seeing Europe is a must when I retire," Jason answered. "Maybe I can hang it up sooner than expected if I don't live in New York. New Mexico and Arizona have interesting communities. After 'Sandy' hit the east coast I'm not so excited about living my later years in this area.”

“I agree," William said. "Arizona's not bad. I haven't traveled much in New Mexico, but Santa Fe was pretty damn nice.”

"I'll keep looking. The southwest seems to draw me in. I don't have ties to New York, like family or close friends, so who knows what I'll do?"

"Call, if you want my help, Jason. I've lived in Flagstaff and Phoenix. Different worlds and both have their good points."

"I'll let you know. Let's talk more tomorrow."

The call ended and William climbed the stairs to the apartment. When William entered the room he saw Leslie already in bed. The sound of the ocean waves crashing on the rocks below became an added sleep aide. Leslie was glad to see William again and the two enjoyed their intimacy under the blankets. Delayed sex was an added benefit to a good night's sleep.

*****

"Breakfast on the Plaza?" William asked Leslie. "Where we ate lunch yesterday works for me, and it's not far from the hotel."

"It's the only restaurant on the Plaza open this time of year," she answered. "Let's get Anne and head out."

After breakfast, the trio walked around the town and visited the few open shops. While sightseeing they heard about a rail strike scheduled to take place on Saturday. The trains would stop running after ten a.m. They headed to the station and booked three tickets to Pisa on the second train out.

The trio returned to their hotel and the sisters prepared themselves for the steep five-mile trek north. They wrapped sweatshirts around their waists for the evening return by boat. After lunch, the sisters started their hike. William returned to the hotel to wait for the NYSE to open.

While in his room William retrieved the company names in his email, read a little, and responded to Facebook friends. After a nap, he turned on his computer around four. Both tortillas seemed to be in the energy sector and were involved in nuclear waste management. Both had different approaches to the storing of the radioactive material with a half-life longer than the time since dinosaurs walked the earth.

When William applied his ability, he saw big jumps in the price of the stocks. This could be a large payday for Jason and The Company investors. What it meant for William's financial gain was not yet determined.

William pushed the button to let Jason know he was ready for the return call. A minute passed before the phone rang.

"Hello, William. How's the food in Italy?"

“I think this is going to be a big day for Mexican food and the tortilla business. Here are some numbers. They seem to be substantial.”

After receiving the information Jason's voice showed his excitement. “This is a big jump! I need to take care of things on my end right away. Thanks for the ingredients. I'll call again next week for an Italian dish."

Jason wanted to get the numbers out to The Company investors quickly. Buying at the current price, before the numbers started to rise, was of utmost importance. The difference could be in the millions.

William's job was finished for the week. It was now after five p.m. and the walk to the train station would take twenty minutes. There was plenty of time to find the girls before dinner.

He arrived in Monterosso around sunset and wandered down the main road towards the harbor. He found the two sisters in a scarf boutique on Main Street having *girl time.* They were trying on all the patterned and colored wraps in every size imaginable.

"Hi, girls. Looks like you're having fun with the local shopping," William said.

"Hi, William," Leslie answered. "This is fantastic. I bought a few warm shawls for the winter evenings in Mexico. Anne found this wrap from Afghanistan made from spun goat hair. It's perfect for Paris winters. I'm buying it for her as an early birthday gift."

"Do you have enough cash? I can see they're not cheap, and I only gave you a thousand Euros."

"I've enough for these scarves, but you'll need to get some more cash because I'm just getting started."

Leslie had no problem making the transition into having money.

“You know I love shopping with you, right?" William's sarcasm couldn't be disguised.

Leslie rolled her eyes and grinned. “Why don’t you head down to the waterfront and have a warm drink while we continue. Get some more Euros, and wait for us in the *Green Fig* restaurant.”

“Okay," William answered. "I'll meet you there in an hour." He headed towards the docks, found an ATM along the way, and got some more cash. He was putting the bills into his wallet when his personal phone rang. It startled William because he wasn't expecting a call.

“William, how are you?" It was Robert. "Enjoying the Italian seaside I suspect?”

“Yes, we are. We're having dinner soon so I've got a few minutes to talk. How'd Karl do? Did he get what he needed?”

“That's why I'm calling. After the diversion with the desk clerk, Karl placed a bug under the front desk near the phone used to call the manager. I didn't send him all the way to Italy just to do that. It was only the first step.”

“What do you mean the first step? I could've done what Karl did."

“The bug was to hear if any calls were made to the manager regarding your arrival. I was right."

“What do you mean you were right?”

“As soon as you left the lobby, the front desk made a call to the manager letting him know you'd checked in. Karl heard the conversation through the bug he put under the manager’s door. You couldn't have done that.”

“Oh, I don't know. Anyway, what happened next?" William felt the hairs on his arm starting to tingle.

“The manager made a call to Jason right away. Jason is monitoring you, William.”

“Really. I wonder what for?” William said.

“I don't know but I think he's watching out for his asset. You may have someone following you.”

“Wow, now I'm an asset." William paused for a moment. "Anyway, we're heading back to Pisa on Saturday to do some sight seeing. Leslie's loving Italy, without the tourists, so we're thinking about stretching our stay.”

“Fine, William. I'll call if anything else comes up. Just watch your back. That's all I know. I haven't linked Jason with the deaths at the hotel or the clinic. Karl might find out something soon.”

“Speaking of Karl, where's he staying? At the Tower Hotel?”

“No, he's staying at a hotel nearby. He was only at the Tower to place and retrieve the bugs. The less the hotel knows about Karl, the better. When you leave Pisa, and nothing turns up, I'm sending him home.”

“Where's home? In Europe or the States?”

“In the States for now. I use him for other jobs. He's too Americanized to live in Germany again.”

“One more thing, Robert. Do you know how The Company figures out how much to pay clients like me? I haven't been able to come up with an answer."

“I do," Robert answered. "Each investor pays into The Company 10% of their earnings into the working fund. The Company, in turn, pays people like you 10% of what they take in. The other monies are used to run the office and finance the research team investigating the businesses listed on the NYSE. You don't have to use any of your earnings so all the risk is theirs.”

“How'd you find this out? Never mind, I don't really want to know. I'm sure you have your ways. Here come the girls. I've got to go. You've got my schedule so call if you need to.”

“Goodbye, or as they say it in Italy, ciao." Robert ended the call.

William put his phone away just as Anne and Leslie reached the front door of the *Green Fig* where he'd arrived ten minutes before. He was sitting alone at one of the empty tables outside.

“I see you're carrying a few more bags since the scarf boutique. Did you find some other stores with 'have to have' items?”

“Yes, dear. Relax. I found a couple of earrings and some wool pants from another store near the harbor," Leslie said. "Anne bought a sweater from Peru. We're both tired, starving, and I need a glass of wine to unwind.”

William and the sisters went inside and sat at a window seat. Night-lights illuminated the waterfront since the sun was now gone for the day.

"I got the tickets for the boat at nine so there's no need to rush," William added.

“Did you finish your business this afternoon?" Anne asked after they ordered dinner. She'd finished her first glass of wine. The second round loosened her up enough to pry some more into William's life.

“Yes, I did. It didn't take long. I had to wait until New York woke up because of the six hour time difference.”

“What exactly is it that you do? I thought you're retired. Leslie never told me about this new job.”

“The reason she never told you is because I was hired after she left to be with you. It's a consulting position. I'm used for my expertise in the area of stock futures. I don’t do much other than give them my predictions how well a stock might do.” William smiled to himself after giving Anne his answer. He thought the response was pretty damn clever.

“They pay you to do that?" Anne asked.

"Yes, the material I read has to do with energy, and how America is shifting to different ways of obtaining it. Europe is way ahead of America in wind and solar.”

“That's true in France. We have nuclear plants, but we still use a lot of solar.”

“In America it's different. Oil is still king. Instead of putting money into alternative energy we're digging deeper for the stuff and getting into areas we know little about. That spill in the Gulf of Mexico is a perfect example.”

“You're right about that," Anne said. "Europe has lots of wind energy. Solar panels are on almost every apartment and office building. The lack of oil has forced Europe into alternative energy. Nuclear is big but they face the same problems wherever you have a plant. What do you do with the radioactive waste?"

"Funny you should mention that," William said. "That's what I did my latest projection on. There are a few companies that are coming up with ways to deal with this problem."

"Is the job worth the effort?" Anne continued her probing. "In other words, do they pay you well?"

"There're some good weeks depending upon the market. I received a bonus and a little cash to do some investigating in Europe. My trip here was paid for, and I got to meet up with you two. All in all, I think the side job is paying off." Again, William was pleased with his skillful reply.

The three finished dinner and caught the ferry to Vernazza. Having to get up early the next day was a concern. They didn't want to miss their train to Pisa.

*****

By sunrise William, Leslie, and Anne were packed and rolling their suitcases up the cobblestone road towards the train station. After boarding the train, William discovered it had Wi-Fi. He checked his emails and posted a few photos of Vernazza, taken by Leslie, on Facebook. William waited until Anne was reading her book before he opened the Cayman account.

"Damn," William said in a low voice. "I'm so friggin nervous I keep hitting the wrong access code." He finally hit the right numbers.

“Holy shit,” he whispered loud enough for Leslie to hear. "They did cough up the big bucks." $830,000 had been added to the account.

Leslie and I are millionaires, he thought. William almost went into shock.

Leslie leaned over to see the computer screen. When she saw the account balance, her eyes widened. She breathed a loud whisper. “What the hell?" She swiftly covered her mouth to avoid drawing attention from Anne or anyone else on the train. “That's ours?"

"Yes," William answered weakly.

"You've got some explaining to do, mister. I can hardly wait to hear about this one." Leslie said.

“As soon as Anne is gone, we'll sit down, and go over everything. Don't say a word to her about any of this. Seriously."

“All right, but I don't want to hear any more moaning when I spend $5 for a latte at Starbucks. The country may run on *Dunkin,* but I now see we can afford lots of coffee drinks, and not break the bank.”

Leslie is right, William thought. Starbucks was now in the budget.

“Before I close this account I need the names of two companies you support.”

Leslie handed the names of the companies to William and watched as he sent $100,000 to each one. She seemed pleased yet, at the same time, perplexed. She'd have to wait until Sunday to find out what William had been up to for the past two weeks.

The travelers arrived in Pisa after eleven a.m. William kept looking at Leslie to try and read her emotions. Was she angry or scared? Maybe both. He'd find out tomorrow.

The taxi to the Tower Hotel took longer than usual due to the strike. The roads were packed.

Luca was on duty when they checked in and stood to the left of the phone that went directly to the manager.

“Good to see you again, Mr. Ray. I hope your stay in Cinque Terra was relaxing.”

Knowing their arrival would be reported back to Jason in a matter of minutes, William made sure his answer remained generic.

“Happy to be back, Luca. This is my wife, Leslie, and my sister-in-law, Anne. I wanted to show them what a wonderful hotel you have, and experience it for a few days. We plan to visit the sights and stay longer in Italy. Tuscany has always been a place I've read about so we may head there afterward."

"Excellent, Mr. Ray. Be sure to visit Massa Marittima. It's a place where Europeans go. Most Americans haven't discovered it yet because they visit the main cities in Italy like Venice, Rome, and Florence. Exploring the smaller communities is worth the trip."

"Thanks, Luca. I'll remember that."

"Do you still have the vase with you?" Luca asked. "I can place it in the safe while you're here."

"Yes, I do." William smiled at Luca. "I'm not sending it back to the States by mail. It'd never end up in one piece, and be a pile of shards by the time it arrived."

After securing the vase the three travelers decided to have lunch in the hotel dining area overlooking the river.

"Let's see the Leaning Tower after lunch. Then we can walk around the other sights and come back for a rest." Leslie was already planning the day.

*****

Late afternoon the group returned to the hotel and the girls decided to stay in the room and talk. William found a spa near the hotel and was able to book an hour deep tissue session with a masseuse named Rafella. Bodywork is just what I need, William thought. Everyone needs a massage after becoming a millionaire.

After William came out of the spa and was walking back to the hotel, he noticed Karl, sitting on a bench, reading another German newspaper. Karl reached out with his right hand touching the bench. He wanted William to sit. William sat down a few feet away, stared forward, and took a sip of the bottled water Rafella had given him after the massage.

“You're being followed so I'll make this short," Karl said in a low voice while holding up the paper to cover his face. “Someone wants to know where you are at all times. There doesn't appear to be a connection between us so let’s keep it that way. I'm sure it's Jason and The Company. It’s dangerous for me to be seen with you. This may be our last meeting. I'm still investigating the clinic. You should get back to the hotel before a connection can be made.”

William stood up, did a side stretch, and proceeded down the street to the hotel. He didn't say a word to Karl.

After reaching the hotel, William noticed a woman in the lobby reading a magazine. She was well dressed, and he remembered seeing her when checking into the hotel. She had changed her clothes but her spiked haircut caused her to stand out from the crowd.

William took the elevator to the room. The girls were awake and talking about their retreat. They were also making plans when they'd see each other again.

"I think we can fly over to visit Anne next spring. She lives near the Louvre, and staying with her in Paris is no problem." Leslie studied Williams face looking for a positive response.

"No problem here. I'd love to see where you live," William said.

“All right then. We'll put the trip on our calendar for the month of May." Leslie looked forward to visiting Anne in her Paris flat.

"How about this idea for our last night in Pisa," William added. "Luca told me his brother is the owner and chef of a restaurant nearby. It's called the *Olive Tree* and Luca said he could get us in before the regular dinner crowd arrived."

The girls agreed to the plan. A little after six they were dressed, and in the lobby to get directions from Luca.

"It will take you ten minutes at the most to reach the restaurant," Luca said.

William quickly scanned the room to see if the spike haired-woman was still around. His instincts had him on high alert, but she was nowhere in sight.

The three reached the *Olive Tree,* and Luca's brother was at the door to greet them.

"Luca told me you were coming. Happy to meet you," he said. "My name is Rondo."

"This is my wife, Leslie, and her sister, Anne. My name's William." The two men shook hands.

"I'm so glad Americans are starting to discover my restaurant. We specialize in authentic Italian dishes but at the same time realize other nationalities don't eat like we do in Italy. Instead of the full course meals you can try several dishes in small amounts. That way you can get the flavor of the food and not overload the stomach."

"We're mainly vegetarians," Leslie said.

"Not a problem," said Rondo. "I'll prepare four separate dishes in petite portions. With a small salad and a bottle of the house wine, you'll have the complete Italian experience."

The three were seated and the wine arrived shortly afterward. In Italy wine is served with every course. The restaurant began to fill, but mostly with the bar crowd. The food started to arrive after twenty minutes. Italians never hurry when it come to a meal.

After dinner, William sat back in his chair to take in the

ambiance of the restaurant. Suddenly he noticed a hairstyle he'd seen before. Sitting at the bar was the woman from the hotel. She was with another woman having a glass of wine.

The girlfriend of *Miss Spiky hair* was facing their table, while the mystery lady had her back to them. William was now positive she was following him. As he and the girls walked out of the restaurant, William gave another glance back at the bar. The girlfriend was watching him, but turned away as soon as their eyes met. "I'll be seeing you again," William said in a low voice.

The cool evening prevented the three from walking around the neighborhood. Neither Anne nor Leslie visited the bar scene, so that was out of the picture. Anne said she wanted to write some emails to her friends in Paris and pack, so he said goodnight and went to her room.

Leslie checked out one of the French foreign movies popular a few years ago. The series of three movies each had a title of one of the colors of the French flag. *Red, White and Blue*. She picked *Red* and settled in for an evening of subtitles.

William fell asleep during the middle of the movie and woke up early with a blanket over him without any recollection of the movie ending. Leslie was under the covers and sound asleep.

While sitting with his thoughts, William started to make plans for the future. He now knew they couldn't live in San Felipe any longer. After what he'd been through, playing Mexican Train Dominoes, Bridge, and visiting the pool would never fill the void after this adventure ended.

Leslie began to stir. It was now early morning, and she wanted to get up at sunrise to make sure Anne got on the train to Paris.

A nine a.m. ticket had been purchased with only one transfer in Milan. The continental breakfast, plus a few egg dishes in the hotel buffet, filled all three of them. A cab to the station gave them plenty of time to say their goodbyes. Kisses and hugs and she was gone.

Instead of returning with the taxi, William went to the car rental a block away from the station. William chose an Alfa Romeo station wagon for two main reasons. Good gas mileage, style, and room for their luggage. William and Leslie decided to drive south to Tuscany and the town of Massa Marittima.

"We're going to Venice," William told Luca as he checked out of the Tower Hotel. His intent was to throw Jason off and leave the spiky hair woman behind. William had now earned his white belt towards becoming a full-fledged spy.

I might as well have some fun playing this game, William thought. I hope that woman enjoys Venice.

Chapter 16

Karl returned to his room with a bag of snacks and a couple liter bottles of Italian beer. A soccer game between Germany and England was scheduled to start in five minutes. He had his shoes off and was relaxing on the bed when the game started.

Downstairs in the lobby, a man walked into the hotel. A driver had picked him up at the train station and drove him to the hotel. The man checked into the hotel and took the elevator to the third floor. After entering his room, he opened his bag, extracted the tools he needed, and turned to leave. He opened his apartment door, proceeded to the staircase, and walked up one flight of stairs. He had the room number of the target. He stopped in front of room 412. The hall was empty. The man could hear a soccer game on the television behind the door. He reached into his coat pocket and grabbed the cloth drenched with chloroform. He knocked.

As the door opened the man quickly placed the cloth over Karl's face with one hand and the back of his head with the other. He pushed Karl back into the apartment and kneed him in the groin at the same time. Karl went down, still holding the gun he was trying to remove from his back holster when he answered the door. It was too late.

Behind closed doors, the body of Karl was dragged to the bed, and placed on top of the covers. The soccer game was left on. The mystery man worked quickly removing Karl's sock from his left foot and injecting the area between the big and second toe. The drug would take a few minutes to work. The mystery man waited.

He reached out with his gloved finger to check the German's pulse. Karl was dead. The man quickly scanned the room for any signs of a struggle, and then backed out of the room and down the staircase to the third floor.

Upon reaching his own apartment, he put the medical tools into his bag and left. The rear exit of the hotel took the man to the alley street where he hailed a taxi. The next train back to Paris was in an hour and he would be on it. Mission accomplished.

Chapter 17

By eleven a.m. the Rays were on the main road going south. The A12 provided the beauty of the Italian countryside, as well as time for William to tell Leslie what he been doing for the last two weeks. Leslie started the conversation.

“We have several hours of driving ahead of us. You promised to fill me in, and I'm ready to burst, William, so let’s hear it.”

“All right, but you first need to swear to secrecy. Are you ready to do that?"

“Does that mean I can't tell anyone in our family?" Leslie seemed worried.

“You can't tell a soul, especially family members. This is for your protection and theirs.”

“What've you done, William? Am I going to be sorry or happy after I hear this story?”

“There'll be no choice until you agree to the silence clause. I'm serious, Leslie. This is bigger than both of us, and you need to trust me.”

“Okay, but I'm not too excited so far. The last thing you told me was about your visit to Herbie and Melinda's to learn about stock trading. It seems you learned a lot more than what you intended. It's like that line in that Nancy Sinatra song. *What You Know You Ain't Had Time to Learn*." Leslie made her best attempt at a joke, to ease the tension.

"Does okay mean you agree to the silence? I need to hear you say it because it's important. Any leaks may put others in danger."

"Yes, I agree, but this danger crap is making me uptight. What'd you do?"

"I'll tell you the whole story, but don't ask any questions until the end. My mind is on overload as it is. Interrupting my train of thought might derail any hope of giving you all the details." The comment was William's attempt at a joke.

William began to unravel his adventure after leaving Peter's home in New River. He left nothing out. The phone call, meeting with Jason in Santa Fe, the Cayman Island account, the conversations, and meeting with Robert. Everything. When he finished he told Leslie the real reason he came to Europe and Pisa. By now she was ready to burst.

"Lay it on me, Leslie. I know you have questions," William said.

"So you're telling me we're now rich because you gave a person named Jason closing numbers of a few stocks on the New York exchange?" Leslie could hardly believe the story she'd just heard.

“Yes, I think that sums it up.”

“William, I don't know what to say. I'm completely at a loss for words.”

After Leslie said this, William thought she could be going into shock. Lost for words was not a term she ever used. She was never at a loss for a verbal response.

“The most redeeming outcome of this situation is your ability to donate to organizations in need. The jury is still out on the idea of helping billionaires make more money. I'll get back to you on that one when my mind finally settles down.”

William drove in silence, making only the occasional comment regarding the scenery of the countryside.

Leslie eventually recovered and asked her first question. “How long do you plan on working for Jason?” Her question broke the silence and startled William.

“I don't know. With Robert in the equation, I've agreed to help out in any way I can until we find out who's involved in the deaths of the two previous clients. Robert's not sure if Jason has anything to do with the clinic. He thinks Jason is only keeping an eye on us or at least me.”

“Is he keeping an eye on you while we're in Europe?"

Leslie's asked.

“I think so. Robert has a man in Pisa trying to find out. I met Karl on the flight to Italy, and as far as I know he's still in Pisa. When I last spoke to him he said he'd remain near the Tower Hotel, and find out anything he can about the clinic.”

“If this business deal gets dangerous can you pull out?" Leslie was ready to pull out right now.

"I could pretend my ability stopped. Jason also assured me I could quit at any time. The problem with either plan is I wouldn't be able to help Robert.”

“So, you're committed to helping Robert? How does that work? I mean, what does Robert expect you to do?" Leslie's tone was a bit hostile in her attempt to cover up her nervousness.

“Not much. All I did was create a distraction for Karl. He's the one doing all the spying. We just need to continue our vacation.”

The spiky-haired woman was not mentioned. William hoped she was on her way to Venice and would be out of the picture.

“I just saw a sign for Massa Marittima," Leslie said. "Do we have a room booked?”

“Finding a room in November is not going to be a problem.

It's the offseason and the rates will be dirt cheap."

"William, you're a millionaire. You don't have to think about hotel rates anymore. Get over yourself."

"You're right. I'm sorry. This money thing takes getting used to."

William took the turnoff to Massa Marittima and drove through more farmland. Soon he could see the town perched on top of a hill. There were stone walls surrounding the towers, and castle- like structures. The road up to Massa took them to a parking center near the main church.

The surrounding buildings had a medieval feel, and the cobblestone streets were too narrow for cars. This was a walking town only. The tourist office was located near the parking lot where William found the Massa Alta hotel. A room, overlooking the plaza, provided them with a first class view of the town square.

After checking in, the *Jason* phone rang. William said, "I've got to take this call, Sweetheart. Go and find us somewhere to eat."

Leslie left and William pushed the receive button.

"William, how are you? You're not in Pisa. My phone says you're in Tuscany in a town called Massa Marittima. Is that how you pronounce it?"

“Yes, I think so. You seemed surprised. Did you expect us to be somewhere else?" William added the quiet jab into the conversation because he'd thrown Jason a curve ball back in Pisa.

“I knew you wanted to tour for a while, but I expected you'd be going to the typical tourist's spots.”

“Like Venice?" William laughed to himself.

“Yes, like Venice or Rome,” Jason said. He sounded perturbed.

“Well, we changed our minds and decided to visit Tuscany. Massa Marittima turned out to be perfect. We're just now heading out to explore the shops and have lunch.”

"Let me get right to business then. I'm sending you another recipe for our next dish. By the way, did you see how well the last meal turned out? We're all surprised.”

“Yes, and I want to thank the different chefs for their contributions. It made me feel my part in the creation of the menu was appreciated. The number of chilies blew me out of the water,” William added.

“We all did well. Before I send a couple of tortilla ideas, my boss asked me if you might be interested in a different type of restaurant. This is not the time to discuss it because you're heading out the door. I'll call later when I can explain it in more detail. All I need to know is if you're open to trying something different."

"How could I say no to at least hearing the proposal?" William said. "It sounds like a subject as important as this should be discussed in person."

"You're right, William. First, let me send you the tortillas. I'll call and arrange a meeting with an employee in Italy. That person can go over the details and see if you're interested. I just need to know where you'll be on Friday."

"Why on Friday?" William asked.

"It will take my assistant a few days to reach you."

"I'll get back to you tomorrow," William answered. "That'll give us enough time to plan our trip."

"That works. I'll let you go. Talk to you tomorrow."

William hung up and went down to the lobby to wait for Leslie to return. William felt his blood sugar dropping. He needed food. A few minutes later, Leslie arrived.

"I found this pottery store near the hotel," she said. "I bought a wall hanging plate showing the Tuscany countryside. It'd look great on the fireplace mantel. They'll even ship it home for us. I only need to pay and give the woman our address."

"Leslie, I think you should have everything shipped to your brother's house in New River. When we return to the States I don't think we'll want to continue living in Mexico. Too much has changed."

The look on Leslie's face went from normal to extreme joy. William knew she'd be pleased. Mexico was not her favorite place to live and she took the news well.

He continued. "I love the slower lifestyle down there, but I know you miss the faster pace in the States. We can decide where we want to be later, but for now, I think Peter's address would be best."

Leslie agreed. From the tone of her voice, William could tell she was more excited about the move back to the States than the plate she'd purchased thirty minutes ago.

"I'm really hungry. Let's eat first before we walk around," William pleated.

"Fine with me, Sweetheart. I want to see more of this city. I love it here. We should stay for a few nights at least," Leslie exclaimed.

A café near the plaza was still serving lunch. They found two different entrees and settled back in their chairs.

"How was the call from Jason? Has anything changed that's caused you more stress? You seem a little uptight."

"I'm not sure. He sent me the names of two companies to

look at, and then he offered me a different job."

"Wait, a different job than the one you're doing now?"

"Yes, but I've no idea what it is. Tomorrow we need to know where we'll be on Friday. Jason plans on sending one of his representatives to talk to me."

"Have you agreed to do this job?" Leslie's voice changed, indicating her displeasure at the idea.

"No, I haven't agreed to anything," William said quietly. "When this meeting happens you should be shopping or doing something else. That way we'll have time to discuss it together and then I'll tell Robert about it."

"Why would you want another job with them, and go further towards the dark side?"

Leslie's reference to Star Wars meant she still had her sense of humor, William thought.

"I want to help Robert, but anything that puts us in danger is where I draw the line."

"I'm happy you've drawn a line somewhere," Leslie said. "You seem to say yes to Robert all the time."

"Can you agree with my taking the meeting alone? I'm only finding out what they want."

“The meeting without me is fine. You know I hate technical stuff. One thing I do want to take care of is an increase in our life insurance. If anything happens to either one of us, I want the girls to benefit.”

William did his best to ease Leslie's concerns. "We can do that. I've already set up the Cayman account, with you as the primary, and our daughters as the secondary recipients. I made that change after the second deposit.”

“You've been thinking this through." Her tension eased a bit. "Keep this up and you won’t need me any longer.”

William knew he had to be careful with his next comment. “Sweetheart, I'll always need you. You know that.”

“Good answer, bucko. We might get through this after all,” Leslie said.

“Where do you think we should be on Friday?" William asked.

"Let's think about it for a while and discuss it later."

The last hours of light found the Rays exploring the streets and marking on a map the stores they wanted to return to the next day. They returned to their room and placed the leftovers from lunch in the office refrigerator. The hotel had a copy of the movie *Blue*, and Leslie was determined to read the subtitles and continue the series.

Just as they set up the movie, William's private phone rang. He motioned for Leslie to continue watching while he went into the separate sitting area.

“William. I can't find Karl!” It was Robert and his voice was in a panic. He hurried through the sentence in such a rush that William thought he was speaking a foreign language.

“Slow down, Robert. I can barely understand you. What about Karl?”

“I can't locate him," Robert replied. "I use a special phone with him, and the connection tells me the number can't be reached. This is not like Karl. He hasn't called for two days. When I tried to call him yesterday a code told me the phone's out of service.”

William's thoughts were racing. “The last time I saw Karl was when I left a spa near my hotel. He said we couldn't have contact again. He was going to hang around Pisa until we left Europe. That was two days ago. What are you going to do?”

“I'm not sure. Karl was my connection to the Tower Hotel and assigned to find the clinic's location. I can get another person, but it'll take some time.”

“What do you want me to do?" William asked. "I have a schedule to keep with Jason and a meeting with one of his people on Friday."

“A meeting? What kind of meeting?"

"The Company wants to offer me another job. I have no idea what it is."

"My head isn't clear right now," Robert continued. "My advice is to take the meeting but in a closer location to Pisa. By Friday I should know more about Karl."

"Maybe we'll cut our trip short and return next spring instead of traveling all over Italy," William said.

“Not a bad idea. Hopefully, Karl is fine, but I don't have a good feeling about this at all.”

“All right, Robert. Keep in touch." William hung up. He felt sorry for Robert, but there was nothing he could do.

The movie was still playing when William entered the bedroom. Leslie was deeply entrenched as she focused on the subtitles while following the plot. She looked up briefly and gave William a glance that asked if everything was all right. He shrugged his shoulders, and told her, using body language, to continue watching the movie.

William went down to the office refrigerator to retrieve the leftovers saved from lunch. There were plates in the room and some small airline size bottles of wine in the cupboard. William heated the meal and poured the wine. The food was almost as good as it was during lunch. The wine helped. Reheated food in a Medieval Italian town, while watching a French movie with subtitles, thought William. We really know how to live the high-life.

William returned to the bedroom and the couple ate in silence. Sleep took over for William before the movie ended.

“Are you awake?" Leslie asked. "The movie's over. We've got to get the last one. Did you watch any of it?”

“No, I missed most of it. The call was from Robert. He can't find his German partner, Karl. Something about Karl’s phone being out of order, and not hearing from him for two days. He also made a suggestion.”

“You mean a change of plans?” Leslie asked.

“Possibly. Winter's approaching, so how about a return in the spring when we come to visit Anne. The weather will be warmer and we can take her with us if she wants to travel.”

Leslie's expression told William she just might go for it.

"Rushing through this country doesn't do it justice," William continued. "It’s like flipping through a National Geographic magazine, and seeing the pictures without getting a real feeling for the place."

“Do you mean we should cut the vacation short, and head back to the States?” Leslie asked.

“No, I still need to take the meeting on Friday. We can remain as long as you want and then head back to New Mexico. We still have to pick up our car in Albuquerque. We can be back in Mexico by Thanksgiving. Another alternative is to enjoy the holiday in New River, and then drive south.”

“That was a quick change. Taking Anne with us next spring is a good idea. Her Italian is almost as fluent as her French."

“So you're fine with the change in schedule because I felt a little rushed," William said.

“The plan's fine. I do think we should stay with Peter for Thanksgiving.”

Leslie and William discussed their trip for a while and then decided to sleep. Leslie wanted to get an early start and revisit the stores on her list.

*****

An early wake-up, breakfast in the small dining room downstairs, and shopping. The morning hours went by quickly. By two o'clock, William decided he'd done enough exploring and adding to the economy of Italy. The New York stock exchange would open soon so he said goodbye to Leslie.

The Wi-Fi at the hotel had a powerful connection. Medieval town or not, the 21st century had arrived. William barely felt that the pressure in his head and was not sure about his ability.

When the market finally opened William tried to concentrate on the first stock. He read the opening numbers, but nothing came to him. He tried the second company and still nothing.

I think I'm done, thought William. A burden had been removed from his shoulders, and a smile crossed his face. What a relief, he thought.

William decided to wait a day before calling Jason. Leslie returned from her afternoon of shopping several hours later, and by then William was awake from his nap.

"How did the market go? Did the companies have any big gains?" she asked.

"I think I may be finished. Nothing happened and the pressure's gone. I tried both companies, and then I fell asleep."

"No kidding. Is it over? I'm actually relieved," she said with a sigh. "We've got plenty of money and we don't need anything right now."

"I agree," William said. "This whole experience has been spooky at best. I feel as if a load of rocks has been surgically removed from my shoulders. I'll wait and call Jason tomorrow. This news may change the job offer, so I may not need the meeting at all."

"Maybe we could just stay in the area for a few more days," Leslie said. "We have a car, so can explore the surrounding countryside."

"Great idea, Sweetheart. If Jason still wants me to talk to his rep, we'll have them come here to Massa Marittima."

"That works. Let's get some dinner and decide where to go tomorrow. We'll have two days of exploring. This is more fun than spending our time driving in a car all over Italy."

Chapter 18

"Still no word from Karl?" Robert asked Alan.

"No word yet. What'll we do?" Alan could see Robert was upset.

"If The Company got wind of Karl snooping around Pisa, there's no telling what they'd do. Can you call the local police station in Pisa and see if anyone died who might fit Karl's description? I have to start with the worst-case scenario."

"Not a problem. It might take a while. Shall I call you if I find something?" Alan asked.

"Yes. I'll be in the living room. Can I get you a beer? I know I need one."

"Thanks, but I'm good."

Robert was on his second beer when Alan called him from the office.

"Robert, I think I found something. Look at this."

Alan had the photo of a person who fit Karl's' description. The police in Pisa faxed it to him.

"It's him," yelled Robert. He couldn't believe his eyes. "That's Karl."

Chapter 19

William and Leslie changed into warmer clothes for the cool evening and found their way back to the same restaurant where they ate lunch. During the meal, they asked the owner, Raul, about places they could visit near Massa Marittima in the next two days. He told them the island of Elba, where Napoleon was sent after his downfall, was not far. A drive to Siena could be done the following day.

When dinner was over and they were back in their room, William tried one more time to focus on the companies. Nothing.

William pushed the button on the Jason phone and waited a couple of minutes before it rang.

"William! This is a late call for you. Aren't you usually asleep by now?"

"Yes, but I was waiting until the day ended in New York. I have some bad news regarding the tortilla business. I kept trying to see the right recipe, but nothing happened."

"You usually call much earlier. I suspected something like this might have happened. I told you a month ago the sight wouldn't last forever. So far your ability lasted the longest of all the other cooks, so you've had a good run."

"Really? Longer than anyone else?" William's chest puffed

a little.

“The condition of the other clients was similar. One day you have it, the next day you don’t.”

“That about sums it up for me. Does this new development affect the meeting with your rep?” William asked.

“Actually no. Your change has come at a perfect time. The meeting is still on if you want it. We only need to know where to meet on Friday."

“Leslie and I've decided to cut our Italian trip short. Winter is making travel a challenge. We'll be staying here in Massa Marittima through Friday and then head back to Milan.”

“All right then," Jason said. "No more traveling for now.”

“Have your person come to the Massa Alta hotel, and I'll reserve a room for them. They could stay overnight, and we'll meet at a nearby restaurant.”

“I'll have her arrive Thursday night, so leave a message at the desk. Include the time, place, and maybe draw a little map.”

“How will I recognize her? You did say *her*, right?”

“Yes, she has a picture of you. Be on time, and find a private table."

“All right Jason, but I'm coming to the meeting alone.”

“That's fine. I'll call afterward, and discuss any future plans.”

“Thanks for everything, Jason. When you retire you must come to this place. It's a medieval town with castles, churches, walls, and great shopping.”

“Thanks for the tip, William. I may retire sooner than expected.”

The call ended. William's head hit the pillow and he fell fast asleep. It was the best nights rest he'd experienced since the blood clot last October. The stress of having the sight was now gone and he felt free again.

*****

After breakfast the Rays gathered what they'd need for a day trip, drove to the town of Livorno, and caught the ferry to the island of Elba. The main town of Portoferraio on the island provided quite a view. William rented a scooter in order to circle the island and Leslie rode on the back. After a quick stop at the mansion estate of Napoleon, they decided against a tour and continued on the road headed towards the opposite side of the island.

While eating lunch near the boat harbor in the small town of Procchio, William's private phone rang. Leslie was using the ladies room at the time. It was Robert.

“He’s dead.” Robert's voice was heavy.

“Who’s dead?”

“Karl. They found him in his hotel room. The police report said Karl died in his sleep from a massive heart attack."

“No shit. Did he really die from a heart attack?” William asked.

“The autopsy confirmed it was cardiac arrest, but they also found a puncture wound in between his big and second toe on his left foot. Traces of a mystery compound were in his blood. I'm having the substance identified here in the States. By the way, where are you now?"

"We are on the island of Elba. We decided to stay in the area for a few days before the meeting on Friday."

William wasn't as connected with Karl as Robert was, but he still felt sorry for the man.

“Oh, by the way, I'm normal again.”

“What do you mean you're normal again?”

"I no longer have the sight. My business with The Company is over. The funny thing is, Jason still wants me to have the meeting with his rep.”

“When did this happen?”

“Yesterday. I couldn't come up with any closing amounts. The pressure in my head is gone. Usually, it goes away and then returns. This time, it never came back.”

“No kidding. And you told Jason?”

“I told him last night. He didn't seem upset at all. He said the change came at a perfect time, whatever that means. He also said I had the longest run of all the clients he's worked with.”

“Welcome back to the real world, William. The ability can be addictive. I love controlling stuff, so it was a disappointment to me when the ability stopped.”

“For me, it was a total relief," William said. "Hooking up with Jason made us a lot of money, and it beat playing the blackjack tables across the country. I'm glad it's over."

“Good for you, William. Listen, I've got a feeling the meeting on Friday has something to do with the clinic. If it does maybe we can find more information about that place, and its location.”

“Why do you think it has something to do with the clinic?” William asked.

“Just a feeling. I get them a lot, and usually, they pan out. If you can get inside, maybe we can really find out what happened to my friends. This whole setup smells like murder, and we've no one, other than you, to get answers."

William thought, just when I thought I was done with the spy business, Robert hits me with the, '*we have no one other than you',* comment.

"I'll do what I can, but if this smells risky, I'm out. The meeting is on Friday. I'll let you know what they want after it's over."

"That's fine. By then I should know what the compound in Karl's blood is. If you discover the location of the clinic, I'll try to get another person on the inside. Whatever is happening, we need to find out what it is."

Leslie returned to the table. "Robert, Leslie's starting to give me the stare. She wants to order lunch. I'll call you after the meeting on Friday."

"William, I appreciate what you're doing. I'm upset about the people who died, so I can't let this go. Also, don't forget, I still have your car."

"We'll fly into New Mexico from Europe after changing planes in New York. We should arrive sometime next week."

"Good, I think you have a stop in Atlanta before landing here. Then you and Leslie can see where I live. Plan on staying for a couple of days before heading back to Mexico. We have a lot to discuss.”

“Talk to you on Friday,” William said. The phone call ended.

“I ordered one of the pasta dishes for us to split," Leslie said. "The extra salad and maybe a dessert should fill us for the ride back to the docks. We need to make the four o’clock boat, and be on the road before dark.” Leslie was thorough.

“Something's bothering you. What is it?" William asked.

“Just when I thought you might be done with all this Robert and Jason business, we get deeper into it. What's going on, William?”

"All I'm doing is feeding Robert information. Nothing more."

“Do you know anything about the meeting on Friday?" Leslie asked.

“No, I don't. When Jason told me about The Company, all he wanted me to do was listen. I'm sure I'll have some time to think about this offer as well.”

“What if they want you to stay in Italy? What'll we do?” Leslie still sounded stressed.

“Let’s not get ahead of ourselves. I really don't know what the job offer is. I agreed to the first job with Jason and look what happened. We're now millionaires. Let's find out what they want and then decide what to do."

William decided not to mention Karl's death. Leslie was barely coping with the meeting on Friday. A death might put her over the top, and that would be hard to deal with.

"All right, William. Let's hurry up with lunch. I'd like to walk around town before heading back."

*****

On the voyage back to the mainland, dark clouds started to gather in the north. Rain could strike before they reached their hotel. Half way back to Massa the storm hit. It was a real downpour including lightening. It felt like a good old fashion Monsoon cloudburst they were accustomed to getting in Arizona.

When they arrived in Massa the rain had subsided. They had dinner at Raul's restaurant and shared their day with him.

"Tomorrow we're going to Siena. I think we can get there in a few hours, Raul, what do you think?" William said.

"Maybe a little longer. Depends on how fast you drive. Americans tend to drive slower than Italians. The people in Italy think they're all related to racecar drivers. My wife even tells me I drive too slow. I, how you say, bite my tongue off?"

"Bite my tongue. It means keep quiet," Leslie said.

“Yes. I just bite my tongue. I drive slower than most who live here but Egypt is not known for car racing. Camel racing maybe." Raul was from Egypt, and his wife was Italian.

They finished dinner, thanked Raul for the visit, and promised they'd be back the next night for dinner.

The next day the visit to Siena was full and rewarding for the Rays. Leslie continued her Christmas shopping, filling up the back seat of the car like Santa's sleigh. The weather cleared, making the trip enjoyable, and by three o'clock they started back to Massa.

They arrived before sunset. Leslie dropped by a luggage store to purchase a trunk for her presents, while William went to the front desk to leave a note for Jason’s representative. The desk clerk said there was a reservation for her, but she hadn't checked in. A small map was included with the note, directing the rep to Raul’s restaurant.

The Rays planned to check out of the hotel the next day after the meeting, and drive back to Pisa. They'd spend one more night at the Tower Hotel and then catch a train to Milan.

The dinner at Raul’s was a happy occasion with promises of a return next spring. Back at the hotel, Leslie rented the last of the French film series, *White*, and planned to watch it while packing. William used the time to catch up with emails.

By ten o'clock the movie ended and the Rays were ready for bed. William would pack in the morning.

Chapter 20

Paul McClure took the reins of The Company in 2005. The twenty-two millionaires were just beginning to work together to form their investment team. Every one of the men had accumulated their wealth by different means. Paul's grandfather, like the Kennedy family during prohibition, smuggled alcohol to the States.

Grandfather Sean and his older brother, Ian, owned a small Irish whiskey distillery near Dublin. They made a modest income supplying the various pubs throughout the region with their family brand. A small amount was being shipped to New York to an Irish pub owned by another cousin. Prohibition shut him down as well as many bar owners. As the saying goes, 'when you're dealt lemons, make lemonade'. In this case, it became Irish whiskey.

The shipping routes in 1922 were already established and now the demand was increased. All the McClure clan needed to do was to ramp up production. First, they bought out two other distilleries near Dublin. They kept everyone working just as they had before. The only difference was the factories did not shut down at the end of the day. An all night shift in all three of the whiskey distilleries more than quadrupled their production. Employment was high and the wages were good.

There was no need to try and hide the whiskey being shipped into the U.S. because Canada was a safe port of entry. After it arrived in Canada the American mafia took over.

Gangsters had their established route into the U.S. and paid top dollar for the cases brought in. The McClure family made millions without breaking the law. They just made a lot of whiskey, shipped it to Canada, and let the mafia do all the dirty work.

The McClure family made sure their cousin in New York received his supply to keep him going. He ran a small *Speak Easy* in a hidden back room bar during the failed attempt at Prohibition. When a man is thirsty he will pay anything for a drink.

By the time the 18th Amendment was appealed, the McClure family had made enough money to purchase estates surrounding Dublin or built large homes in Martha's Vineyard in Massachusetts. Grandfather Sean had moved to the States by then, while brother Ian ran the Irish branch of the business. Two more distilleries were built in Ireland. Five Irish whiskey plants were now shipping thousands of cases every week, supplying the thirsty hordes in America after the 21st Amendment appealed Prohibition in 1933.

Paul McClure, the second son of Sean, was educated at Notre Dame, a good Irish University. He wasn't interested in the family booze business. He took his inheritance and started investing in the New York Stock exchange in the 60's. Paul got together with a few other friends and began an investment club. By the eighties and nineties, they were becoming a force in the market.

By 2003 The Company was made up of twenty-three multi-millionaires and membership had closed. In '04' the first people who could predict the future and impact the stock market, reached the attention of Paul and his group. They established a network of spies in the medical world and were now in the *brain bleed* business.

People like Jason Burns were hired to manage the population who had the sight, while the research team provided the managers with names of the stock companies to study. World events were watched carefully. Everything affected the stock market. Storms, wars, elections and even drinking water were all part of the game.

The Company invested with little risk. They had the winning lottery ticket each week. Most of them invested in a few companies that took a loss in profits, thus diverting suspicion away from them. Their gains greatly outnumbered their losses.

A fund was created to pay the clients who were making them the richest men in the world. People like William and Robert made hundreds of thousands of dollars with their ability. Money was not the issue. The Company members wanted more.

*****

Paul McClure's phone rang. It was Smith, the head of his security team.

"Mr. McClure, we've taken care of the problem."

"Good job, Smith. Did you give the police in Pisa what they would need to make this go away?"

"The man's death was documented as a heart attack and the authorities are shipping the body back to Germany."

"Do you think he was working for someone?" Paul asked.

"We're not sure. All we know is he hung around the Tower Hotel but stayed in another one nearby. He was asking a lot of questions regarding our two previous clients at the Tower, but we don't know if he found out any information. We believe the location of the clinic is still secret. If someone out there is snooping around, they might send another person to follow up."

"Let me know if anything else happens. I'll take care of this on my end."

The call ended. McClure had a decision to make and decided to do so without putting it to a vote. As soon as the dosage problem was taken care of, he would shut down the Italian operation. A new location was in the beginning stages and much closer than Europe. Someone might have found out about the clinic in Italy so shutting down was a smart move.

Chapter 21

The next morning William arrived early at Raul’s restaurant and found a seat in the back corner near the bathrooms. Nobody likes to sit near the bathrooms so William knew they wouldn't be disturbed. Ten minutes later a woman walked in and William recognized her right away. As she approached the table, William stood up and held out his hand.

“Hello, my name's William Ray. How was your trip to Venice?”

The woman held out her hand with a questioning look on her face.

“My name is Sonja Mastnak. How'd you know I came from Venice?”

“Because I sent you there. Please sit down. It's rude of me to put you on the defensive.”

Sonja sat down and the waiter brought them each a cappuccino to sip as they got to know each other.

“Sonja, I'm not trying to upset you, but I know you've been following me since Pisa. Maybe you're new at the 'tailing' business, but I want to give you some advice.”

“Some advice? Okay, I’m listening,” she said, barely concealing her anger.

“Change your hairstyle when doing undercover work. You've got a trendy haircut, and it looks great. Problem is, people like me notice things like that. By the way, the Venice escapade was fun, wasn't it?"

“Sending me to Venice was fun? Maybe for you,” she said.

“I told the Tower Hotel I was going there. I realized you'd find out and follow us.”

Sonja still seemed perturbed. “You're right Mr. Ray. I'm not a professional spy. I was hired to keep an eye on you the entire time you were in Europe. You're valuable to Jason and The Company he works for. I started following you in Milan when you boarded the train to Pisa. I sat in the next car so you didn't notice me. I'm sorry if I made you uneasy, but I'm really here to protect you.”

“Protect me from what?" William raised his voice.

“Please, Mr. Ray. Try and keep it down. You've got a gift or should I say, *had*? Jason told me you're back to normal. The timing couldn't be more perfect. What I'm going to tell you concerns the opportunity to recreate your previous state.”

“Recreate it? What do you mean recreate it? How do you make a medical accident happen again?” William was getting worked up.

“That's exactly why we've been monitoring you since the beginning. A few years ago all The Company could do was find people who had the sight. Each person they found was presented with the same options. Work for The Company or use the ability on your own. Many joined, and after a few weeks their condition was gone.”

“What about those who didn't want to work for the Company? What happened to them?”

“We monitored a few of them. Some did well on their own, while others headed to the racetracks or casinos. After their condition terminated, alcohol and drugs often took over."

"Did they all keep quiet about their ability?" William asked.

“Mostly. One person bragged about what he could do and word spread. When he arrived in any gambling site he was blackballed. He disappeared while staying in Vegas.”

“Disappeared? What do you mean he disappeared?”

"We think he's buried somewhere out in the desert. Casinos take their moneymaking ventures seriously. Anyone with a gift like yours was warned if they were caught. Those who didn't put a stop to their activities vanished. Jason researched your stay in Lockland and noticed how well you did. He told me you got out just in time.”

“Really? I kept my winnings low. I wasn't given any warnings.”

“The casinos were aware of you. Had you stayed and won more money you might have become fertilizer for a Saguaro or Ocotillo.”

“You don't beat around the bush do you, Sonja." William took a deep breath. "Now that we've cleared the air, can we get down to business?"

"Sure, Mr. Ray." Sonja was smiling because she had put William in his place.

"It's just that we're traveling today. Do I need to tell you where we're going, or do you already know?" William was pissed Sonja knew so much about his life.

“Jason said you decided to cut your vacation short and travel back to the States. You'll need to return the car so I assume you're driving to Pisa.”

“Not bad, Sonja. Change the hairstyle, and you'll make a great sleuth.”

“Okay, William. Point taken." She paused. "Here's the proposal.”

Sonja dropped her voice to a loud whisper. “Two years ago The Company got tired of looking for people with this ability.

They didn't shut down the search division but instead started another branch. It's known as the Clinical Study Department, and they opened a secret lab outside of Pisa."

"You said secret. Do you know where it is?"

"No, but let me finish. The decision to open an operation in Italy happened because of the financial collapse in Europe. The clinical work remained private and bribes kept anyone from asking too many questions. Italy's good at keeping silent when it comes to paying people off."

"And that's why you didn't start the clinic in the States?" William asked.

"Yes, too many whistleblowers and righteous people are in the States. When the clinic started in Italy it conducted experiments, which were considered experimental and unsafe."

"Unsafe. You mean people got hurt?" William asked.

"I don't know for sure and neither does Jason. The truth is the first few years involved mostly research. They were working by themselves. The other departments had no idea what they were doing."

"Why are you here? Shouldn't they send one of their own representatives?" William asked.

"First they want to find out if you're interested in their

offer."

"Okay. Go on." William said.

"Anyway, because Jason is the only person you've had contact with in The Company, they're using his division to present the idea to you. There's been a breakthrough."

"Breakthrough? What does that mean?"

"They developed a drug with the ability to replicate your condition. They first tried experimenting on paid volunteers. Nothing happened. They discovered that the drug is effective only on those who previously experienced the sight. Something to do with the way you're wired."

"So you're saying I'm a hot commodity?" William asked.

"Yes, as far as I know. I don't have all the facts. Like I said, the clinical division doesn't share. Jason only knows what I've told you."

"So he's in the dark as well?"

"Yes, we both are. Anyway, here's the proposal: Because you're already in Italy, The Company would like you to tour the clinic. They'd be able to give you more information. The Company is opening another lab in Mexico."

"Mexico? I live in Mexico."

"The Company realizes that Mexico is another country where money speaks. All they ask is for you take a quick tour, and meet the head doctor. He'll fill you in on what they're doing. You can decide later if you want anything to do with them."

"When would they like me to take this tour? We're planning on leaving Italy in a few days."

"When did you say you'd be in Pisa?"

"Later today. We're staying the night and taking the train to Milan tomorrow."

"I'm sure they can arrange for a tour after you reach Pisa, so you can still catch the train to Milan. The Company would take care of any expenses that interfere with your schedule."

"How about tomorrow morning. I'd be fresh and we can catch a later train."

"I'll arrange it. Jason will call and let you know when. Are you planning on staying at the Tower Hotel again?"

"Yes, we'll be there tonight."

"All right, William. That's it. This has been an interesting meeting. Thanks for the hairstyle tips. Following people is not my real job. I just happen to live in Italy and speak the language. I'm actually a Canadian."

"What's your real job?"

“I work as a research specialist, and discover people like you in Europe. It's similar to what Jason does. Potential clients don't appear often so I have a lot of time for other endeavors. In the summer I'm in Florence showing tourists around.”

“Do you have a card? My wife and I are returning next spring. We didn't get a chance to see much of Italy due to the weather.”

Sonja gave William a card with her private phone number. She also left a ten-euro bill on the table for the two coffees.

"I plan to stay one more night to look around Massa Marittima," Sonja added. "I've never been here before because it's off the tourist path. This is a fantastic town to take special groups."

Sonja and William shook hands. She turned and walked out the door just as Leslie came in.

Leslie spotted William in the back of the restaurant and hurried over to him.

“Was that the person you had the meeting with?” Leslie asked. She motioned towards the woman who passed her in the entrance.

“Yes, her name's Sonja. Let’s get out of here, and I'll fill you in later. We may see her when we come back to Italy next spring.”

“See her again? You mean you accepted their offer?”

“No. She's a tour guide in Florence, and we can use her services next year.”

“A tour guide working for Jason in Italy. What a great cover."

“No, I think the touring part is her own business," William said. "The job with Jason is part-time. She needs to be available for The Company at the drop of the hat so being a guide gives her the flexibility.”

William and Leslie walked to the car in the plaza parking lot and ten minutes later were on the road heading north towards Pisa.

“Well, Mr. Spy Man, what happened in the meeting? Are we staying in Italy longer or heading back to the States?” Leslie was ready to say goodbye to Italy and head home.

Rain started to fall. Not a heavy downpour but a light mist.

“Tomorrow morning I'm going to take a tour of a clinic outside of Pisa. They are opening a similar clinic in Mexico. They may use me again."

“You’re kidding me? Mexico? I thought you wanted to move from Mexico?”

"I do. The new clinic's located there, not us. The doctor

will fill me in. Neither Jason nor Sonja knows anything about either clinic."

"Am I going with you?"

"No, I need to keep you safely out of the picture. I'll feel better doing this alone."

"Fine with me. I'd rather say in the hotel and read. Just let me know if a Dr. Frankenstein works there. I hear he's planning on building a million-dollar man somewhere in Europe. This may be the place."

"Funny, Leslie. Oh, look. An Osteria is coming up on the right. I'm ready for lunch."

William pulled over and parked. The rain had let up and the lunch crowd was arriving.

While having lunch William left a message on Robert's cell. He'd give him another call when he reached Pisa.

*****

"How was your stay in Venice?" Luca asked. He was on duty at the front desk.

"We decided to visit Tuscany instead," William answered. "Long- distance driving with winter coming didn't seem like a good idea. We took your advice and visited Massa Marittima."

“You got to see Massa? I'm so glad for you. Not many Americans know about it. I hope you enjoyed your stay?”

“Leslie couldn't get enough of the place. She did most of her Christmas shopping there, and we plan to return in the spring. We'll visit more of Italy when the weather's better.”

“You're right, Mr. Ray. We're starting to get rain and cold winds. How long are you here this time?”

“We leave tomorrow. I'm dropping off our luggage as well as Leslie before I return the car. We'll catch a taxi to the train station if no more train strikes are scheduled.”

“None are planned,” Luca answered with a smile.

“We'd like to visit your brother’s restaurant tonight. Can you make reservations for around eight?”

“No problem. The rains will keep the crowds small so seating should be fine. I'll call Rondo, and tell him you're coming.”

After dropping off the car William had enough time to relax, while Leslie washed her hair to remove the travel dust from the drive. When she came out of the bathroom William said, “I made a reservation to return to Rondo’s restaurant tonight. Sound good?”

“Fine with me. Do you need to call Robert before we eat? It must be around nine in the morning over there.”

Just then The Company phone rang.

“William, my phone says you're in Pisa. Did you like Tuscany?” Jason asked.

“Actually we did, Jason. We had a great time, but we're ready to head home. The weather's turning cold.”

“Sonja called and said you're going to take the clinic tour. She also told me you gave her some good tips on how to stay undercover. I'm sorry if she made you uncomfortable. It was only for your protection. She speaks fluent Italian, and can kick ass if necessary.”

“No problem. I had fun sending her to Venice. I figured she'd find out our destination from the front desk. How would she know which hotel we were in?”

“Through your credit card," Jason said.

William remembered Robert telling him the same thing in Texas.

"A person has to pay for the service," Jason continued, "but the knowledge is invaluable, especially tracking someone like you. The Company takes particular care with their clients and wants them safe.”

William thought for a moment. “How does one go off the grid?”

“It's getting more difficult all the time," Jason answered. "Access to security cameras is even possible. Face recognition systems are so good that one would have to get plastic surgery before going underground."

"No knife is going to touch my face. I'm happy with what I've got. I'll just continue looking the way I do and stay retired."

“Good for you, William. I may be joining you. I'm approaching fifty and want to travel. This job is getting to me.”

"I wish you all the best if you do, Jason.”

“Thanks, William. I'm calling to let you know that a car will pick you up at nine o'clock in front of your hotel. The tour should take about three hours, travel time included, so you can still catch a train by one o'clock to Milan.”

“That works. We don’t want to arrive in Milan too late.”

“We have no one watching out for you so don't get into trouble. Sonja seems to have found a new town for her tourist business. She's in love with Massa Marittima and is setting up a few hotels to book for next summer. That woman's a workaholic.”

"We may use her services when we return in the spring. Thanks for the call. If I agree to work for the clinic in Mexico will someone else take over as my contact?”

“I have no idea, William. The research division is an

unknown. Even their location is a mystery. I've never been there."

"No kidding. So far the phone you gave me hasn't melted. I guess The Company wants to keep in contact with me. This has been an adventure for sure. No one could have made this up."

"You're right, William. Enough said. I'll call you later when you get back, so have a good tour and flight."

William's next call was to Robert.

"Hey, Robert. It's William. I'm in Pisa."

"I got your message," Robert said. "How'd the meeting go with the rep?"

"I just got off the phone with Jason. The meeting went fine."

Robert listened as William repeated all the information he'd received from Sonja. When the part about past clients using the drug was mentioned, Robert exclaimed, "Wow, now I'm really interested. I've still got a bad feeling about the research. Why would they keep it hidden from other divisions?"

"No idea," William said. "Maybe I'll find out on the tour. Jason also hinted he may retire soon. I get the feeling something is bothering him, but he's not able to talk about it."

"That's interesting." Robert thought for a moment. "You're taking the tour, right?"

“Yes. Tomorrow. I don't know what they want, but Sonja said the doctor would fill me in. I'll have time to think about it before I give them an answer. I'll call you when I'm done."

"Phone me around the same time tomorrow. I'll be waiting. This is wild. The ability to reproduce the sight is a game changer."

“Yeah, but a game changer for who? The Company will no longer have to wait for a client to appear. They could use this ability all the time.” William's voice was tense.

“They could," Robert added. "That’s why it’s a game changer,”

William continued, “Their ability to buy low, sell high, and never lose would increase their worth tremendously. Forget Bill Gates and Carlos Simms. There'd be nothing to stop them from financial domination.”

“William, that's exactly what I mean. There's no limit to what they could do with this power. Murder would be nothing to a group of men about to control the world markets.”

“You're worrying me, Robert. Do you think I should still take the tour tomorrow? I told Leslie I'd get out if there's any danger. Am I too late?”

“You're fine. Karl was the spy. They're more interested in using you again. At this point, they'll probably show you around, and let you decide."

"I don't know if I'm interested in doing this again." William felt the stress building in his upper back.

"Hang in there for a while longer. We still don't know the extent of their capabilities. They still could be in the trial and error part of their research. They must be getting close because they're expanding to Mexico."

"Okay, Robert. I'll call you tomorrow. I should know something by then."

"Oh, one more thing, William. The person I sent to investigate Karl's death is still in Pisa. I'll have him tail you from your hotel so we'll know the clinic's location. He's good at what he does so you won't see him at all."

"Fine with me. Make sure he doesn't have a spiked haircut." William was being smug.

"What do you mean by that?"

"I'll tell you later. It's a funny story."

William hung up and pocketed his phone. In ten minutes both he and Leslie had on their coats and were ready for the short walk to dinner. Luca gave them an umbrella in case the rains returned. Winter was knocking at the door, and the Rays were glad to be heading back to the States.

Chapter 22

At 9 a.m. William was standing in front of the Tower Hotel holding half a bagel from breakfast. As he took the last bite, the car from the clinic arrived and the driver got out. He came around the car and opened the door for William.

“Hello, Mr. Ray. My name is Pablo. I'll be your driver.”

“Glad to meet you, Pablo. Where do you want me to sit?”

“In the back, please. You'll notice the windows are blacked out, and I'll be putting up a barrier between us after we get on the road. It is a policy of the clinic to protect their location. Don't worry. I'll have voice contact with you. The drive takes about 45 minutes.”

William's mind was racing. Blacked windows and no idea where he was going, worried him. Would he be the next victim?

"I don't know my way around Pisa anyway so it makes no difference.”

“All right, Mr. Ray. You're safe so enjoy the ride. There is a mini bar in the back seat. I made some coffee earlier. It's in the thermos attached to the left door. Cream and sugar are in the small refrigerator on the right.”

The time passed quickly for William. He tried to listen to noises outside the car to form an idea where they were going but nothing stood out. They arrived at the clinic fifty minutes later and William could hear a metal gate swing open.

Pablo said something in Italian to the person operating the barrier. No one was going to get into this place without permission. Pablo opened the car door, while William let go a sigh of relief. He'd arrived safely.

The building looked like a small villa built in the 1800's. The all-stone structure took on the appearance of a fortress as well as a home.

A man in a white coat came down the hallway towards the front door. William thought it looked like a reenactment of some sci-fi flick complete with costumes. Maybe Leslie was right and Dr. Frankenstein does work here.

"Mr. Ray, I'm happy to meet you. My name is Dr. Yee. I'm the director of the clinic."

"Good to meet you, Dr. Yee," William said as he shook his hand.

The doctor appeared to be Chinese-European. He had the characteristics of a Chinese male in his eyes and skin tone, but his six-foot height wasn't typical of most men from that part of the world.

"I assume Pablo took good care of you? Sorry about the

secrecy, but we're careful regarding our research. You do realize how valuable our work is?”

“I understand how secrecy could be important. I have one question for you."

"Yes, and what is that?" Dr. Yee asked.

"You used the word research. I was told you had a breakthrough and duplicated the same condition I experienced. Isn’t that right?”

“Yes and no. We've had some success recently and we're now learning more about the correct dosage for each patient. The drug itself is still fairly new.” Dr. Yee continued to talk as the two men proceeded down the hall.

“We created the compound in our own lab. Getting the correct dosage is of utmost importance."

William wondered if Robert's two friends were given an overdose? That may have been the reason for their deaths.

“First let me show you around and I'll attempt to answer any questions.”

Dr. Yee led William through a second inner door and down a long hallway. William could see someone sitting behind a glass wall at the head of the corridor monitoring people coming in and out the building.

"There are three private rooms used for our clients," Dr. Yee said.

William looked into one of the rooms and saw a hospital bed as modern as anything he'd seen in the States. Dr. Yee said he had two nurses assisting him. No patients were presently staying at clinic according to the doctor, but a client was expected to arrive from Switzerland later in the week.

There was a small lab on the second floor with two technicians also wearing white coats. Neither of them looked up when Dr. Yee and William entered the room.

"Does anyone live at the clinic or do they have homes outside the compound?" William asked.

"They all live in Pisa and are driven to the clinic by Pablo. He's been with us since we first started four years ago. We screen everyone and pay them well for their services."

"So the nurses and the technicians don't drive here on their own. Have you had any problems with outsiders, or people asking questions about what you're doing?" William probed.

"Not so far. Officials help in this area. As long as we're not a threat, they're happy to ensure our privacy."

"What would be my role if I worked for you? I'm still not sure I want to experience this ability again."

Dr. Yee looked directly into William's eyes and paused before answering. “There is another clinic starting in Mexico as we speak. We're keeping its location secret as well. It may be a while before your services are needed. I believe they want to do a CAT scan and find out why your condition lasted so long.”

“Really, a CAT scan? That's it?”

“Maybe. This will be presented to you at a later date. Give it some thought, and later you can tour the clinic in Mexico when it's operational.”

Williams paused before saying anything. “So nothing has to be decided, and I can make a decision later?"

“Basically, yes. The lab is now working on perfecting the dosage amounts.”

“How long will the drug affect a person?” William asked.

“The effects last a little longer than two weeks. The compound can be used only once a year. The stress on the brain is substantial and could prove to be fatal if repeated too soon. Safety is our main concern.”

Yeah, I’ll bet, thought William.

“Have you had any clinical accidents or mistakes during the research?”

“We've had some close calls, but were able to correct the

technical difficulties immediately. The beginning 'trial and error' situations are in our past."

"This is a large villa. Do you use any other rooms for research?" William asked.

"No. Mainly the two floors are used. We have living quarters for myself and another doctor. He'll be heading up the clinic in Mexico."

"Well, I admit, it's a good start. What is the goal of The Company when this compound is ready?"

"That is a question I can't answer. I signed on to this project because I'm interested in brain research. I plan on opening my own clinic when the project is finished."

"No kidding. Your own place."

"Yes. After The Company has the compound I'll be awarded a bonus. It will be enough to start my own brain research. I won't be needed here to administer the drugs. That can be done with a nurse."

"Any idea what The Company's future plans are?"

"No, and I prefer it that way. This is a stepping stone project for me. Mankind has begun tapping into unexplored areas of the brain, and you're a perfect example."

"You got that right," William answered.

“I believe we can discover ways to stimulate the brain to cure other diseases such as Alzheimer's or even cancer. We're only touching the surface in this area. Viewing the future is not an interest of mine. I don't share the same goals as The Company.”

William's thoughts about Dr. Yee were starting to change. The man saw a way to finance his own research. William wondered if The Company would release him when he was done? The project was worth billions in the open market. Signing a non-disclosure agreement may be enough for Dr. Yee, but would it be enough for The Company? Could he be the next casualty?

William asked, "Will Jason be contacting me or does the research division have their own handlers?”

“I don't know who'll be contacting you," Dr. Yee answered. "I've shown you all there is to see. My range of knowledge ends at the door.” From the tone of Dr. Yee's voice, William could tell he was done with the tour.

“We'd better see if Pablo is still around because I need to get back. I wish you all the best,” William said.

Dr. Yee walked William to the front of the villa and placed a call to Pablo. A few minutes later the car pulled up with one of the nurses in the back seat.

“Marta is just finishing her shift and needs to return to her apartment. Is that all right with you, Mr. Ray?’

“No problem, Pablo. No reason to make two trips when only one is needed.”

On the ride home, William noticed a worried look on Marta's face. She didn't say much. William thought it might be due to her limited English. William sat back and closed his eyes for a little nap. Suddenly he felt Marta’s fingers touch his. She was sliding something under his hand while keeping her gaze forward. She said nothing. William slipped the paper into his pocket and continued the silent ride towards Pisa. Five minutes later the car stopped and Marta got out.

“This is home I live," she said in her broken English. "Thank you for car ride.” She looked deep into William's eyes and gave him a nod. She then shut the door.

The car continued for another ten minutes and arrived at the Tower Hotel. William thanked Pablo for his services and went inside to find Leslie. His heart was beating rapidly as he reached into his pocket for the note. It had Marta's name on one side, and a phone number. On the other side she wrote: "Call me. More news I have."

Marta was taking a chance, William thought. How does she know I won't turn her in? Whatever it is, the risk must be worth it.

William knew Robert would have to call Marta because he and Leslie were leaving Italy tomorrow. It also dawned on William that it could be a setup, and Marta was working for The Company to feel him out. This double agent shit was getting to William.

William found Leslie, gathered their luggage, and proceeded to the cab at the front of the hotel. They arrived at the station with enough time to tag their bags, buy tickets, and drink a cappuccino.

After boarding the train and finding their seats, Leslie asked, “How was the tour? Any deep dark secrets the world needs to know about?”

William gave Leslie a description of the tour. "Nothing seemed to be out of the ordinary and I won't be needed until sometime next year."

William didn't tell her about the message from Marta. He was afraid it might upset her so he decided to keep that detail to himself. He planned to pass the info on to Robert, and let him deal with it. The Rays were not in the spy business.

After eating a late lunch in the dining car, Leslie decided to nap. By now it was early morning in New Mexico. William proceeded to a lounge area at the front of the car and called Robert.

“William. I've been waiting for your call. I found out what happened to Karl."

"Really, what was it?" William asked.

"The substance injected into Karl was a cocktail of stimulants causing him to have a heart attack. Someone murdered him and the Italian police didn't investigate his death. They wanted no part of it."

"Robert, my guess is they were paid off. Maybe the German authorities will follow through with an investigation. Let me tell you what I found out before Leslie wakes up."

William described the tour to Robert. Nothing regarding the clinic's location was revealed other than it being between 45 and 55 minutes from the hotel. William described the interaction with Marta and gave Robert her phone number and message.

"All I can tell you is she seemed nervous. I'm turning this over to you because we can't stay in Pisa. Marta doesn't speak fluent English so you'll need someone who speaks Italian. Something was bothering her. Whoever she talks to needs to be careful."

"Why's that?" Robert asked.

"She's probably taking a big risk passing on information so let's not spook her. I don't think Dr. Yee would like any of his employees giving out any secrets."

"We'll be cautious. It seems you won't be needed until the clinic is operational in Mexico. That could be awhile. I'll see you when you arrive in Albuquerque. Call the day before so I can pick you up at the airport. "

"Sounds good," William answered.

"I should have some information regarding Marta by then," Robert said. "My contact in Italy was able to follow you in the limo. We now know where the clinic is located, and my associate told me the security was tight."

"It is. No one is getting into that place without permission. I'll call you from Atlanta." William looked out the window. "We'd better hang up. We're approaching a tunnel and may lose connection. See you soon."

William shut his cell phone as the train entered the tunnel. Lights went on and remained on for the rest of the trip. William walked back to his seat just as Leslie woke up.

"Where'd you go? I opened my eyes and you were gone," she said.

"I made a call to Robert and told him what I found out. He had his assistant follow me so Robert now knows the clinic's location. He has all my information, so it's up to him to figure out what to do with it."

"Good. Then maybe we're done with this business?" Leslie said firmly.

"All we need to do now is to fly home, visit Jon in Atlanta, and pick up our car in New Mexico. We can be in New River by Thanksgiving."

"Fine with me," Leslie said. "Let's start planning where we want to move to." Leslie was ready to make the transition back to the States as soon as possible.

Milan was the next stop. The Rays departed from the train, caught a taxi to the Alto Hotel and checked in. The Air Italia direct flight to New York left at eight in the morning, and from there they'd catch a connecting flight to Atlanta.

The one night stop in Atlanta, and dinner with their nephew provided William the opportunity to give Jon the special olive oil he purchased in Italy. The visit was short, and Leslie promised they'd return and stay longer. Both William and Leslie were eager to get home.

Chapter 23

The flight to Albuquerque landed around noon. Robert arrived in his SUV knowing William and Leslie had lots of luggage.

“Glad to meet you, Leslie. How was the trip?" Robert asked.

“Happy to meet you as well, Robert," Leslie said. "William's been busy with you on the phone, and now I finally get to meet you in person.”

“Welcome to New Mexico. I used to live in Utah, but this is my home now."

The porters loaded the SUV with the luggage, and they were soon on the road to Robert’s house.

During the 30-minute drive to the two-acre estate William and Leslie listened to Robert's news regarding the investigation. The German authorities were not going to investigate Karl's death. It seemed The Company's influences extended into Deutschland. Also, Robert’s associate in Italy finally arranged a meeting with Marta.

"It seems she only wanted to speak with you, William," Robert said.

“What does a nurse have to do with the investigation?"

Leslie asked. "I didn't hear about her before." There was concern in her voice.

“I didn't want to worry you," William said. "She slipped me a note with her name and number. The note said she had some information.”

Robert interrupted. “Leslie, William is trying to keep you out of the loop as much as possible. We don't know exactly what we're dealing with. There're a few mysterious deaths that may be connected to the clinic. We think they happened during their research so we're being careful."

Leslie didn't answer. She hoped William was finished working with Robert, and a normal life lay ahead for both of them.

As they arrived at Robert’s home, the conversation about the clinic ended. William transferred the luggage to their car, which was located in one of the four garages alongside the western ranch style home. All they would need was their overnight bags.

The guest room was located off the pool overlooking a beautifully manicured backyard. A mixture of cactus and desert shrubs completed the southwest landscape. A couple of rows of solar panels lined the property's boundary facing south. Robert had also installed two windmills to capture the desert breezes.

“I really like this place. I had no idea you were into alternative energy,” William said.

“I need a good power source to run all my electronic toys and information center because I work from my home. I'll give you a tour after you rest. Carla is my cook and she is making some sandwiches. Would you like guacamole and chips to go with the egg salad?”

“Are you kidding?" William said. "Leslie lives on avocados. You've made her day for sure.”

William and Leslie retreated to their room after lunch. William wanted to see more of Robert’s house but needed to rest first. After a short nap, he woke and found Leslie reading.

“Did you sleep?” he asked.

“No, I'm too wound up. Thinking about moving has me excited. I can't stop thinking about it.”

“Let’s try to make this transition as painless as possible," William said. "Where to move should be our first step. After that, we'll figure it out.”

They both dressed and returned to the open living area that looked out towards the pool. The sun was setting and the water reflected the orange glow of this event, visible from the living room. Robert entered through a door on the south side of the house that opened to the living area.

“Did you both get a nap? Travel can really tire you out.”

“I slept but Leslie is preoccupied with planning where to move. A community between three and four thousand feet we feel would work. A little elevation in Arizona is essential to survive the summers.”

“I know what you mean. Albuquerque is around 5,000 feet and it makes a difference in the summer. I may be able to help. There are a few communities in the hills behind Tucson. I assume you want to stay in Arizona? I'll get the information, and print it out if you want. The developments might be exactly what you're looking for.”

“Sounds perfect,” Leslie said. “Looking for the right place can be a chore, and we'd appreciate any help we can get.” Leslie was now warming up to Robert.

“We should come up with a plan for the future," Robert said. "First of all, I want you to see my office, and show you how I operate. I've been in the investigation business for a while. It started out as a hobby after I retired from The Company.”

“Do you get a lot of work?” William asked.

“The list of high-end clients is endless. I took on the first jobs because I was bored and needed something to do. Income was not the issue. After a few successful jobs, word got out. I now work a full-time investigation business.”

“You said you do this out of your home, and I saw a few

dishes on your roof. Do you have access to satellites as well?"

"Come into the cave room. This is where it all happens," Robert said.

Leslie and William entered the large work area, and William gave a gasp as he entered. Four huge screens were mounted on one wall with a table computer in the middle of the room. The office in the TV show, Hawaii 50, looked similar. This was no rookie operation, William thought. Robert is a high-end investigator with the equipment on the cutting edge of technology.

"I don't want to draw attention to my operation from the outside world. The alternative energy resources keep the power companies in the dark as to what I'm doing here. My power bill would be off the charts, and nosy people would start poking around. I'm only on the grid for my house needs and charge batteries for my office equipment."

"This is amazing. And no one knows you have this stuff in your house?"

"I'm isolated as you can see," Robert answered. "I have neighbors but we are spread out in this part of town.

"This is friggin amazing," William exclaimed again. "I had no idea you're so involved in the spy business."

"Investigating, William. Spying is just a part of the job.

Only a select few have seen my operation. Because we're working together I didn't want to hide anything from you. I know what I'm doing. If the research portion of The Company is killing people, I plan to put a stop to it. All three men were friends of mine. I owe it to their families to find the killers."

"Like I said before, Robert, I'm willing to help as long as we're not in any danger."

"You have done a lot so far, William. Because of you I now know the location of the clinic. I'll show you on the screen to your left."

Leslie and William sat in two chairs below the monitor as Robert did a Google earth type search. First Italy appeared. He typed in a location and the camera zoomed into the city of Pisa. Finally, the villa clinic was visible.

"Damn, look Leslie. There's the driver and the car that drove me. His name is Pablo." A man was seen walking from a car to the front door of the clinic.

"The video you're seeing is from earlier today. It's now around one in the morning in Italy and everything is dark. I have the monitor recording the clinic in the daytime. My assistant comes in and reviews all the activity. The Company has no clue I'm watching their every move."

"This is so cool, Robert. How'd you do all this?"

“William, as I mentioned before, there are people in the electronic world who sell their wares and services to whoever meets their price. All one has to do is find them. It’s as simple as that.”

“I’m glad you're one of the good guys, Robert."

"Nothing is expected from you until the Mexico clinic is operational, right? If I had the name of the doctor from Mexico, I'd be able to track him.”

“Dr. Yee never told me his name. Does your office include a face recognition program?”

“Of course. That's one of the first systems I purchased. It's invaluable in this business.”

“My only suggestion is to monitor who comes to the clinic. Dr. Yee said the Mexico doctor visits all the time.”

“Good idea, William. See, you're a natural.”

“Staying one step ahead of my kids as a teacher is a full-time job. Maybe it was investigation training, and I didn’t even know it.”

“Maybe," Robert said. "Anyway, I think we're in a *wait and see* period. My assistant in Italy will meet Marta soon. We're taping the clinic 24/7. If Jason calls, let me know. If you're right about Jason, he might be ready to re-evaluate his connection with

The Company."

"Do you plan on contacting him?" William asked.

"I might. He knows who I am. You said he's thinking of retiring? I wonder if he's getting suspicious of the clinic?"

"He might. He's a decent guy. If he knew people were getting killed he might want out and be done with them."

"The Marta meeting could give us something we could use. Something will eventually break this investigation wide open. We just need to be patient."

Leslie and William decided to take a walk around the property and stretch their legs.

Robert had another job and stayed in his office. "Carla has dinner set for six," Robert said. "Be back by then."

Leslie had been quiet during the conversation, but she now let fly with her concerns as soon as they were away from the house. "Where do you think this is headed, William? I was blown away with Robert and his office. He's living a life found in thriller novels."

"Yeah, I noticed you were quiet. I'm as overwhelmed as you are. Let's leave tomorrow for your brother's house and help him get ready for Thanksgiving. That's all we can do."

Leslie nodded her approval.

“This information is off limits to anyone else," William added. "As far as the family knows we sold our lot in Flagstaff and the money paid your retreat and vacation.”

“And if we move to a new home? Where does that money come from?”

“That's none of their business. Let's take a drive to Tucson after Thanksgiving and see what the communities are like.” The last statement made Leslie really happy.

“The sun sets around five, and it's a long drive, so we'd better get an early start," Leslie said. She was ready to start the transition back to Arizona.

The evening with Robert went smoothly. After dinner, they retreated to the living area overlooking the patio. The pool lights were on and radiated like a beacon in the desert.

"Carla will have breakfast ready for you in the morning. I usually eat late but I'll be up to say goodbye."

“Oh, one more thing, Robert," William added. "We need a tax accountant. All this income will appear on the tax radar when we draw on the Cayman account, and I could use some help. Do you have anyone you could recommend?”

“My accountant is fantastic. His name is Jones. I'll get you his card. He has offices in New Mexico and Arizona. He'll advise and give you the breaks you're eligible for. Trust him, he knows his stuff."

"Thanks, Robert. The accounting of money can be really complicated, but not the spending. Leslie has that down." William received a poke in the rib from Leslie and it really hurt.

Early breakfast worked for William, while Leslie took fruit to eat later. The sun rose and so did Robert. He walked William and Leslie to their car and asked them to call when they got to Phoenix. He was becoming a good friend but neither one knew where their relationship would take them?

Chapter 24

The holidays passed with little progress in the investigation. Robert mentioned they might experience a *wait and see* period. During this time frame, the Rays made their move from Mexico to Tucson, buying into one of the developments recommended by Robert. The move was completed before Christmas and all the family spent the holidays with them in the new home. The gifts were distributed from Leslie's European shopping spree and everyone was pleased with the results.

It was now February. Leslie's mother, Doris, had moved in with them in January and found the dry weather much to her liking. Leslie now had a project, which was to keep her mother happy.

A call from Robert broke the life of normality the Rays were presently experiencing.

"William, how are you?" he asked.

"Good to hear from you, Robert. It's almost like a dream that we were running around Italy a few months ago. What's up?" William had a feeling the waiting period was over.

"My assistant made contact with Marta. She was reluctant to meet with him. After a month of continual probing, she finally gave in."

“I tried to tell you she was nervous," William reminded Robert. "I'm glad she made the effort to finally talk.”

“It seems our Dr. Yee and his crew were doing more than what he told you. Marta said the early research at the clinic included homeless patients. They were paid to take part in the study. Dr. Yee didn't tell you what happened to these first patients, did he?"

"No, not a thing." William was now a little worried.

Robert continued. "According to Marta, a few of them died. Because they had signed a release allowing the clinic to perform the tests, Yee and his crew were off the hook. Also, these patients had no family, so nobody attempted to find out what happened to them.”

“So people died during the first tests?" William's head started to hurt. He waited a few seconds before he asked, "how many died, and what did they do with the bodies?”

“There may have been as many as six according to Marta. People were paid to dispose of the bodies, no questions asked.”

“What about now? Does Marta know anything about your two friends?” William knew there had to be a connection.

“She remembered them. She said they also signed a release form and were compensated for their participation in the tests.

They died during the period the clinic was trying to determine the correct dosages amounts. One person previously had a stroke, while the other experienced a weak heart. The drug may have aggravated these weak areas in their bodies and they died because of it."

"Why was no connection made between the clinic and their deaths?" William asked. "It's obvious to me."

“The clinic paid off people. They still have something to hide, and don't want anyone poking around their research. Marta also said there were a few successful cases, and those people left soon after the compound was administered.”

“What happened next?” William asked. He felt excited about the investigation once again and wanted to know everything.

“I don't think she knows that these people and The Company were connected with the stock marked. All she remembered was that the clients left the clinic after the tests proved to be successful.”

“I wonder how long their ability lasted?" William asked.

"Dr. Yee told you the effect could only be repeated once a year. If the condition lasts two weeks then only twenty-five clients, or one every two weeks, would give them control of the market, 24/7.”

“That is a major concern if you are trying to stop them," William said. "Were you able to find out anything about Karl?”

“That's the only thing I don't have." There was anger in Robert's voice. He wanted to avenge his friend's death. "The drug found in his system tells me he was murdered. There's still no proof the clinic is connected. We really need a contact on the inside, and maybe the clinic in Mexico is our only hope. Have you received any calls from them?”

“No, not yet. Did you call Jason to see if he'll help?” William was not sure he liked where this conversation was headed.

“Yes. He was happy to hear from me, but I didn't pass on any information. He said he was retiring and would like to talk about New Mexico. It seems he likes the area. He may confide in us when he separates completely from The Company.”

“I got the same feeling," William agreed. "He's been thinking about retirement for a while.”

“He's flying out here next week to look around. I offered my home in Santa Fe, and he accepted. I plan to visit with him while he's here and see what information I can get from him.”

“Robert, that's a big move. Jason knows a lot more about The Company than either of us do."

"You're right, William. By the way, are you living in

Tucson, or just visiting? My phone shows me you're there now. Did any of those developments pan out?"

"We bought a house in one of them," William said.

"Really? Do you like your place?"

"Yes, we moved in right before Christmas. We went with the two-car garage, single story stone model, with the red tile roof. It's a common style in the area, with a small patio, and room for flowers. Leslie's mother moved in with us, and loves to grow roses."

"Good for you, William."

"I'm still waiting for the clinic in Mexico to call regarding the CAT scan. In May we leave for Europe," William continued. "We're going to travel with Leslie's sister and see more than we did last year."

"If The Company phone is still working they'll call," Robert said. "Let me know right away when the CAT scan is scheduled."

"I will. You'll be the first person I'll call. You also know where we live now."

This last remark was in regards to Robert's ability to track people. My phone gives Robert my exact location, William thought. His satellite computer can zoom in and relay pictures of us in the yard. Robert made a mental note to cross off nude sunbathing in the patio. He'd mention this fact to Leslie as well.

Chapter 25

Paul McClure gave the order to have the clinic closed in Italy. The completed research allowed Dr. Yee to collect his bonus check, and continue with his own study in Singapore. The staff was given severance pay and the villa was put on the market. All the research was boxed up and sent on to Mexico.

No one else turned up in Pisa asking questions at the Tower Hotel. There was no longer a connection between the clinic and The Company. As far as Paul McClure was concerned, he'd covered his tracks. The Company would continue to operate but use past clients instead of having to find new ones.

The money for the secret project would continue to flow. The next generation of Company members could still influence the world. It was important for Paul McClure to ensure the plan before he handed over the CEO reins to his son. He had raised him to see the world as he did. *Those with financial means needed to be in charge*. When the water project was in place, the Company members would make their move.

*****

On April 1st The Company phone rang. “Hello, William. It's Jason. How have you been? Why aren’t you in Mexico? Have you moved?”

"Wow, that's a lot of questions. We moved last December

to Arizona, and we seem to be doing fine. How about you?"

"No kidding. I'm moving too. I'll be a neighbor one state over." Jason spent ten minutes bringing William up to date on his new life.

"I'm retired from The Company and you're my last contact. The clinic is going to pay you $750,000 for a picture of your brain. Not bad for a simple CAT scan. A doctor from Mexico will fly to where you are to complete the scan. By the way, my phone tells me that would be Tucson."

"That would be correct, Jason," William answered. He was expecting the call from Jason regarding the scan, but the news of him moving out of New York was new to him.

"After this call, I'm leaving New York and heading to Santa Fe. I purchased a house and I'm looking forward to the move."

"You're actually retiring? Good for you Jason. I can't believe it."

"I fell in love with Santa Fe and realized I could live well in the Southwest," Jason said.

“We'll have to meet up soon, Jason. When can they do the scan? We're heading back to Europe next month so I have a four-week window to get this done.”

“I'll let The Company know your schedule. They told me

the new clinic is finished and the doctor would be ready to do the scan right away. I guess they like your brain."

"I like it too, Jason. Anyway, how does it feel to be retired?"

"My stress level has dropped. I contacted an old client in New Mexico, and he persuaded me to retire sooner rather than later. He even helped me find a place in Santa Fe."

"Fantastic, Jason. What should I do with this Company phone? Will it melt after we hang up?"

"No, the phone will be your contact with the Mexican doctor. He's your new case manager."

"Case manager? I hope I became something more than a case to you, Jason. We'd love to re-connect after your move. I'll give you my personal phone number."

After exchanging numbers, and a little more sharing about the Southwest, the two men said goodbye and hung up. Two minutes later Williams regular phone rang. It was Robert.

"William, hi. Did Jason just call you?"

"Yes. How'd you know?"

"I'm in the spy business, remember? I can track Jason's calls because of the monitoring device I planted in his phone. He visited me in Santa Fe, and while he was in the shower, I bugged his phone. It now tells me who he called. Before I could only tell where he made the call. He suspects nothing. We also had a talk and he told me the reason why he retired."

"What'd he say?" William could hardly wait to hear the reason.

"He believes The Company was involved in some shady dealings in their Italian clinic. He also knew about my friends who died at the Tower Hotel."

"Why would he start telling you all this? What'd you say that got him started?" William asked.

"He believed the actions of the research wing are out of control. I then told him my suspicions about The Company's involvement in murder."

"What'd he say to that?" William hung on to every word.

"He seemed relieved. He thought he was alone with the information. When I told him about my investigation of the Italian clinic he told me everything he knew."

"Really? Does he know about me working with you?"

"No, you're my ace in the hole. He said if the clinic shuts down, and The Company collapsed, he wouldn't care. Murder is not a part of who he is. If it turns out that The Company sanctioned the killings he said he'd start working with me."

“Robert, you're amazing. You're able to get Jason to join us. That’s a huge accomplishment.” William knew Robert was persuasive because he used his charms on him.

“What else did he say?” Robert asked.

William repeated the conversation he had with Jason.

“Did he mention using you to try the compound?” Robert asked.

“No. The clinic doctor will talk more about that. When he comes to Arizona you can get his ID. You have that face recognition program, right?”

“William, I knew you had a knack for spy work. I was going to do that, but I'm glad you brought it up. Which TV shows do you watch?

“NCIS, Criminal Minds, and Burn Notice. Are any of their tricks relevant to what we're doing?” William asked.

“A few. Bugging the doctor somehow may work. I'll get someone to place a device. We should have no problem finding out exactly where the doctor works in Mexico.”

“Any more news regarding the Italian clinic?” William asked.

“From the video surveillance cameras, we've noticed a bit more activity. We've seen a couple of vans pull up to the front of the villa and load boxes. It seems like they're packing up and closing down the place."

"Really? Closing it down? Jason never mentioned anything about that," William said.

"He may not know anything. My person in Italy hasn't been able to make contact with Marta either. Her phone's been disconnected, and she has been absent from work the past three days. Her name's been removed from her apartment mailbox, and the neighbors haven't seen her for a week."

"Does she have family?"

"Not in Italy. She's actually Peruvian and came over to Italy to work as a nurse. We think she was hired because she has no local connections. Marta may have gone back to Peru. She worked for The Company for several years and probably saved enough money to retire."

"Do you think we could find her in Peru? She must know why the clinic's shutting down." William asked this question because he had an idea he wanted to run past Robert.

"I think so. She might feel more comfortable talking to someone about the clinic when she is home. She'd feel safer being near her family. I'll put a trace on her and find out where she lives. It shouldn't take more than a few days."

“Leslie and I always wanted to visit Peru and Machu Picchu. If you want us to talk to her, let me know. We could mix the vacation with a little business.” William was serious about visiting South America and hoped Robert would need him for this side job.

“I'll keep that in mind. Marta took a liking to you, William. She only saw you once but trusted you enough to give you her number. If you interview her, she may supply us with more information than she gave my man in Italy.”

“Well, let me know how I can help. We have the time. After Europe, the month of October or November could be set aside. It'd be spring in Peru, right?”

“Yes, it will," Robert said. "Call me when the doctor from Mexico makes contact. You may be the only person on the inside if Marta is gone. Dr. Yee isn't going to divulge anything, and he's using his money to run his own brain research clinic somewhere else.”

"I'll call when I hear anything, Robert. Talk to you later."

William could feel himself falling deeper into this game of *cat and mouse* with The Company. Why anyone needed all that financial wealth was beyond him. How much money was enough? This wasn't about monetary gain. It couldn’t be. William thought something bigger was their goal. Maybe Robert would eventually find out from Jason."

*****

The next day The Company phone rang. William was alone in his patio and answered it.

“Is this, William Ray?”

“Yes, it is.”

“My name is Dr. Peter Gupta. I think Mr. Burns told you I'd be calling.”

“Good morning, doctor. Yes he did. I've been expecting your call.”

“Great. Then I don't have to go into a long story. I'm calling to set up the CAT scan in Tucson. Mr. Burns said you're leaving for vacation in May, so I wanted to get it done on Monday or Tuesday of next week. Will that work for you?”

“Yes, I can be available.”

“Good. I'll fly into Tucson to set up the scan. The hospital will call, and give you the date and time.”

“That'll be fine. You said fly so you're not driving?"

"No, not this time. Also, did Jason tell you I'll be your phone contact from now on?” Dr. Gupta asked.

“Yes, he did. I did have a question. Why am I important to your research, doctor?"

“You're an unusual case, Mr. Ray. Your condition lasted two weeks longer than any other patient. We'd like to find out why.”

“I'd like to find out as well," William added.

“Thank you for your co-operation, Mr. Ray. I look forward to meeting you in Tuson.”

Dr. Gupta hung up. William reached for his phone to call Robert.

“Robert, he just called.”

“Who?”

“Dr. Gupta. I'm having the CAT scan next Monday or Tuesday. Gupta is flying in from Mexico and the hospital will call to set it up. It’s happening, Robert.”

“Fantastic. I’m glad you called, William. I've some major news so hold onto your seat.”

“Am I going to like this?”

“I think so."

“Okay, Robert. Let's hear it.”

“The clinic in Italy has shut down. Everything's been moved. Dr. Yee left the villa, and is no longer on our radar. Many crates have been shipped to Mexico, probably containing the research. We were able to zoom in and read the address on one. A city in Mexico called San Miguel."

“Are any of the nurses still there?” William asked.

“Marta returned to Peru, and lives in the city of Cusco, the old Inca capital. We may want to contact her but first things first. We have no more people on the inside with Marta gone and Jason retired. You're our only hope right now, William.”

“That’s a lot of pressure. You sure there's no one else?”

“Your connection with Dr. Gupta and his clinic is all that's left.”

William sat for a moment trying to collect his thoughts. He was glad Leslie was not around. She'd freak out if she heard his answer.

“You know the position you are putting me in is a difficult one, don’t you?”

“Yes, and I'm sorry. I really am.”

William knew The Company would stop at nothing when people got in their way. Karl was proof of that. William waited a few moments before giving his answer. Finally the words cleared his throat.

“I may regret this, but here goes. I’m all in.” William imagined pushing all his chips into the center of the table. Retirement had taken a new turn.

Robert didn't say a word. He didn't really expect the answer William gave him.

Finally he said, "Really? You're in? Way to step up to the plate."

"I'm not comfortable with any of this, but I have to see it through," William said.

"Good call, William. I'll have someone ready on Monday."

"I'll call you when I know the exact time," William answered.

"Do you know the name of the hospital?"

"St. Joseph's Hospital. It's located to the east of I-10."

"Good. I may be able to find someone to help us. A tech working in the CAT scan lab would be invaluable. I'll see what I can do." Robert said goodbye and hung up.

Chapter 26

April fourth: The phone rang. "Hello. This is St. Joseph's Hospital. We are calling for a William Ray."

"This is William Ray."

"We have a CAT scan appointment for you at seven a.m. on Monday the seventh of April. Will that time work for you?"

Shit, William thought. They're paying me 3/4 of a million dollars to take a picture of my brain. I'd make a two a.m. appointment work for that amount.

"That'll be fine. Do I need to come early to fill out any paperwork?"

"No, the front desk will have everything ready. A lab technician will walk you through. Please 'fast' and don't take any medications or drink coffee after midnight the evening before. Are there any questions?"

"No questions. I'll be there at seven. Thanks for the call."

William decided to arrive on Sunday night with Leslie and check into a hotel near the hospital. They'd do some shopping after the scan. $750,000 could buy a lot of stuff.

William called Robert. "Robert, hi. The scan is scheduled for Monday at seven in the morning. Is that enough time?

"It has to be. I have a lab tech that'll report any findings. She can be the tech for any day and has the weekend to fix the schedule."

"How'd you do that, Robert? You have an answer for everything."

"The tech needs the extra cash and she'll give us what we want."

"Okay, Robert. I'll be there on Monday. It's amazing what money can buy."

"Complete the scan and we'll see what happens," Robert said.

"Will do." The two friends hung up.

Facing Leslie was going to be difficult. After 21 years of marriage, he knew this would be a hard pill for her to swallow.

*****

"What do you mean you told Robert you were all in?" Leslie was furious. "What does that mean? I thought we were going to keep this spy stuff to a minimum and live like retired teachers." Leslie's reaction was understandable.

"All I'm doing is having a CAT scan on Monday and getting paid for it. Robert is managing the spy work. There's no informant working on the inside anymore. The nurse in Italy returned to Peru, and the clinic in Pisa shut down. I'm the only connection to the clinic in Mexico."

"When does this end, William? The money is fine, but are we becoming like the men in The Company? Will we ever have enough?"

"I don't think it's the money with them," William answered. "They're killing people and we don't understand the reasons. Robert is trying to put a stop to that."

"Okay, William, but here is the deal. If you're continuing to work with Robert, we need to increase your Life Insurance. You're playing with fire, as far as I'm concerned. If I'm left alone caring for mom, I want the financial backing to do it easily. I'm sorry, but this is how I feel about this whole mess. I'm not Indiana Jones's girlfriend and you're not Indie. Being practical is all I've got left."

"Don't I look a little like Jones from the side?" William may have thrown more fuel on the fire.

"Not funny, William. I'm serious. Go ahead. Do the CAT scan on Monday, but let's be practical. If you think you can stop a company of multi-billionaires from getting what they want, then good luck. We'd be like a fly on the wall to them. One swift smack and you'd be gone. They'd simply move on to the next person."

William was tired of arguing. "All right then. Let's get ready for Monday. Will mom be comfortable staying alone or does she want to come on Sunday? We have to stay overnight because my appointment is at seven."

"In the morning?"

"Yes."

"I think she'd rather go with us. She needs a little excitement."

"Also we need to start planning for Europe," William said. "I can e-mail Sonja who runs the tours. Remember, she's the lady who followed me in Pisa, and worked for Jason. She'll book our rooms anywhere in Italy and show us around. Will that work?" William had to come up with something to distract Leslie.

"You do that, William." Leslie was still angry. "I'm ready for another vacation after what we've been through. Moving to the new house was really stressful."

"You're right. Start planning the trip and I'll make sure your brother can stay here with mom while we're in Europe."

*****

The Rays made the drive into Tucson on Sunday morning. After checking into the hotel the three decided to walk around.

"Hello," William said after his phone rang. It was Robert.

"William, I see you're in Tucson. Are you ready for the

scan tomorrow?"

"As much as I can be. Wait a second." William told Leslie that he had to take this call, and he'd meet them back at the car. They agreed and walked towards a quaint clothing store.

"Are you set up for this?"

"I believe so. The tech I hired is operating your scan."

"We're staying a few blocks from the hospital. I'll be in and out by ten. I'll let you know more about Gupta after I'm finished."

"Good job so far. I do have a little news."

"What's that?" William asked.

"We now have Marta's address in Peru. She wasn't hard to find. She went right back to her family's home in Cusco, and is now in an apartment a few blocks from her mother."

"Robert, I'll repeat what I said earlier. If you need me to go to Peru for an interview, let me know. Leslie and I'd love to see that part of the world."

"I'll let you know," Robert said.

"I'll call you tomorrow." William hung up and walked back to the car. He sat in the front seat, and closed his eyes, trying to calm his thoughts.

Twenty minutes later the car door opened. Leslie and Doris

had returned and were ready to unwind back at the hotel.

"What did Robert say? Is everything all right?" Leslie asked.

"The only news he had concerned the nurse from the clinic in Pisa. He found her living in Cusco and has her address. I volunteered our services if she needed to be interviewed. You still want to go to Peru don't you?"

"Of course I do. The land of the Inca is definitely a must see." Leslie might not like William working for Robert, but she did enjoy seeing the world.

*****

William was up by six. He dressed and walked the short distance to the hospital observing the early morning rituals around town. Starbucks was full, both at the drive-up window and the walk-in area. A bran muffin and a Grande cappuccino latte would be perfect right now but would have to wait.

"Hello, I'm William Ray. I'm here for a CAT scan with Dr. Gupta."

"Yes, Mr. Ray. They're ready for you now. I'll have Miss Marks take you to the lab on the 2nd floor. All we need is your name and address."

"Do you know how long this will take?" William asked.

The smells from Starbucks still lingered and he was hungry.

"The doctor rented the lab for several hours. He's scanning your brain as well as another patient from Mexico. You're scheduled first so you should be finished before nine."

William gave the secretary his name and address. He then followed the assistant to the elevator and took it to the second floor. Another person in a blue gown came into the room and showed him to a dressing chamber adjacent to the CAT scan. He removed his shoes and shirt and put on a white top that hung to his knees. His blood pressure was taken, and William was now ready for the morning procedure to begin.

"Mr. Ray, my name is Megan, and I'll be operating the scan. All I need from you is to hold as still as possible. The machine is loud so we'll be playing some music inside the chamber. We have three choices. Bach, Beatles or Country. We call ourselves the BBC of CAT scan music. No Heavy Metal or Rap, so there you have it."

"Beatles for sure. I like their music."

"Beatles it is. All you need to do is lay back and I'll guide you through the session. Some people suffer from claustrophobia, so if you want to close your eyes, then do so. That'll help."

Finding himself in the narrow chamber was unsettling even though he didn't have space issues. William remained calm and relaxed as *Hey Jude, Norwegian Wood,* and *Yesterday* played in surround sound.

After thirty minutes, Megan's voice came over the speaker. "All done. Remain where you are until you are out of the chamber. I'll give the all clear. Hope you enjoyed your flight."

William was transported to the front of the scanner, and Megan was there to greet him. She helped him sit up and swing his legs off the table onto the floor. "That wasn't so bad was it, Mr. Ray?"

"No, not really. Great choice of music. Are you doing the scan for Dr. Gupta's next patient?"

"I am. I signed on for the morning shift, and someone else takes over at noon. Your clothes are on the chair, and your shoes are underneath. Dr. Gupta wants to talk with you in the visiting doctor's office at the end of the hall. We won't have your x-rays for a while, but he would like to meet you."

Megan showed William to the office.

"Hello, Mr. Ray. I'm Dr. Gupta. I'm glad to finally meet you. I hope the scan was not difficult?" The men shook hands.

"No, it wasn't." William studied the face of Dr. Gupta trying to get a read on his personality. If he still had his old condition he could have read Gupta's mind.

"I can assure you the scan will be valuable in our research," Dr. Gupta said.

"I hope so. Are you in contact with Dr. Yee in Italy? I met him last year when I was in Pisa. He showed me around his clinic, and told me a little about the work you're doing."

"As far as I know Dr. Yee completed his work in Italy and has gone on to do his own research. The clinic there is now closed and everything has been shipped to Mexico. We're doing our best to sort out the files and continue with the study. Our hope is that your scan will give us more data."

"The clinic is closed?" William pretended to be surprised. "Are you the only one doing research now?"

"At the moment. We're having positive results, and Mexico offers the best location to continue this work. Perhaps you can come down for a visit sometime."

"I would love to tour the clinic, but I'm hesitant about becoming active again."

"I understand," Gupta said. "Many past patients have turned us down."

"The secretary mentioned you brought another patient from Mexico," William said.

"Actually the woman has a similar story as you. She's still

active so we plan to compare her scan with yours."

"Really. I'm surprised The Company didn't think of that sooner," William added.

"This research is relatively new. I can tell you more if you visit us after you return from Europe," Dr. Gupta said.

"We're leaving in May and could be gone a month. Who knows how I'll feel about reactivation then." William had no interest in working for The Company again, but he wanted to keep his foot in the door. Information might come his way that would help the investigation.

"It's been a pleasure to meet you, Mr. Ray. I hope to see you again."

The two men shook hands and William left the office. As he approached the scan lab, he noticed Megan walking towards him, accompanied by another woman. Both were speaking Spanish. As William passed, he nodded to Megan, said hello, and thought the number, 760-554-0269. Hopefully, the other woman would pick it up.

The number was William's AT&T phone number with the *Call Mexico* plan. He still used it to make contact with friends in San Felipe. He hoped the woman would recognize the prefix.

The woman looked curiously at William as though she

mentally had received the numbers. William nodded to her. Would she remember the digits? He held up his right hand with his thumb in his ear and the baby finger in his mouth. It was the international sign language for 'call me'. With luck, she'd understand.

William kept walking. As soon as he was out of the hospital he made a call to Robert.

"Robert. Something new has come up."

"Really? Are you done with the scan?"

"Yes, but I have something you should be aware of. Dr. Gupta brought an active patient from Mexico. Megan is scanning her brain to make a comparison with mine. If Megan is going to copy my x-ray then she should duplicate the woman's as well."

"This is interesting. I'll get the message to Megan right away," Robert said. "By the way, we now have a tracking device planted on Dr. Gupta. Megan was able to place it on his coat when he was using the bathroom. It's as small as a dime and will disappear when he has his coat cleaned. That should give us the location of the clinic when he returns. The man I sent to Tucson gave it to her."

"The information regarding the other woman is all I've got. I'll let you go so you can get in touch with Megan. Good luck."

William hung up and walked to Starbucks down the street

for a muffin and coffee. He had done his part. With any luck, the Mexican woman would give him a call. Suddenly it dawned on William that if she did call he had no idea what to say to her? He'd also forgotten to mention the incident to Robert.

William's mind was racing with all the possible scenarios. He called Leslie to see where she was.

"Hi, Sweetheart. Have you had breakfast?" William asked.

"We just sat down in the hotel dining room. Want to join us?"

"I had coffee and a muffin a few minutes ago. I have another idea. You two eat and meet me back at the room in an hour. I need to visit a spa I saw on my way to the hospital. They do chair massages."

"How'd the scan go?"

"It went fine. Dr. Gupta brought a woman from Mexico to get a scan as well, and she's still active. I'll tell you about it later."

"All right. We'll meet you back at the room," Leslie said. "Love you."

William stood in front of the spa, sipping on the last of his coffee. There was an opening for a chair session. He signed up for 30 minutes of upper body work.

William returned to the room five minutes before Doris and

Leslie arrived. They were soon packed and checked out of the hotel. They drove to Trader Joe's, purchased two weeks' worth of food, and headed home. Normal life felt good.

Chapter 27

The next day Leslie and William spent time mapping out where they wanted to tour in Italy. An email to Sonja let her know their schedule.

"I'm happy you remembered me," she wrote back. Sonja also thanked William for introducing her to Massa Marittima, where they first met. She said she'd already conducted two tours there, and the clients loved it.

"Give my regards to Jason if you see him," she emailed.

William answered, "I'll call and give him your message."

After completing their travel schedule, William called Jason.

"Hi, Jason. It's William."

"William, it is good to hear your voice again."

"I scheduled time with Sonja to tour in Italy, and she wanted me to say hi."

"The last time I talked to Sonja, she told me you might use her services. How's she doing?" Jason asked.

"The tour guide business is keeping her afloat. She said there're no more Company jobs for her since you retired. Dr. Gupta informed me about the Pisa clinic closing. San Miguel is the new research center."

"San Miguel? I've heard of that town," Jason said.

"I just had a CAT scan in Tucson and met Dr. Gupta. Do you know him?"

"Met him once. He visited the office in New York when he was being interviewed for the job in Pisa. I don't think The Company uses American doctors."

"Why's that?" asked William.

"They don't want any employees who might have a problem with their research. They want people to do their job, get paid, and move on. I never did find out much about the clinic in Pisa," Jason added. "I've heard rumors of misconduct, but nothing for sure."

"Can you tell me what you heard?" William's inquisitive mind kicked in.

"No, I rather not. I'm now working with someone conducting an investigation. I'm helping him when I can. I only worked with clients with the 'sight', like you."

"Who are you working with?" William knew the answer but wanted to keep Jason in the dark regarding his connection with Robert.

"A past client who lives in Albuquerque. I have no more

connections with The Company because I retired."

"That's interesting. My involvement's been minor as well. They paid me for the scan and offered me compensation to reactivate."

"Just be careful, William. I know these men and they're powerful. Our involvement helped us financially, but it also made them rich. It was a tradeoff for sure. I'm content with what I earned, but these men are different."

"In what way?"

"They're never satisfied. I've never understood their motives. Controlling others is a major objective for them."

"What do you mean?" William felt he was finally getting some information from Jason that could help the investigation.

"I mean life's already complicated enough and these men want to control the financial world?" Jason said.

"I'm glad you got out when you did. Are you in any danger?" William asked.

"I hope not. As long as my name doesn't resurface then I'm safe. I did my job well. Any information I pass on needs to be kept secret."

"No problem on my part. Anyway, I just wanted to call and reconnect," William said.

"Be sure to say 'hi' to Sonja when you see her."

"I will. If I come across anything, does that former client you mentioned need help?" William asked.

"I'll give him your name and number, and ask him to call you. Will that work?"

"That sounds fine. It'd be good to have someone to report to."

"Thanks for calling, William. We'll get together when you get back from Europe."

Both men hung up. William sat back in his chair and counted the seconds. When he reached ten the phone rang. He knew Robert too well.

"Hello, Robert? I was expecting you," William said with a grin.

"You knew I'd call?"

"I just got off the phone with Jason and you're monitoring his phone. Damn right I knew you'd call."

"William, the sleuth from Tucson. You're getting good at this. What's new with Jason?"

"He should be calling to give you my name and phone number. I told him I wanted to help with the investigation. He said he was working with a former client who lives in Albuquerque. Not too hard to put that piece in the puzzle. I also have something to tell you."

"What's that?"

"I sent a mental thought to the Hispanic woman at the hospital. I gave her my Mexican phone number. She may or may not call but if she does I don't know what to say. Any ideas?"

"You did what?" Robert asked.

"I mentally sent her my phone number, and she looked at me like she understood."

"Does she speak English?" Robert asked.

"I don't know. That's why I sent her the numbers in Spanish. She spoke Spanish to Megan so if she does speak English I won't know until she calls. Any ideas how I should handle this?"

"Introduce yourself first to help her feel at ease. Let her know you're a past client. There's a chance she speaks English. What did she look like?"

"She was probably in her thirties, and well dressed in the sense that she wore nice city clothes."

"Do you remember if she wore a wedding ring?" Robert asked.

"Damn, I didn't notice. A good sleuth would have. I better add that to my list of things to improve on," William said.

"She's possibly from a family with means and speaks some English. Also, she's traveling to the States so she must have a permit or passport. Only Mexicans with the financial backing are issued those. I'll put in another call into Megan, and see what she knows about this woman. If she does call, earn her trust. What she's going through may be scary to her."

"Sounds like we have this call covered," William said. "I'll let you know if anything materializes."

"Talk to you later, William. Have a good trip."

William hung up. He realized he hadn't checked the Cayman account since his CAT scan. He typed in his access code. There it was. $750,000 deposited yesterday.

William thought, not bad for a couple of hours out of my busy schedule.

*****

A few days passed since the CAT scan with little change in the life of two retired teachers in Tucson. On Wednesday morning William's Mexico AT&T phone rang.

"Hello," William answered. Silence, then a click, and the phone went dead. The number was a Mexico prefix William hadn't seen before. He waited a few minutes deciding whether to call the number or wait. If it was a call from the woman from the hospital, he didn't want to scare her. She needed to call again. Two minutes later the phone rang.

"Hello, this is William Ray."

"Hola, Mr. Ray. My name is Marie Ortiz. I call you because you sent me number to my head. I see you in hospital last week. Why you want me to call?" A tone of fear was in her voice.

"Hi, Marie. I was in the hospital having a CAT scan just like you. I used to have the same ability you have right now. I wanted to tell you not to worry, and that you'll be normal again."

"You can tell future like me?" Marie said. She sounded excited.

"Not anymore. I had the ability for more than six weeks. I'm normal now. It was scary at first. How about you? Can you still read people's thoughts?"

"Yes, I can hear people talking in heads. Also numbers. Dr. Gupta, two weeks past, find me in hospital in Mexico City. I had blood medicine for making blood not so thick. Made me have brain problem. I tell doctor about hearing thoughts of people. My doctor called Dr. Gupta and come to me about working for him. They pay me *mucho dinero* to see numbers for stock market."

"I had a similar story. I had a blood clot, was given a blood thinner, and it caused a brain bleed. I worked for the same Company as you do. Do you have the visions all the time?"

"Yes, I do. I sometimes wish thoughts stop. Dr. Gupta paid me more money to come to Arizona for brain picture. He wants to see my brain and other person. Maybe that is you?"

"Yes, it was. Do you know what Dr. Gupta is doing with these pictures?"

"No. He tell me *nada*. I'm happy with the money, but I know nothing."

"Where are you staying in Mexico?" William asked. He was pleased Marie was relaxed and talking to him so freely.

"I live in San Miguel and travel to clinic for experiment. I receive money for tests. I do nothing more with stock market. I like clinic better."

"I wanted to talk to you so I'm glad you called," William said.

"I was hoping someone else was like me," she said. I want to talk to them. Sometimes I'm scared."

"I know, Marie. It's a special ability. The brain heals the pressure, and it goes away. Will you be all right until you're back to normal?"

"Yes, I think so. I left family in Mexico City. I call them, but no visits until test are over. My family is happy with money I send them. More dinero than we earn with family restaurant for many years."

"I know, Marie. The Company paid me lots of money too."

"Can I call again if I am worried, Mr. Ray?"

"Yes, you can. Can I call you if I have questions?" William decided not to press her for information and scare her. She was alone and William provided her at the moment with some degree of comfort.

"I think so. Only person outside clinic who knows what is happening to me is you. My family does not know. They not understand. They have strong belief in Catholic religion and may say I have devil inside me."

"It's best to keep this quiet, Marie. Let the Company do the tests if you feel safe. People outside the clinic won't understand. When the tests are finished you'll have enough money to live for a long time without working. Can I use this phone number when I call?"

"Yes, it is my own phone."

"Also, Marie, can we keep our conversation quiet from Dr. Gupta? He might not like you talking about this to other people."

"Yes, I think so," Marie answered. She was glad she had called William and felt so much better than she did ten minutes before.

"Good. I'll be away for a month. You can call me on this number when I get back. I may tour the clinic then. If you're still there can I visit you?"

"Yes, please do. I enjoy this talk."

"I suggest you keep the condition quiet from your family. I didn't tell my relatives either."

"I think you know a good answer, Mr. Ray. Thank you for talk. Call me if you make more questions."

"I will, Marie. Good-bye"

William now had contact with a person on the inside. He didn't know if she'd be much help. Right now she needed assurance she'd be normal again.

Chapter 28

A call went through to Robert. William hoped his contact with Marie would help with the investigation.

"Hello again. Guess who just called?"

"The woman from the hospital who also had a CAT scan."

"Damn it. Can't sneak anything by you, can I?"

"Not really. Tell me about her," Robert said.

William repeated the conversation he had with Marie. When Robert was told she was mostly involved in research, he paused before answering.

"Isn't that interesting?" he finally said. "Where is she now?"

"She lives outside the clinic in San Miguel. Her family doesn't know about her ability. She says they're religious and might think she's possessed."

The comment brought back memories for Robert. It seemed to him that if religion couldn't explain a situation, they labeled it as the work of the devil.

"That sounds like my experience with the Mormon Church," Robert said. "Good work, William. You didn't scare her off. She might be helpful down the road. Megan did her job and made copies of both your scans, but Gupta never told her anything about the research."

"I don't think Gupta is going to tell anyone anything," William said.

"There must be an end game to this somewhere," Robert continued. "I'd like to know what they're planning on doing with all that cash? Simply making more money cannot be the goal. They must have another objective. We just don't know what it is."

"You may be right, Robert. I thought of that too. Maybe you should change the focus of the investigation, and find the bigger picture."

"You're right, William. I just may do that." Robert still had his ace in the hole and Jason might be the one who could tell him more about The Company and their real plans.

Robert finished the conversation with William and hung up. He needed to meet with Jason and see how committed he was to the investigation. So far, Company member names were unknown. He was not sure if Jason knew any of them, but he needed to ask. He placed a call.

"Hello, Jason. This is your neighbor, Robert."

"Hey, Robert. Good to hear from you. How was the winter in Albuquerque? We got a few feet of snow up here."

"Sixty degree winters aren't difficult to handle. I'm heading your way to open up my house. Are you available for lunch anytime this week?"

"Of course. I'd really like to see you too. How about tomorrow at *The Green Burrito* around noon? I still can't get enough Mexican food. I've got a feeling you have something to ask me. Am I right?"

"You know me, Jason."

Robert kept his conversation to a minimum. He still didn't know if The Company was monitoring Jason.

"I'll meet you there," Jason said.

"Sounds good."

After hanging up, Robert began to think of all the questions he would ask Jason. No more beating around the proverbial bush. Jason was either in or out. It was time to get to the real reason The Company was socking away all that money. Greed could not be the only answer.

Robert drove to Santa Fe that evening instead of waiting for morning. He wanted to wake up in town, and take his time getting ready for the meeting. At 11:30 a.m. he walked to the restaurant a few blocks away.

The Green Burrito offered outdoor seating as well as indoor tables. Robert arrived early so he could find a suitable spot and privacy. Jason arrived twenty minutes later and found Robert finishing his first beer of the day.

"Robert, It's good to see you again. Don't you love the summers up here?" Both men shook hands.

"I do, Jason. I just can't stand the snow so my winter home is really my permanent residence. I try to visit as much as I can every summer. How've you been?"

"This community suits me. I'm still unwinding from New York and getting used to the lifestyle. Winters here are nowhere close to the New York cold. I also have some good news. I met a woman."

"Wow, this place is really paying off for you. How'd you meet?"

"She's an artist and owns a gallery just off the plaza. I was looking for some pictures for my walls, and what she displayed in her gallery suited my tastes. After several visits, I got to know her and eventually asked her out for coffee. One thing led to another, and now we're seeing each other all the time."

"Did she ever ask you about your previous life in New York?"

"Yes. I told her I worked for a company doing stock market research. She never asked me anything more about it. Her name is

Rosa. The financial sector is the furthest thing from her mind because artists look for beauty in the world. We seem to have a lot in common as well. I took up photography, and plan on framing a few pictures for her gallery."

"Jason, I'm impressed. A woman and a hobby and you've only been here a few months."

"I also drink less and sleep a full eight hours every night. The city life is something I could never return to."

Robert could see how relaxed Jason appeared.

"Do you want a drink?" Robert asked. "I really like this local brand of beer."

"I'll have the house lemonade. An occasional beer in the evening suits me best."

"I have a few more beer drinking days ahead of me to make up for my Mormon past," Robert said.

As the two men caught up with their lives, Robert kept waiting to ask a question regarding The Company. After they ordered, Robert decided to cut the crap and get to the real reason for lunch.

"Jason here is why I wanted to talk to you. As you know, the clinic has closed down in Italy and is now operating in Mexico in a town called San Miguel. A new doctor is running the show, and everyone in Italy has moved on."

"You've been busy since our last meeting," Jason said.

"Yes, I have, and it's getting serious. I found out that deaths were involved in the research part of the clinic. Several homeless people were killed in the beginning. Two past clients I knew were rehired and they both died." Robert's voice started to rise.

Jason sat quietly and didn't say a word.

"I sent a man to investigate, and he was murdered in his hotel room in Pisa. We believe the Italian police, as well as the German authorities, were paid to cover up the murder. I can prove someone killed him, but not who."

"Robert, I'm aware things happened in the clinic, and that's the reason I got out. They operated like a rogue branch of The Company, and answered to no one."

Jason knew a lot of information that would help in the investigation, but he needed to be careful regarding his own safety.

"You knew about the deaths?" Robert's voice raised another notch.

"Yes, but not directly. The manager of the clinic has a separate office. His division is in a different building. All I can give you is a name, and where you'll find him. Their operation is secret. I wanted out when I heard about the deaths. I knew those two men who died, as well."

There was a look of sadness on Jason's face when he mentioned the previous clients.

"I'm sorry to put you in this position, Jason, but murder is murder. I have to do what I can to stop them. Any name's a start. An address, or where they hang out, would also help."

There was a long pause before Jason spoke. "Here goes," Jason said in a whisper. He looked around the patio. "I hope you know what you're doing. The head of the clinic is Mark Jones. He used to work for the CIA. He had an office in one of the Twin Towers, but that was before the clinic was up and running. He just happened to be out of the country on 9/11."

"That was lucky," Robert said.

"Yes, it was. Because of that disaster the division restarted their research from scratch. Everything was lost. He happened to be the only one out of the office at the time. A whole new staff was hired, and worked down the hall from us before moving to the Chrysler building."

"Is that where this Jones is now?" Robert was taking notes. He wanted to be sure he had all the facts in order to help Alan research this Jones character.

"Yes. He has three people in the New York office. The

doctor in the clinic is the only person he deals with, so Dr. Gupta is the go-to man in Mexico."

Did you know Jones?"

"Not really. Jones is a member of an all men's organization in the city called *Ron's*. The club labels itself a cigar-smoking business. Most of the members used to work for the government in some way. The only reason I know about it is because Mark asked me to join."

"You don't smoke do you?"

"No, I don't. Red neck attitudes, and a few overheard conversations regarding where they think a woman's place should be told me this was not a crowd I wanted to hang out with. That's the extent of what I know about Jones."

"Do you have any idea where he lives?"

"He has an apartment downtown. The New York nightlife fits his style, and he hangs with different women every night. He's cut from the same cloth as the 'Good Ole Boys Club'. Be careful. He has the size and meanness of a linebacker. He's not a nice guy. If murder is involved he'd be the one to do it." Jason paused. He'd given Robert enough information to mount his attack on The Company.

"I'll find him. I can access his personal files and get his

picture. This is a great start, Jason. I know you're starting a new life in Santa Fe. I would like to call if I have any more questions."

"Okay, but only to meet. Lunch or dinner discussions in person are best. I know The Company is still monitoring me. My knowledge will eventually be declassified, and I'll hopefully be free from them."

"Jason, thank you for your help."

The two men finished lunch and shook hands. Robert drove back to Albuquerque. He needed Jason in the investigation and hoped more names would turn up in future. He and Alan had work to do.

Chapter 29

The Air Italia flight from Phoenix left around ten, and flew directly to Milan. Leslie and William were now continuing their vacation that was interrupted by weather the year before.

"When does Anna arrive in Florence?" William asked.

"She'll be there to meet us at the train station," Leslie said. "Here is our itinerary for the next few weeks. Just us, Anne and the cities of Italy."

The return trip to Europe would keep the Rays busy for a month.

*****

While William and Leslie were in Europe, Robert put his plan into action. Mark Jones, after being vetted by Alan, looked dangerous on paper. He was not a Boy Scout by any definition of the term. His training in Special Forces, and skills in killing people put him in his own class. He also spent a few years protecting businessmen in foreign countries where oil was involved. The Company hired him to manage the new research division just before 9-11.

Jones was the perfect man for The Company. Human life meant little to him. Robert did not know if his two friends died because of Jones, but he was going to find out.

After Dr. Gupta and Marie returned to Mexico, Robert knew the exact location of the clinic because of the bug Megan placed on Gupta's coat. Alan programmed the satellite reception to show the new clinic building in San Miguel. Up until now most of the activity in Mexico was moving crates inside. Nothing was visible behind the outer walls.

Robert needed to attack Mark Jones in order to infiltrate The Company. Even though he'd lost Karl, there was still another option. In New York City Robert knew a woman who was perfect for the role, because he'd hired her before. Jones was a womanizer and Julia was hot. Her five foot seven-inch frame was kept in shape with a strenuous workout program. She was expensive, but he knew she could manage the job.

Robert dialed Julia's number. "Julia, hi. This is Robert Woods. It's been a while."

Julia was employed by Robert as an investigator to work on four different assignments over the past two years.

"Robert, how are you?" She was always glad to get a call from Robert.

"Fine. I have a job if you're interested. The person lives in the City so you won't have to travel. I need information from him, so we might have to go with the 'truth serum' approach. Does any of this sound interesting?"

"Robert, you really know how to sweet talk a woman. I've been trying to hook up with you for two years, and this is how you greet me?" Julia had a crush on him. She had plenty of men asking her out, but she was attracted to Robert. She knew he was single, but not sure if he was straight.

"I'm sorry, Julia. I guess I'm a little wound up with this project. I need your service because this person is a womanizer. I know you and I'm sure you can handle him." Robert knew she was interested in him, but tried to keep their connection professional.

"Have you met this guy?" she asked.

"No, but I've got a file I can send you. Will that work?"

"Maybe. Since you won't come to New York, fly me to New Mexico. We can discuss the file there. I'd even give you my discount rate. How does that sound?"

Robert never allowed employees to visit his Albuquerque home. Maybe a visit to his Santa Fe house would work, he thought. That would keep his spy center a secret.

"Ok, Julia. You win. I'll fly you to Albuquerque and pick you up at the airport. We'll drive to Santa Fe. This time of year the higher elevation is much more comfortable."

"I'm available right now." Eagerness was in her voice. "Wire me a ticket, and I can be there by tomorrow. I might like

New Mexico more than the Big Apple. I've never visited the Southwest. Who knows where this may lead?"

Robert knew Julia was a woman of strong desires. He'd talked to her over the phone many times and met her personally on two occasions. She was competent, beautiful, and not afraid to let Robert know how she felt.

"Okay, Julia. I'm sending your ticket right now. Pack light with just a carry-on. Also, a jacket or sweater because high elevation nights can cool off."

"Will do Robert, but I was hoping you'd keep me warm." Julia was playing with Robert. She was determined to put a dent in his *business only* approach to her.

"You're cute, Julia. Behave yourself, and save all that energy for this job. I'm afraid you'll need it. This Mark Jones guy is a real asshole, but he's smart."

"See you tomorrow, Robert." Julia hadn't given up. She'd make her move when the time was right. In her mind, Robert didn't stand a chance.

Robert hung up and took a deep breath. Julia was getting to him. His mind started to wander as he envisioned tomorrow night in Santa Fe. He had to keep this professional. She'd managed to get a rise out of him, and it took a minute before he returned to normal.

*****

Alan kept busy with the research on Mark Jones. He'd located Jones' apartment address and uncovered his social pattern based on his credit card charges. On Thursday nights he seemed to hang out at a club called Max's. It was a meat market pickup bar for those who didn't want to be alone on Friday or Saturday nights. This is where those, who lived a fast paced lifestyle, made connections with the opposite sex. *Women and men both came to score.* This last bit of information was posted on the web comment section describing nightclubs in New York.

Men, like Jones, didn't want attachments, only dinner and maybe a follow-up encounter if the sex was good. After that, back to the club for another conquest. *So many women, so little time*, seemed to be the mantra for guys like Jones.

Robert made a list of what he thought Julia would need if she cornered Jones. He went to his office refrigerator. A drug used to paralyze Jones was in one packet. A syringe, with enough *truth serum* to make an elephant talk, was also included. The last item was an injection that would blank Jones' memory for the previous twenty-four hours. Robert was ready to start his attack on The Company.

*****

"Delta Airlines flight 1452 from Atlanta is now unloading

at gate A-12. Those meeting passengers are instructed to wait for them near exit 4. Thank you for flying Delta." The loudspeaker clicked off. The flight from New York had to make a stop in Georgia before landing in New Mexico.

Robert waited for Julia as the passengers came down the escalator from the 2nd floor. She was easy to spot. Blond hair resting on her shoulders, skin-tight black leather pants, Dorothy-red high-heeled shoes, and a white blouse, exposing enough cleavage to make heads turn and look. Robert knew right away he was in trouble.

"Robert." Julia spotted him when she was half way down the escalator. She waved. "I'm here." It was quite a show.

Robert waved back. At the same time, five men in the forty something age group turned towards him. They wanted to see the lucky guy they would change places within the blink of an eye. Robert was turning red. Even a few women were staring at him.

He greeted Julia, allowing her to kiss him on the cheek. He then took Julia's carry-on bag and quickly escorted her to his car in the parking lot.

"You certainly know how to make an entrance," Robert said after all the blood that had rushed to his face, returned to the rest of his body.

"What on earth do you mean, Robert?"

"I mean, every single guy in the waiting area had you on his radar."

"Oh, that. I'm just practicing for my role when I deal with this Mark Jones person. You mentioned he was a womanizer, so I thought I'd give him a good target. I've been around men like him before, and I know what they like. I'm really just role-playing. How'd I do?"

"My guess is a few chiropractors will have some adjustments to make tomorrow, judging from the heads you managed to snap around."

"Why Robert, thank you. Is that a compliment? I just wanted to make sure I still have what it takes to draw some attention."

"Julia, you're a handful. If I didn't know you I would have been fooled by that performance. We have a few hours drive ahead of us. Are you hungry?"

"No, I'm fine. Since you flew me, first class, the airline fed us during the flight. You really know how to treat a woman, Robert." Julia gave him a wink. She was already starting to break through his defensive shield.

Robert knew he'd hired the right woman for the job. She knew how to play men and would have Mark Jones eating out of her hand when she was finished with him.

Julia eventually settled down after her airport performance. It took time after her sexual hormones were fired up.

During the drive, Robert filled Julia in on Jones's position with The Company. The possibility he may have killed one of Robert's employees told Julia a little more about the man. He was trained in Special Forces and capable of anything.

The couple arrived in Santa Fe around two in the afternoon and went straight to Robert's home.

"So this is where you spend the summer season. I have to say the temperature up here sure beats the 100 degrees we just drove out of. At the same time, I didn't mind the dry heat. The humidity in New York is miserable in July," she said.

"The Southwest has a few communities that are summer friendly," Robert said.

"Are you going to show me around this place? First, let me slip into something that'll work here. Can we eat somewhere near that square we drove through? This is really exciting." Julia didn't wait for an answer to any of her questions.

Julia went into the bedroom and came out ten minutes later after transforming from Cher to the girl next door. This was the person Robert was attracted to. She was dressed in jeans, sandals, and a long sleeved blouse. She'd pulled her blond, shoulder-length hair into a ponytail and looked perfect for the artist community.

Robert's home was just a few blocks from the town square, and his favorite restaurant called the Hilltop Inn. It was the same location where William met Jason many months ago. The patio offered a chance to sit outside and feel the warmth of summer.

A short walk brought the couple to their destination. They were seated in a corner of the patio under an umbrella. It was past the noon rush hour so they were almost alone.

"Well, what do you think?" she asked. "Can I pull this caper off?"

"I have complete confidence in your abilities, Julia. That's why I hired you. I just want to make sure we're on the same page. Here's his file or at least what we've been able to dig up. Jones has a routine he follows, and the best place for you to make contact would be at a nightclub called Max's in the City. Do you know it?"

"Yes, I've heard of it. It's where the horny women go to meet the horny men." She gave a quick laugh at her answer.

"That sounds like the information we received," Robert said. "Jones' picture is in the file, but you may have to show up a few times to contact him."

"You keep saying 'we'. What does that mean?"

"I have an assistant who does most of the research. He's a computer science student."

Julia was relieved it wasn't another woman. "What exactly are we trying to get from this guy? Are there certain questions to ask him when he's primed?"

"We want the names of the people above him. In other words, who's his boss? Also, does he know their goals? I suspect these investors have a secret agenda."

"Investors? Like in the stock market? Is The Company made up of people who invest?"

"Yes. It's an all men's group according to my source. What they're doing with all their money is one of my main questions. Jones may or may not know the answer, but I'm sure he can provide us with some names." Robert paused. "Next; did he have anything to do with the death of a German by the name of Karl? He was the man I hired to spy on them in Italy."

Robert waited before asking his last question. "There were two clients who died in Italy after visiting the clinic. Ask Jones if he had anything to do with their deaths."

"I better write this down. You certainly have a few scores to settle with this creep. After we get the answers, then what? Kill him?"

Robert could see Julia did not like Jones, and taking him out would pose no problem.

"As much as I'd like to, we'd better not upset the apple cart. Just erase his memory and get out. I want to be sure you're safe."

The drinks arrived, followed by the trout special. Julia liked beer as much as Robert did. By the time they were halfway through the meal they each ordered another variety of beer. Anything dark was a safe bet.

After they finished their meal, the business mindset of Robert had changed. He could walk around town with Julia, or consummate their relationship, and see where it would go. The alcohol set the mood for the couple.

She said, "Maybe we can go back and have a nap before we explore the town? What do you think, Robert?"

Robert knew what she meant by a nap and could feel his manhood rise for the occasion.

"Whatever you want to do, Julia." It was the beer speaking and Robert decided not to get in the way.

The short walk home took only minutes. Both Robert and Julia quickened the pace, knowing what lay ahead. Their excitement was in the moment, and adrenaline pumped through their bodies at an accelerated rate. When they got to the stairs they ran to the door. There was not going to be any small talk. As soon as they got into the house the animal in both of them took over.

Within minutes clothes lay on the floor in a pathway to the main bedroom. Naked bodies were joined in passion after two years of verbal foreplay. The buildup brought both to thirty minutes of groping and exploring what each wanted in the encounter. Mouths and lips were used to bring each other to sexual heights not realized before. They were lost in the moment and neither were looking for a rescue team to find them.

Chapter 30

The Rays and Leslie's sister, Anne, were still in Florence. Sonja was their tour guide in the city and was having an after dinner coffee with them on the main square.

"I'm planning a side journey in four days with some German tourists to Massa Marittima," Sonja said. "After you visit Venice maybe you can join us."

"I think Leslie has us in Massa around that time. What are the dates again, Sweetheart?"

"We should be there in five days," Leslie answered.

"We're leaving for Venice tomorrow," William said. "Did Jason get in touch with you?"

"He sent me a card thanking me for my service," Sonja answered. "He mentioned something about The Company not operating in Europe. Is the clinic in Pisa closed?"

"Yes, we think so. Mexico is the new location. I may still do a little work for them when I return to the States. I'd like to talk to you about The Company later. Maybe in Massa, we could sit down and chat."

William could see Anna focusing on their conversation. Any more information would bring up questions from her.

"Have a good trip to Venice and we'll meet up in Massa," Sonja said.

Sonja got up from the table, gave everyone a hug, and the French double cheek kiss. William and the sisters stayed a while longer sipping the decaf cappuccino after the meal.

In the background, they could hear a voice singing an opera aria. It bounced off the tower walls that surrounded the plaza. From their table, they could see a street beggar belting out her song. On the way back to the car, Leslie added a ten-euro note to the woman's cup and thanked her for her performance.

"Are you still involved with The Company that paid you all that money, William?" Anne waited until they reached the B&B before the questions began.

"Yes and no," he answered. "They paid me for a CAT scan to see how my brain works."

"Sonja said there was a clinic in Pisa. Sorry to repeat your conversation, but I couldn't help overhearing it."

"Anne, I need to be blunt. I can't tell you anything. Something happened to me for a while, and the experience was long and complicated. No one except Leslie knows everything. We have to keep it that way. Maybe someday the whole story will be told, but not now. All I can say is it's in everyone's best interest."

"Wow, William," Anne exclaimed. "This is exciting. A real mystery and someone I know is involved. Keep me in the loop. I'll want to hear about this one for sure."

By now Leslie was starting to feel a little uneasy. She added, "William is only playing along with The Company. He doesn't have much to do with them anymore."

"All right then," Anne said. "No more questions. Let's get some rest. Venice tomorrow."

Chapter 31

Robert and Julia were still asleep, and it was now after five. They had spent a lot of energy in bed. The learning process took several attempts to get it right. Not that they weren't getting it right with each attempt, but they wanted to keep trying just to be sure.

Fifteen minutes later Robert awoke and looked at the clock. He stared at this beautiful woman who had completely drained him. He thought about her and the assignment and knew this could get complicated.

Julia stirred and rolled over. "What time is it? I feel we've been asleep for a while."

"About five-thirty. We could walk around the square before having dinner."

"Yes, I guess we could, or continue where we left off, and have a late meal."

Robert didn't need another prompt. He felt Julia's hand wrap around his manhood and their lips met at the same time. A late dinner was planned for that evening.

*****

Ninety minutes later Robert escaped to the shower. He was ready to eat something and talk for a while. Julia was a wild woman and he loved it. She joined him in the shower after a few minutes and they took turns soaping each other. They needed to remove the smells of their love- making before going out into public.

"Where are you taking me for dinner, Robert?"

Robert was already out of the shower and half dressed. He needed to keep ahead of Julia by moving into the bedroom. There was no telling what she'd do if they were standing naked together in the bathroom.

"Do you like pizza? We have an Italian restaurant that specializes in Tuscan cuisine. The owner is from New York, and some say his Italian food is better than anything in the Big Apple."

"This I've got to see. I love Italian food. Let's find out if the rumors are true."

"We can walk to the restaurant since the air's not too cold. Just bring a light sweater and you'll be warm."

The two lovers left the house, and made the short walk to *Romeos*, just off the main square. Julia slipped her arm into Robert's, and let the warmth of her body spread through their connection. Robert loved her wanting to be close to him. He didn't know how their relationship would play out, but he was willing to explore it for a while longer.

The restaurant was jammed with customers. Seating for

two was available in the back, along the wall with all the pictures of Italian landscapes. A bottle of Italian red from Tuscany seemed appropriate. A thin crust pizza was ordered with chicken, and four varieties of vegetables covering the large platter. The meal was set over a small flame that kept the pizza warm while they ate and drank. Neither wanted the evening to end.

"When do you want me to start this assignment, Robert? The sooner I complete it, the faster I can fly back to New Mexico."

"I'm really in a bind," Robert said with a sigh. "This assignment is dangerous and I don't want anything happening to you." Robert was between a rock and a hard place. Julia was the only one he knew who could pull this off, and she was now the last person he wanted for the assignment.

"Robert, this kind of job really gets my juices flowing. It's one of the many reasons I'm attracted to you. I want to be more involved with what you do. Let me complete this job, then we can see what happens next."

She made perfect sense. Robert would have to use her to finish the assignment. He also thought about having her work with him in Albuquerque. They'd be a great team. Two hot lovers fighting the injustices of the world together. Hollywood could make a mini-series. *Robert and Julia.* The show would have to be on HBO. They were too steamy for prime time.

"You've never seen my house in Albuquerque, Julia. Before you fly back to New York I want you to see my home and the level of my operation. I could use a full-time partner and right now I can't think of anyone more suited than you."

"Robert, you are such a romantic. You really know how to sweep a woman off her feet." Julia continued teasing him. She was interested in his proposal, but leaving the Big Apple would be difficult. New York was like a drug fix. Julia was not sure if she was ready for the detoxification that would follow.

"Julia, I want you to meet someone. I just spotted him at the bar with his new girlfriend. I used to work for him. I think I told you what I was involved in several years ago. Anyway, he just retired and moved to Santa Fe. His name's Jason."

"He has a new girlfriend? Is there something in the Santa Fe air that makes a man commit to a woman? I think I'll bottle a few gulps and take them back to New York. If this high elevation air works, I know women who'll pay top dollar to try this on their boyfriends."

"Okay, Julia, behave. I'd really like you to meet Jason."

Robert and Julia approached the bar just as Jason turned around.

"Robert, what a surprise to see you. I'd like you to meet my friend, Rosa."

"The pleasure is mine, Rosa. This is my friend Julia, who's visiting from New York. We've known each other for a while, and I finally got her to fly to the Southwest and experience small town living."

Julia spoke up, "What Robert means to say is I finally got him to fly me to New Mexico. It was an all out effort on my part." She paused and looked at Jason. "You sound like you're from New York as well, Jason. Am I right?"

"That'd be correct. I managed people for a living. Now I'm retired and learning about photography."

"And doing quite well, I might add," Rosa said. "I'm thinking of displaying a couple of his wildflower pictures. He has potential, and I want to encourage him."

"We just finished dinner and are headed home. Julia needs to get back to New York soon. We may be seeing more of her in the future. How about you two?"

"We're waiting to be seated," Jason said. "Can I call you later, Robert? I have some information that may help you in your investigation."

"You have my secure number?" Robert asked.

"I do. How about tomorrow night? Will you be home?"

"Of course. Call me then." Robert said.

"Nice to meet you, Rosa," Julia said. "I may be coming back to this area real soon. My high altitude air business may take off in New York, and I'd have to return to fill a few more containers. I'll explain more next time I see you."

Rosa and Jason had a puzzled look on their faces. Robert rolled his eyes, letting them know not to take Julia's comment seriously. She had a sense of humor only a mother or a lover could understand. Robert was not her mother, but he was doing his best to fulfill the other position.

"Good to meet you as well, Julia," Rosa said. "Come by my gallery the next time you're in town, and you can tell me more about the air business. Robert knows where it is."

"Will do," Julia answered as she gave Rosa a wink.

"Talk to you tomorrow, Jason," Robert said.

Julia and Robert left the restaurant. Now, all they had ahead of them was more passion and hot sex. The last twenty feet of the walk home found them again running down the sidewalk.

Clothes were removed while they made their way to the bedroom. Hard nipples and a stiff organ were in play. A question raced through Robert's mind before he landed on the bed next to Julia; Do I need a prescription for Viagra?

*****

The lovers woke around seven in the morning. They wanted to be on the road by nine. That didn't hold them back. Morning sex was better than a cup of coffee. Thirty minutes later they were having their first cup of Joe and throwing clothes into suitcases. Robert had a couple of omelets bubbling on the stove, and bread in the toaster. They were ready to leave fifteen minutes before nine.

Little conversation transpired between them for the first part of the drive. They were re-visiting their actions covering the past twenty-four hours. The flame between them was like the out of control brush fires that burn California every summer. There was plenty of fuel. It just needed a spark, and the trip to Santa Fe to provided that.

"We should be in Albuquerque in about an hour." Robert's voice finally broke the silence. "I live on the east side of town. I need to tell you more about myself. After that, I want to hear about you."

"I thought you knew all about me from my file?" Julia asked. "I know you research people before you hire them."

"True, but the file doesn't tell me everything about a person. I'd like to know more than what a file says."

Robert covered his previous life in Utah and explained in

depth how he became involved with Jason and The Company. His previous life in Utah and the Mormon Church fascinated Julia, so she didn't utter a word during his monolog.

"Your turn, my dear. Who influenced you the most when you grew up, and how did you become an investigator for hire?"

Julia used the rest of the trip to describe her early years. Her need to find justice for the underdog played a big part in her development. Her father was a cop in New York City. He eventually became a detective, and Julia learned some investigative skills from him. Her mother died when she was eight so dad was her role model.

At age twenty-five, she enrolled in the police academy and learned martial arts. After three years of walking a beat, she decided she could contribute more as a private investigator. Criminals and their slick lawyers used the court system to get off, and this flaw in the legal system disillusioned her.

Working for Robert was a breath of fresh air for Julia, and she looked forward to her jobs with him. She became more attracted to him with each assignment.

"Anyway, Robert, I hope I got my point across as to how I feel about you. This has been the best information gathering assignment I've had, and we hardly left the house."

"Your point's been made," Robert said. "I'm glad you

suggested coming out here. I had no idea how this would play out."

Julia thought for a moment. The last two days were a lot to take in. "I'm excited about seeing your home in Albuquerque, and going over the final plan regarding Jones. He sounds like a real bastard, but I've dealt with his kind before."

"Here we are," Robert said, as he pulled into the driveway. Carla was at the front door to greet them.

"Carla, I'd like you to meet my friend, Julia. She'll be here for a day before she flies back to New York."

"Buenos Dias, Julia. I'm happy to see that Señor Woods has a woman friend in his life. I was afraid he was going to be a lonely bachelor forever." Carla never held back from what she was thinking.

"Carla is like a mother to me. She speaks her mind, so not much is hidden by formalities."

"Good to meet you, Carla," Julia said. They shook hands.

"I'll be serving lunch in an hour," Carla said. "You have time to clean up after the drive."

Robert took Julia's bag and dropped it off in the master bedroom. Julia walked through the back sliding glass door and stood by the pool. She noticed the solar panels along the south border of the property, and several windmills spinning in the distance. They were partially hidden by large palm trees.

"You seem to have enough alternative energy to run this house all by itself. What do you need all this power for?" Julia asked as she took in the landscape and pool area.

Robert took her hand and led her into the main office where the large screens and computer table was located. Julia stood at the door of the office as her gaze swept from one side of the room to the other. She was stunned. Robert finally broke the silence.

"This is the hub of my business. Alan is my assistant and is usually here, but he's visiting his parents."

Julia continued to stare at all the equipment. Finally, she was able to speak. "Robert, I had no idea you had this much hardware. The cops in New York would be jealous. Do you realize you may have one of the largest equipped private spy businesses probably in America?"

"I tried to tell you I'm pretty serious in my work. This is one of the reasons I need a partner. It's getting difficult to manage alone. Alan does research and monitors the satellite computer, but there are many duties I need help with."

"Robert, I'm blown away. You have a beautiful home and a top of the line investigation business. You've peaked my interest for sure. Let's get cleaned up for lunch and discuss this later."

Julia was ready for a continuation of Santa Fe in private. Robert wasn't going to block any plans she had for him. As soon as the bedroom door was closed, Robert felt Julia's hand reaching for his belt. Pants were removed and within seconds the warm feeling of oral sex filtered through Robert's entire body. Clothes were removed and the re-exploring of each other's sensitive areas began again. Julia wanted every possible moment she had left for Robert to be inside her. She'd be gone tomorrow and didn't know how long until she'd see him again.

Chapter 32

Robert had a hard time saying goodbye. When he drove Julia to the airport he didn't say much. She had a job to do. A long kiss and she was gone.

Julia studied the Jones files on the flight back to New York. She concealed the drugs in her cosmetic bag to get past inspection. She wanted to finish up with Jones as soon as possible and get back to Robert.

She and Robert agreed to work as a team. She had everything she wanted and more. A job she loved, and a guy she wanted to do it with. Julia didn't know if it was love, but she felt the relationship heading that way. She would know more when the physical passion leveled out and she could see their relationship clearly.

When Julia got back to her apartment in New York, she cleared her calendar on Thursday nights. There was a good chance Jones would be attending Max's to score another notch for his bedpost. Julia would be wearing the same outfit she wore when she arrived in Albuquerque. Jones didn't stand a chance.

*****

The day before, Robert called and left a message for Jason to return his call the following afternoon because he knew he'd be occupied with Julia until then.

The phone rang and startled Robert who was daydreaming about the last two days with Julia. "Robert, hi. This is Jason."

"Hi, Jason. Thanks for calling. I had no time to talk last night."

"After meeting Julia, I'm surprised you let her go back to New York," Jason said.

"She has a job to do. We're planning on running my business together, so she has a few ends to tie up in the City. It's a big change for her. You must have gone through a similar transition when you moved out here."

"Yes, I did, but I was tired of the fast pace of New York. The energy level in Santa Fe suits me. Anyway, let me tell you what I've found out."

"All right. Do you have someone on the inside feeding you info?" Robert asked.

"No names. If anyone in The Company finds out about me, I could be the next deceased ex-employee. Anyway, here's what The Company wants to control." Jason paused. After what seemed like an eternity to Robert, Jason spoke. "Water."

Robert didn't say anything right away. He couldn't believe what he'd heard. Finally, he said, "Water? Are you kidding?"

"Water. It's as simple as that. The real question should be

'why'? Why control water?" Jason waited for Robert to respond.

"Okay, I'll bite. Why control water?"

"What do humans need to survive?" Jason asked. "Air, food, and water. Shelter is a distant fourth. Man started out in caves, and we still have a few of those around. We can only control the quality of our air. Food, or the lack of it, is keeping the population of the world in check. Water is the third item that man needs in order to survive. Control water and you can impact the world."

"Are you kidding? How do they expect to do that?"

"Company investors are pouring money into the construction of desalination plants around the world. Man is destroying water resources at a fast rate. One of the few remaining ways to get drinkable water will be to extract it from the ocean."

"Aren't the Saudis doing that already?"

"Yes. They've done it for a while. They're the ones selling their technology to The Company. The Company investors see this as a way to have a say in the planet's future. A number of these plants are under construction on different continents. Africa and Asia are the main locations. South America has just come online."

"Why is the clinic so important?" Robert asked. "Do they need to keep making money to fund this venture?"

"Yes. The world population couldn't give a rat's ass about stock exchanges. They're too busy trying to survive in most third world countries. Controlling water would get international attention." Jason waited for Robert's response.

"So that's their ultimate goal," Robert said. "Control human drinking water and you have the world on its knees. These guys are frigging nuts."

"I'm afraid so, Robert. It's not going to happen in our lifetime, but the younger members in The Company might have real power. In other words, they'll have a say in how the world runs without being a government. They'll become 'the man behind the curtain'."

"This is insane. All along I hoped it was just the money. Now they want to have a say in how the world runs? Hitler wanted the same thing, and tried it through his 'master race theory'. This is just another form of that same madness." By now Robert was pissed off.

"I'm afraid so. Impacting the financial world is just a step in reaching that goal. Stopping The Company from putting a team of future seers in place would be a start," Jason said.

"Stopping them? Easier said than done." Robert knew he'd need help. What could an investigator from Albuquerque do against this group of fanatics?

"Right now that'd be my objective if I were you," Jason said. "Stop the money flow, and you stop the water project, or at least slow it down."

"Jason, you've raised my incentive another notch. I need to change my approach."

"You take out Jones and I'll give you another name," Jason said. "I only know a few Company names and they'll be difficult to reach. They travel in tight circles. Jones will be an easy target compared to the others."

"Deal. After Jones is gone I'll take out each name you give me. One at a time is all I need. They won't know what hit them." Robert was still angry, but now he had a clearer picture of what he was up against.

"How are you going to eliminate Jones? No, don't tell me. The less I know, the better. Call me when the mission's completed," Jason said.

"Good idea, Jason. Stay neutral and you'll be more effective. I'll call you when Jones is gone."

"Sounds good."

"Be sure we use this secure line. After Jones is gone, The Company will look for leaks, and we don't want them to find either of us," Robert said.

"Let me know when you come to Santa Fe again. Also bring Julia when she's back from New York. I'd like to spend an evening with the four of us."

"Will do. Thanks, Jason." Robert hung up.

Chapter 33

"Call me when you're heading my way. I want to show you around Paris when you get there," Anne said to Leslie.

Leslie and William planned to visit Anne after seeing a little more of Italy. Next stop for the Rays was a return to Massa Marittima.

"Expect to see us sooner rather than later, Anne. William wants to eat lunch on top of the Eiffel Tower and walk through a couple of museums. We've had a good tour of Venice and Florence and think we should save southern Italy for a trip all by itself."

Anne boarded the train. She was thankful for the time they spent together, and for the paid vacation.

"That was the best time I've ever had with Anne," Leslie said. "I expect Paris will also be fun, but seeing something new with her was really special. Thank you, William."

"What'd I do? I'm just along for the ride and enjoying the sights."

"I mean thank you for having a blood clot. Without that none of this would have happened."

"You're thanking me for having a blood clot? Are you kidding?" William said.

"What I mean is, you made this happen. Your involvement with The Company is not what I would have done. You had the courage to see it through and look where we are now. Thank you."

"Well, since you put it that way, I accept your compliment. This investigation is still not over. There's not much more for me to do. I don't plan on being a client again."

"Good," Leslie said.

William continued. "If they want to take pictures of my brain and pay me, no problem. Fly to Peru and interview Marta, no problem. Taking down The Company? That's Robert's job."

"Finally, you're starting to agree with me," Leslie said.

The last leg of the drive was spent listening to a Beatles album and enjoying Tuscany. *The Long and Winding Road* fit their mood as William and Leslie headed through the countryside that took them back to Massa Marittima.

Chapter 34

Julia had her work cut out for her. Max's was located in an upscale section of the city about a mile from Times Square. Young men, in the thirty to forty age group, made it a regular stop after work. Expensive handcrafted beers and exotic bar drinks were sold at a price affordable only for those making a high-end salary. This kept the middle-class drinker in his or her own neighborhood drinking Bud light or Coors. Appetizers and other food items were catered from the deli next door. This was an expensive meat market, and any woman entering needed to realize she was on the menu.

The *ladies*, who did show up, ranged from high-end hookers to women looking for sex with no strings attached. Bodies, sculpted at the local gym, pretty much set the scene for the negotiations that took place every night. Hook ups were observed but never stored in anyone's memory because it changed every week. What happened at Max's stayed at Max's.

Arriving early, Julia remained in her car parked across the street. She didn't want to waste her talents on a no-show. She knew she could get any man in Max's to buy her drinks. She had a mission and Jones had to arrive before she'd go into action.

Around nine Julia noticed a man, matching the picture of Jones, getting out of a cab in front of the bar and enter the club. This is it, she thought, as she exited her car and walked across the street towards the front entrance.

Max's was nearing capacity so a doorman was in place to make sure the numbers did not exceed city regulations. When two men leave, two are allowed in. Women were never held to the rule of waiting. They were the reason for Max's in the first place.

Heads turned as Julia made her entrance. The open shirt, gold chain crew stood by the door so they could have first crack at the client list. *Hands off* was the bar policy, but hanging tongues could not be monitored. The drooling began as soon as Julia walked in.

Jones had a favorite seat where he could see the women walking into the bar. He had just slipped the previous occupant a twenty to find another stool. His size and demeanor also indicated he wouldn't take no for an answer. He now occupied his personal throne and turned towards the door as Julia made her way towards the bar.

Julia knew he'd seen her. She sat on an empty bar stool, four seats from Jones. She knew the hook-up had to be his idea. He'll come to me, she thought, and then he's going down.

Within minutes the bartender announced to Julia that the man on the end of the bar wanted to buy her a drink. Glancing toward Jones, she nodded her approval. Another twenty-dollar bill emptied the seat next to Jones. She was now in place to take this meeting to the next level.

*****

Robert was home. It was Thursday night and he assumed Julia might be in the middle of the operation. She promised to call him as soon as the job was complete. Around eleven in the evening his private phone rang. It was Julia. It must have been one in the morning in New York.

"How did it go?" Robert asked.

"I'm fine and how are you, Robert?" Julia had to work on Robert to change him into someone who greeted her with a loving comment and not business.

"I'm sorry. How are you, Sweetheart? I miss you."

Julia knew Robert would get better.

"I miss you too," Julia said. "I think I have everything we need from this clown. He's everything a woman would not want in a relationship. Putting him in his place was an honor."

"You're okay? I'm glad this is over. Did you get what we need?" Robert's voice remained worried.

"Everything and more. I think we've got enough information to take him down. I'm flying out tomorrow with the tape. Let's get some sleep and talk tomorrow night. I'm really tired."

"That is your last job like this. My stomach has been in knots the whole time. I'll email a ticket for a late afternoon flight. You can be here by dinner."

"Good. That'll give me time to pack a few things and tell my roommate to find a new tenant. I plan on keeping the apartment and lease it to her. See you tomorrow evening."

*****

The connection flight through Atlanta landed around five. Robert was there to meet Julia. He held up a sign that read: *Most Beautiful Woman in the World.* Several single women approached Robert before the flight landed because they thought he was advertising. When Julia saw Robert and the sign, a big smile crossed her face.

Now that's the way to greet a woman, she thought. There may be hope for you yet, Robert.

They embraced and gave each other a passionate kiss. A woman, standing behind them, saw the sign and turned to her husband. "Greet me like that next time, and who knows what might happen when we get home."

Robert drove over the speed limit during the thirty-minute drive to his house. They both knew what they would be doing for the next hour. It was eight days since Julia left Albuquerque, and both were more than ready to take up where they left off.

Bags were left in the car. Julia ran ahead of Robert and into the house. She sped past the empty kitchen and into the master bedroom. She was naked by the time Robert entered the house. She grabbed him as he walked into the bedroom. A ripped shirt and torn pants found Robert in the same state of exposure as Julia. They embraced as she mounted him standing up. She had wanted him inside her for the past week. She was home and it felt good.

An hour later the two lovers emerged from the bedroom, dressed only in bathrobes. There was no use getting dressed this late in the evening when they'd be returning to their previous level of exposure after dinner.

"Let's heat one of these pizzas, and have it with the salad Carla left us. She's visiting family for two days, and prepared a few things so we wouldn't starve."

"I know how to cook, Robert. The pizza sounds fine, but tomorrow night you get to taste one of my meals. Will Carla get offended if I invade her kitchen?"

"I'm not sure. Women can be protective of their territory. Carla may be fine with someone else cooking. I'll heat the pizza and then you can tell your story. I'm dying to hear everything," Robert said.

The meal was prepared and the wine poured. The evening air was perfect for eating outside by the pool. By the second slice of pizza, Julia was ready to fill Robert in on the Jones encounter.

"Getting Jones to notice me wasn't difficult," Julia started. "Within minutes, after entering Max's, he'd purchased me a drink, and cleared a seat next to him at the bar. This guy had bypassed his brain and was using an erection to make his decisions. An hour later he was ready to take me home. He'd arrived at Max's in a cab, and I had my car, so I drove."

"He lives downtown, right?" Robert asked. "Alan traced the address of Jones. I just want to make sure he's living where he took you."

"Everything matches up. Let me get through the story first, and then we can do the question and answer thing."

"Okay." Robert filled their wine glasses.

Julia continued. "By the time Jones finished a drink in his apartment, the paralyzing drug I slipped him, took effect. He knew something was wrong, but couldn't do anything about it. The injection of the truth serum into his neck took a few seconds, and soon he was putty in my hands. I started the questioning right away because I wanted to get out as fast as I could. Here is the tape." Julia pulled the recording device from her purse and pushed the play button.

"Are you Mark Jones?"

"Yes."

"Do you work for a company in New York City?"

"Yes."

"What do you do?"

"I'm the head of a research clinic located in San Miguel, Mexico."

"What do they do there?"

"We've developed a drug that can re-create the ability to see the future."

"Can anyone use it?"

"No, only past clients who've had this ability."

"What can these clients do?"

"They can see the closing highs in the stock market."

"Do you know the names of any of these people who are benefitting from this inside information?"

"I know three of them personally."

"Can you give me their names?"

"Peter Marks, John Calhoun and Paul Orbit."

"How do you know them?"

"They're in a private men's club with me."

"Are these the only men you know?"

"Yes. The other twenty members protect their identity, and don't let anyone know who they are."

"Are there only twenty-three people who make up the group?" Julia asked.

"Yes, as far as I know."

"Is making money their only goal?"

"I've heard they're investing a portion of their earnings into desalination plants."

"Why would they do that?"

"I'm not sure."

"Is this a good thing you're doing?"

"That depends on what you mean by a good thing. I get paid well, and that's a good thing."

"Has anyone been hurt by this research?"

"The clinic in Italy had some setbacks. The first trials were done on street people, and a few died. During the trial and error period, a couple of clients developed problems. They suffered a heart attack and a stroke. We also discovered an investigator who was snooping around and he had to be eliminated."

"Did you know the name of this investigator?"

"Karl Swartz. He was German."

"Do you know who he was working for?"

"Not yet, but we're still investigating. We think it's someone based in the States."

"Do you plan on visiting the clinic in Mexico soon?"

"Not unless there're any problems."

"Why did The Company close the clinic in Italy?"

"The German investigator made them nervous. They decided to move to another location, closer to the States."

"Is there any other information you need to tell me?"

"I don't know. You're the one asking questions."

A click was heard on the tape. "That is all I could get out of him," Julia said. "I injected that other drug to erase his short-term memory after I got him onto his bed. He was out like a light."

"Do you know what this means?" Robert asked.

"No, not really."

"It means we have the names of three of the investors from

The Company and a complete confession by Jones. We may have the power to shut down the clinic."

"Robert, we're dealing with some evil men. They're not going to take this lightly. They'll tie up any prosecution in the courts, and buy their way out."

"I don't think we can take them head on either, Julia. The three men, mentioned in the tape, would be interested in hearing what Mark Jones has to say. I think, after hearing it, Jones won't be around for long."

"What happens to Jones is his own making," Julia said. "Having someone else take him out would keep us out of the mix. Let's put this aside and talk more about it tomorrow when we're rested."

"I agree. Mornings are best for making plans. Let me have your wine glass and plate," Robert said.

Robert cleared the table out by the pool. When he returned, Julia was in the water, waiting for him to join her. Sex in a swimming pool was a new experience for Robert, but not for Julia. They'd make the journey to the bedroom eventually, but right now the clear, warm water was where they would join in their lovemaking.

*****

The sun cleared the mountain range in the east. Robert got out of bed and quietly made his way to the office. He didn't want to wake Julia. If he did, another session of sex could be expected, and he needed to get his idea in motion.

Alan was expected to arrive in the office around noon. Robert wrote down the three names from the tape. He needed all the info on these men as soon as possible and that would keep Alan busy.

After leaving the instructions, Robert went back to the bedroom. He knew Julia would be awake by now, and expecting him to perform his manly duties. Robert was already hard as he entered the sleeping chamber. He was right. Her naked body was waiting for him, lying on top of the covers, and ready for the morning exercise session. Breakfast would have to wait.

Chapter 35

The visit to Massa lasted two days. William and Leslie had dinner with Sonja at the restaurant of their friend, Raul, and touched base one last time. The Rays were ready to visit Anne in Paris.

The next morning, the drive back to Pisa was un-eventful. The Tower Hotel was just as they remembered it. Luca was on duty and greeted them like relatives returning home.

"William and Leslie. Good to see you again. Seven months have just flown by."

"Hello again, Luca. It's good to be back again. We're on our way to France and had to drop by. We want to eat dinner at your brother's place tonight. How's everyone been?"

"We live a simple life in Italy. There have been a few changes. The restaurant is doing well and Rondo is having another child in a few months. He can afford to grow his family now. Also, I have a partner."

When someone used the word partner, William took it to mean they're gay and found someone of the same sex.

"Congratulations, Luca," William said. "We're really happy for you. Life is much more fun to go through with a partner. Isn't that right, Sweetheart?"

Leslie looked right at William and gave him one of those looks that said, *don't be a wise-ass.* "Where did you meet your friend?" Leslie asked.

"Actually right here at the hotel. He applied for a job as a driver and doorman. He had good references from a company that used to be based in Pisa. As a matter of fact, he is driving up to the front of the hotel right now."

William turned to see a familiar face enter the front door, carrying a suitcase in each hand. "Pablo. Is that you?"

"Mr. Ray. I had a feeling you'd show up here again. Luca said he was expecting you sometime in the summer, and now you're here."

"Leslie, I want you to meet Pablo. He was the man who drove me last year when I visited the clinic."

"Glad to meet you, Pablo." Leslie shook his hand.

"I need to help these people check into the hotel and into their rooms. We can talk later."

William agreed and turned to Luca. "Did you know I met Pablo last year?"

"Yes, of course. He was the driver for several people staying at the hotel during the last few years. I noticed him then but he seemed too busy to approach. When the clinic shut down he was without a job. He came in one day, and that is when we connected. We met for coffee, and things seemed to click. I hired him, and he's been with us for a few months now. He told me a few things about his previous job. I think you were the last person that Pablo drove from the Tower Hotel to the clinic."

William wanted to ask Pablo some questions about the clinic, but he didn't know where the man's allegiances lay.

"What room do you have us in?" William asked. "We need to rest up before dinner."

"The third floor facing the river. What time do you want to eat? I'll call Rondo to reserve a table."

Leslie let Luca know eight o'clock would work. They had a late lunch on the drive from Massa.

William didn't unpack. He was tired from the drive, and was on the bed and asleep within twenty minutes. Leslie took time to remove a few clothes from her bag and grab the novel she was reading. Books helped relax her mind.

When William woke up, Leslie was sleeping. He decided to go down to the lobby and stretch his legs. Pablo was just pulling into the front of the hotel as William entered the lobby, so William approached him.

"This hotel has turned out to be a good job for you, Pablo.

I'm happy you've found a partner to be with."

"Mr. Ray. You were the last person I drove from here. No more clinic clients came to the Tower Hotel. I ended up driving the employees to and from work and helped pack up the medical equipment. They started to shut down a few weeks after you left."

"What was the reason for the clinic closing?" William asked.

"There were some rumors about someone spying. I don't know many facts. A few days later a strange man showed up at the clinic. Dr. Yee instructed me to drive him to another hotel near here."

"Could you tell what nationality he was," William asked.

"He spoke English with a French accent. That's all I know. A day later a corpse was discovered in the hotel where I took him. It was a different man who died than the one I dropped off."

"How about the man who died. What do you know about him?"

"I heard the dead man was a German national. The person I dropped off at the hotel must have taken a taxi when he left because I didn't pick him up. He never came back to the clinic and I never saw him again."

"Do you think the clinic had something to do with the

German's death?"

"A lot of strange things happened during my time as a driver. I transported several homeless people to the clinic. Not all of them left the building. Also, two American men, I took to the clinic died in the Tower Hotel. The cause was said to be natural. These deaths made me think that the clinic was doing things to people that might not be good. I was glad the clinic was closing even though my job would be gone. What went on inside was kept secret."

"Do you have any contact with the nurse named Marta. I think she was from Peru."

"No. I took her to her apartment about three weeks before my job ended. She said something about going back to South America. She also seemed relieved the job was ending. She was ready to see her family again."

"What happened to Dr. Yee? Do you know where he went?"

"He was the last to go. After I dropped Dr. Yee off at the airport I was instructed to return the car to the dealer. I think Dr. Yee was flying to Singapore. I was wired my last paycheck, and that was the end of my job."

"Pablo, you have been a great help. A friend of mine is investigating the clinic, and what they were doing. This information is helpful. I think you're in a better situation now."

"Thank you, Mr. Ray. I hope the information can help. If the clinic killed people I'm glad I'm working somewhere else."

William shook hands with Pablo and said goodbye. He went back to the room just as Leslie was waking up.

"Is it dinner time? I'm starting to get hungry," she said.

"We have about an hour."

"Where were you?" Leslie asked.

"Talking to Pablo. I need to make another call to Robert. I found out more about the clinic and what happened to Karl and Dr. Yee."

William repeated the conversation he had with Pablo. Leslie's eyes widened when William mentioned the mystery man going into the same hotel as Karl. When William finished the story, she sat on the bed in quiet reflection.

William then called Robert. After the initial hellos, the same information was passed onto him. While William talked to Robert he could hear a woman's voice in the background.

"Is someone with you, Robert?"

"Yes, my new partner. Her name is Julia. You'll meet her when you visit next time."

"We're going to dinner now, but I want to hear how you two met," William said.

"You will. By the way, good job in finding out about Karl and his murderer. I may never find out who this assassin is, but I'll try and access the security cameras in the hotel. If I can identify his face we may find him."

"Good luck, Robert. We leave for Paris tomorrow. We should be back in the States in a week."

"Call me when you get home. I'll update you then. I have to go. Julia is being naughty again and wants my attention."

William hung up and turned to Leslie. "That was interesting. It sounded like Robert has a girlfriend as well as a partner in his business. I heard her in the background."

"That sounds fantastic. Now he may not need you as much," Leslie added.

"You're right," William agreed. "Let go to dinner."

Dinner with Rondo went smoothly and promises to return in the future were made. After the meal, the Rays retired early to their hotel room. They wanted to get enough rest before the long train ride to Paris.

The train departed the station early the next morning. In Milan, they changed trains and arrived in Paris by dinnertime. A taxi to Anne's apartment, and up three flights of stairs, gave them a view of Notre Dame in the distance.

For the next few days, William and Leslie took in the sights of Paris, eating lunch at the top of the Eiffel Tower, and spending hours walking around the Louvre. William was starting to feel like a normal citizen of the world again.

Chapter 36

Alan did a thorough job researching the three company members mentioned in the Jones tape. A week later he sent edited copies to each name by special delivery. Finding their personal home address posed little challenge for Alan.

Peter Marks was the first on the list. He was a young man when he inherited his wealth from a father who made millions during the Vietnam War. His father manufactured chemicals and supplied the military complex with a defoliate spray called Agent Orange. The chemical was used to kill plant life. The idea was to kill the jungle in the areas where the Vietcong were hiding. No jungle, so no place to hide.

John Calhoun made his millions as a co-founder of a company in the Silicon Valley located near San Francisco. Many of the Internet startups made the members multi-millionaires overnight. Calhoun accumulated his wealth and got out. In 2008 he met a few members of The Company who used people like Robert and William to turn their millions into billions.

The last person on the list was Paul Orbit. He'd been a banker in his early years and decided to open his own branch in California. Bear Bank was a front for what he actually did. Two large drug cartels from Mexico needed his services to launder their money. Mr. Orbit later sold his bank and joined The Company a year later.

"Alan, good work on the research," Robert said. "My only question was how you found out about Paul Orbit and his money laundering business. If you found out, then the Federal Government must have known as well."

"This guy was a little more difficult," Alan said. "I had to break into classified files. It seems some big names in government were involved. If Mr. Orbit ever appeared in court, a senator or two would be exposed. The case was classified as top secret because of National Security. In other words, business as usual."

"Who are these people?" Robert asked. "I bet there are more skeletons in American politics than a season of Bones."

"Do you watch that show too?" Alan asked. "I get a good laugh each time I see it, but they do seem to get all the body parts right."

At that moment Julia walked into the office. She was eating a sandwich and had made one for Alan and Robert. Carla was busy, cooking beans for dinner. It was Mexican night.

The three sat in front of the clinic satellite screen. Now that the research lab had been moved to Mexico, the action was live.

"Any word on how the three men reacted when they received Jones' tape, exposing them?" Julia asked.

Alan shook his head. "Not yet, but I did put a call to your

roommate in New York like you asked. I faxed her a picture of Jones last week. She dropped by Max's on Thursday to see if he showed up. She called on Friday and said he was a 'no show'."

"How is Cathy? Did she talk about anything else, or just report to you?"

"Pretty much a report. We talked a little, but mostly about technical stuff. She's taking a night class on computer systems. I told her she could call me anytime if she needed help."

"Watch out for her, Alan," Julia added. "She's a wild woman. That's one reason I liked her so much."

"I'm pretty shy when it comes to women, Julia. There's little chance a wild woman would give me a second look."

"Oh, I don't know about that. Sometimes it's men like you who are the ones Cathy's attracted to. She likes attention and a quiet man in the background is what works for her."

"Anyway, she said she'd go to the bar again next Thursday. Said something about Max's being a real 'meat market'. She could only stand being there for as long as it took to drink a glass of wine."

"If Jones didn't show up, then something must have happened," Robert said. "The Company members strive to keep their identity private, and now someone outside their circle knows their names. Are you sure the packages can't be traced back to us?"

"Not a chance. The closest they'll get to trace anything is to a Chinese bookstore in Hong Kong. I use them as the sender for any mail we don't want to be tracked back to us. Want to know the name of the shop?"

"You have a sick sense of humor, Alan, but ok, I'll bite," Robert said.

"Wong Fook Hing Book Store. I think they sell books in English as well as Chinese. I got their name from the Internet."

"Alan, you're sick. That is so off the wall I like it," Julia laughed. "A good sense of humor is attractive to a woman, Alan. Don't sell yourself short. I know ladies who would love to be around a funny guy like you."

"Thanks, Julia. I try. Probably the girl I meet will have to be in Starbucks working on her computer. I go there sometimes to see if any pretty geeks show up. Maybe I should start an Internet group. I saw one on TV called 'Christian Mingle'. How about one called 'Geek Mingle'. There are thousands of computer geeks out there who would like to meet other computer nerds. Why not make it easier for them. You have just given me a great idea, Julia. Thanks."

"I didn't say a thing. You came up with that all by yourself. If you do get it off the ground and need some financial help, let us know. That sounds like a great idea."

"All right, but let me get back to work. We're getting off track."

Alan glanced up at the computer screen and noticed some activity.

"Look," he said. "Something's happening at the clinic."

While all three watched the satellite screen, a black limo pulled up at the entrance of the clinic. The front door opened and a heavyset man got out and opened the back door. Mark Jones stumbled out. The first man from the front seat supported him, while a second assistant got out. Each took hold of Jones under the arms and escorted him into the clinic. Jones was unsteady and stumbling like he was drugged. He did not struggle with the men supporting him. Within minutes they were inside the clinic door. The car pulled away leaving the courtyard empty.

"What the hell do you think we just witnessed, Robert?" Julia said as she squeezed his hand.

"I don't know. I suspect Mark Jones won't be coming out of that clinic alive. From the stories we've heard from Italy, people disappeared, and were never heard from again."

"Is that what we just saw? The end of Mark Jones?" Julia gasped.

"We need a copy of that video, Alan," Robert said. "This could be used as evidence or a safety net. We may not be able to take The Company down, but if Jones is reported missing, the authorities could receive a copy, and do the follow-up work themselves." Robert paused. He thought about their next move.

"The three men on the tape are also up a creek," Robert said. "I doubt The Company will kill them, but I'll bet they distance themselves from them. Three down and twenty more to go." Robert stopped talking in order to think. Julia left the room to get drinks for everyone.

"Do you really believe The Company will remove these men?" Alan asked. "They know too much, and part of their earnings are going to that water project you mentioned."

"You're right," Robert said. "They might not kick them out. The Company just took a hit, but it's like a rock hitting a hornet's nest. They're going to be pissed, and looking for someone to sting."

Just then Julia returned with beers for Robert and herself. Alan preferred lemonade. Robert pondered over all the ways The Company could find out about them. Julia was first on the list.

"Where's the car you used when you went to Max's?" Robert asked.

"I left it with my roommate in New York. She drives it around when she needs it."

"When you went to Jones's apartment, where did you park?"

"Close to the front door. Why?" Julia was worried.

"Max's and Jones apartment will have surveillance cameras. The Company will trace where Jones went, and who visited him. It'll take time for them to figure this out. If the cameras pick up the license plate or have a clear shot of your face leaving with Jones, they'll have a lead."

"I completely forgot about that," Julia said. "He was the one who approached me in the bar. As far as any information on the camera, I'm Jones's weekend date. Can we get to those cameras, or are we in trouble?"

"How long were you in the apartment with Woods?"

"About ninety minutes. Maybe two hours. Long enough for a 'Wham, Bam, Thank you Ma'am' encounter. The type of women Jones picked up never stayed the night."

"We have to separate you from this guy. We first need to call your roommate, because she could be in danger and so could you."

"And do what?" Julia asked. Panic was now in her voice.

"Does your roommate have any other place to move to?"

"She has a mother in Queens," Julia answered.

"Call and tell her she needs to get out of the apartment. I'll pay for her expenses. Also, have her sell the car. Take a loss if you must, just do that right away. Don't let her use the car anymore."

"This is getting scary. I've never seen you so worked up before," Julia said. She started to feel sick.

"This could be serious. If you fax all the owner's papers to Cathy, she can sell it, and get another one. Also, she needs a phony identity. Alan can FedEx a new driver's license to her. We don't want the company tracing the car back to her either." Robert's investigator's persona had kicked in, and he was in *survivor mode* regarding Julia and Cathy.

"Last of all, you have to let your apartment go. Your car probably has your New York address connected with it. Right?"

"Yes," Julia answered slowly.

"We need to eliminate your past as fast as possible," Robert continued. "The apartment should be easy to sell. The realtor doesn't need to know where you live now. We only have a couple of weeks before The Company starts putting the pieces together."

Julia was going into shock.

"Getting Cathy to a safe place, and removing any car or apartment with your name on them, should bring their search to a halt," Robert continued. "Do you think we can do this?"

"I had no idea that joining up with you would bring all this change. You really owe me big, Robert. Why didn't you think of this before?"

"Julia, I'm really sorry. You saw how fast they reacted to Jones. I'm sure they have an investigative team working on this, but I bet they're not as high tech as we are."

"Do we have enough time to pull this off?" Julia asked.

"I hope so. They'll try to find out who sent the three members those tapes. If I were The Company I'd research the lifestyle of Jones and follow any leads. Going to his apartment makes you a suspect."

"I'll call Cathy right now. Can I use your phone so my call can't be traced?"

"Here it is. I'm really sorry, Julia. Being wrong and preparing for the worst is better than being right and face the consequences."

Julia made the call to Cathy and explained as much as she could without exposing Robert's business. Being in danger was all Cathy needed to know.

*****

By the next day, the plan was in motion. Cathy knew someone who owned a used car lot. She thought she could get rid of the car quickly and erase Julia's name. Alan sent the car papers and a new driver's license that afternoon.

The apartment would easily sell. Cathy had a friend who'd give Julia a fair price. A quick sale, with no inspections, and she could close in a couple of weeks. Cathy planned to move in with another girlfriend. She had no intention of moving back with her mother.

"When this is done I'll ease up," Robert said. "Putting you and Cathy in danger was never my intention."

"Are you sure the drug I gave Jones can't be reversed? You know, the memory one," Julia said.

"Jones has no memory of you or giving up the names of The Company members. We deleted your voice from the recording when you asked questions. We didn't include the part about the killings that took place in Italy either. We have copies of the complete tape, and I put them in a safe deposit box. If anything happens to any of us, the tapes will be sent to the FBI, Homeland Security and some other governmental body. I haven't figured out which one yet."

"We have to keep Cathy safe," Julia demanded.

"We'll take care of this," Robert promised, trying to force a smile.

Using William to work for the clinic was now out of the question. It was too dangerous. The Company would be on high alert. Robert had the phone number of Marie, in Mexico. The problem with contacting her had to do with Marie being watched.

With no one on the inside, only Marta was left. Robert knew where she lived in Peru. William volunteered to make a trip to Cusco during South America's spring or summer and meet with her.

The plan was laid out. William and Leslie were now home and could be contacted regarding a Peru visit. Robert would make the call tomorrow morning. Right now he was ready to take Julia into town and relieve some stress.

Robert called a spa, not far from his house, and booked two ninety-minute sessions. The couple planned to be back in time for dinner. It was Mexican night and Carla might feel slighted if they missed the meal.

Julia was overwhelmed by everything. She had no idea investigating The Company would mean she'd have to give up her life in New York. Basically, she went underground like a person in witness protection. She needed to change her name, and disappear altogether. It's a good thing she liked Robert as much as she did. She hoped there'd be no regrets down the road.

Dinner was at seven. Robert and Julia arrived home from

the spa around six. They had enough time for a *quickie* and a shower. Sex was still the main course in their relationship.

An hour later Robert and Julia sat out by the pool drinking a Negra Modella and eating Carla's home cooked meal. Carla was home with her family, and Alan had a night class, so the house was all theirs.

As the sun set, large thunderheads gathered in the south bringing in the possibility of monsoon rains dumping moisture from the Gulf of Mexico. Darkness eventually stretched across the valley floor.

The pool lights went on and the 90-degree water beckoned. Both Robert and Julia felt relaxed after the massage, sex, dinner, and beer. A dip in the water and more aerobics would wrap up the evening for the couple. Morning would come early enough, and there was much to do.

*****

William was up early as usual. If he slept until five, it was a good night. This morning found him at his computer at half past three, clearing out the spam, old messages, and answering the ones worthy of a response. His phone rang around seven.

"William, Robert here. Just trying to catch you before you're gone for the day."

"Hi, Robert. It's been a few weeks."

"Have you both recovered from your trip to Europe?" Robert asked.

"I think so. How's the investigation going? I bet this call has something to do with that."

"You know me too well, William. Quite a bit has happened since we last spoke."

Robert proceeded to tell William everything that had transpired including the information about the water treatment plants. The removal of Mark Jones, from his position in The Company, and time on earth was also covered in detail. Robert felt justice had been served with the Jones removal.

The suggestion that William cut his ties with the clinic was well received because he was not interested in working for The Company again. Money was no longer an issue. The Company was looking for the mole in their network, and any past employees were certainly on that list.

"What about my phone and Dr. Gupta? Should I wait until he calls and then tell him I'm finished working for The Company?" William asked.

"That's a good idea, William," Robert said. "Let him call you. Right now they're in a bit of an upheaval. They're pursuing any leaks because they don't want to lose their 'Golden Goose'. They'll go after any leads they get. I'll let Jason know what's happened to give him a 'heads up'. The only connections they have between Julia and me are the two flights she made to Albuquerque last month."

"Do you think they can get access to surveillance tapes at the airport showing Julia and you together?" William asked. "I know government authorities can get permission to view them. Do you think The Company has that much clout?"

"Shit. I forgot about that. Damn, William, are you sure you were a teacher all those years? You're really good at this spy stuff."

"Too much TV, Robert. Is there any way The Company can get to you through those tapes?"

"Money can buy anything, Robert. I'll work on this problem right away. Anyway, here's the reason I'm calling. How does a visit to Peru sound? It has to be soon. It's almost Fall here, but it'll be spring in South America. We know where Marta lives, and she may be able to give us some more information."

"Peru? Leslie and I've talked about it."

"I'll fly you round trip and get you some cash for expenses. How does that sound?"

"Robert, you have a deal. I'm sure Leslie will love to tour

Peru. I'll talk to her and get back to you tomorrow. This sounds like another adventure for sure."

"All right then. I'll expect a call tomorrow. Julia is now with me full time and is a huge help in this investigation. We don't think we can stop their desalination venture, but maybe we can slow down their income."

"You're probably right. Just keep doing what you can and maybe we'll get lucky," William said. The conversation ended and he hung up.

Leslie came into the kitchen and started making coffee. "Was that Robert on the phone?"

"Yes. He filled me in on the investigation. A lot has happened during or trip."

"Robert usually wants you to do something for him when he calls. What does he want you to do this time?"

"The good news is he thinks we shouldn't get involved with the clinic in Mexico. The situation could get dangerous. The Company's been exposed, and they're now looking for any possible leaks or people who have been involved."

"Like us?" Leslie's voice went up a notch.

"I don't know, but probably. Any past employees are on that list. I was relieved that Robert suggested I distance myself from them. The Company eliminated the person who was running the clinic in Italy and Mexico."

"By eliminated you mean killed?" Leslie's gasped.

"Robert believes so." William filled Leslie in on the conversation.

After Leslie heard the whole story she asked, "What does he want from you? I heard you mention something about Peru."

"Robert wants to give us a paid trip to Peru, and have a meeting with Marta. He figures she might tell us more about what went on in Italy now that she's safe and near her family."

"Where does she live again?" Leslie showed some interest. Peru was on her bucket list.

"Cusco. He's including shopping money for you, plus trip expenses. How about it? A paid trip later this fall and we could visit Machu Picchu as well. I only need to talk to Marta and see if she can tell us more about the clinic in Italy."

"How long would we be gone? Leslie asked. "I'm just settling into a routine. The only reason I'd even consider this is because we both have a desire to go there."

"Doesn't the shopping interest you at all?" William asked.

"Maybe. If we go, can we do it at the end of October or early November? I want to be home for the holidays."

"That means we have a month to get ready," William added. "I think we can make this happen. Call Peter and see if he can set up the remodel job with the neighbor next month. Then he can stay here with mom."

"I'll call and see if he's available. You work it out with Robert and I'll take care of the duties on the home-front."

The Rays were again in travel mode. Dates were set and Leslie's brother adjusted his schedule to do the remodel job while they were gone. A credit card and e-tickets were sent to William the following week. The busy life of two retired teachers was once again in full swing. Who knew where this Peru journey would take them?

Chapter 37

Alan was able to get past the firewalls of The Company members and track email messages that related to what was happening. There was a senior company member named Paul McClure that did the correspondences regarding the business. He sent out the closing numbers of the stocks to each investor. One email to the members said *the problem has been eliminated.* Alan seemed to think the comment referred to Mark Jones.

The three members were separated from The Company while an investigation into possible leaks was conducted. The loose lifestyle of Jones and his dating different women was also a part of the search.

By the middle of October, the connections between Julia and New York were eliminated. Her car was sold, and no forwarding address was available. Her apartment was in escrow. Even the agent didn't know who the seller was or where they lived. Julia's new location in New Mexico was hidden.

The last possible connection between Julia and Robert remained on the airport surveillance tapes when she flew into Albuquerque. A call was made to a friend who worked in airport security. He owed Robert a favor regarding an ex-wife who was cheating on him. The friend was able to gain access to the tapes on the dates when Julia flew to New Mexico. Any videos images, where Robert face could be identified, were blurred.

Credit cards were canceled and any other forms of ID, with Julia's old name, were eliminated. Julia kept her first name but she now went by Julia Barker. She had a new drivers license and an American Express card. She never left home without them.

Robert's team focused completely on the investigation. Mark Jones never resurfaced, and satellite videos showed two large boxes being removed from the Mexico clinic early one morning and taken away. That was the only connection pertaining to the possible demise of Mr. Jones.

The young Mexican woman, Marie, was seen entering and leaving the clinic several times. Robert decided to make contact with Marie through Megan, the lab tech from Tucson. She was always ready to earn an extra check.

"Hola, Marie. This is Megan from Tucson. Remember me?"

"Yes, I do. How are you?"

"Muy bueno."

Megan spoke in Spanish and asked Marie if she had a visa to visit the States. She said she did. Megan asked if Marie would be interested in visiting the States again and do some Christmas shopping. Megan said she would pay for the flight and hotel room.

Marie agreed to the visit. She'd made a connection with

Megan, while in Tucson, and decided to make the trip before returning to Mexico City. Christmas shopping would be something to look forward to.

A visit by Marie in three days was set up in Albuquerque because it was a larger city and had a direct flight from Mexico. It was also where Robert and Julia lived. Megan decided to find out as much as she could about the clinic in a private conversation in person with Marie, instead of on the phone.

"Julia, what should we have Megan ask Marie when the two meet? Robert asked. "I don't want to spook Marie with a lot of questions."

"Have her ask Marie how the clinic's been treating her? Also, has anything out of the ordinary happened? Those two questions may help Marie open up. We have to remember, Marie is getting paid a lot of money, and she doesn't want to lose her paycheck from The Company. We may not get much from her, but who knows?"

"Can you call Megan and coach her. It's much better if women talk to each other instead of a man trying to tell a woman what to do. It's never worked for me."

"You're a funny man, Robert. I'll call her, but I still want to remind you that you owe me big time."

"Spoken like an angry woman. It's a good thing I love you."

Julia paused. Her expression was one of surprise. "That's the first time you said that to me, Robert. Do you really mean it?"

"Of course I do. I didn't know how you felt about me."

Julia responded immediately. "You don't think I'd move in with any man who I was not in love with, do you?"

There was a pause and the room went silent. Suddenly Robert got up, looked at Julia and said, "All this talk has gotten me excited."

Robert swooped Julia up in his arms, cradled her, and carried her off towards the bedroom.

Carla watched the laughing couple shuffle past where she was working and thought; these gringos are almost as passionate as Mexicans. There may be a chance for them after all.

As Robert was carrying Julia past the kitchen, Carla called out, "Dinner is at seven so don't be late."

*****

Marie flew into Albuquerque on Monday after she shipped her possessions from San Miguel back to Mexico City. The two-day visit to New Mexico, and shopping with Megan would be a nice diversion before returning to her family.

After departing from the plane, she walked towards the exit with her one small suitcase. She was staying for two nights so she traveled light. While looking over the sea of people meeting the passengers, Marie spotted Megan near the front of the crowd. They gave each other a hug when they greeted each other.

"¿Como esta, Marie?" They both spoke in Spanish for a few sentences.

"Can we speak in English, Megan? I need the practice. I'm happy for you to meet me, Megan. This is a nice thing for you to do." Marie was beaming.

"A friend of mine bought your ticket," Megan said. "His name is Robert and he's interested in studies of the mind. I told him we could meet for lunch tomorrow if that's all right?"

"Of course. Where are we going first?" Marie was excited she had another trip to the States. "My CAT scan in Tucson was my first visit, but I was with Dr. Gupta the whole time, and did not go anywhere. This trip is my reward to myself for all that time spent at the San Miguel clinic."

"Let's drop by the hotel room and leave your bag," Megan said. She was as excited as Marie to get a vacation trip. "We can go to Old Town and have some lunch. There's shopping there, but mostly it's for the tourist wanting Mexican made things without having to go to Mexico. I believe you'd rather visit the downtown mall and stores not found in Mexico City."

"Yes. I want gifts for my whole family, and that means

mucho shopping. My family is large!"

"I know a different place for clothes and shoes. I saw them the last time I visited Albuquerque. They are called *Factory Outlet Stores* and they sell many items for a lower price."

"That sounds good for me. *Comida* and shopping."

After lunch and several hours in the stores, the two women returned to the Hotel Albuquerque and their room on the eleventh floor. They dumped their purchases in the corner near the window overlooking the city. A glass of wine helped both to unwind. Megan asked Marie about the clinic, and by the second glass of wine she received more than she expected. The question, *is there anything out of the ordinary that happened at the clinic,* seemed to get Marie started.

"Yes," Marie said. "One day I was in a room filling out paperwork when some men entered the building. Two of them were helping a man walk to the end of building and downstairs to the lab. He not walk good. A nurse say that man was boss of clinic, but live in New York. It did not look like they treat him well."

"Did you ever see the man again?" Megan asked.

"No. Dr. Gupta said man did not feel good. He needed to go to lab to receive care. I left clinic, and never saw man again."

Megan waited before taking another sip of her wine. Then

she took a big gulp.

"One more thing," Marie said. "On last day at clinic, before I fly here, another man visited. He say his name is Joseph Thomas. He talked to me and say he is new director of clinic. He was nice. That was only time I see him."

"Joseph Thomas. Is he from New York?" Megan asked.

"I think he live in New York, but a nurse say he come from Boston. He had funny way of talking English."

"Yes, the people from Boston are proud of the way they talk. It's called a 'Boston accent'," Megan explained.

The rest of the evening was spent catching up with each other's life at home. By eight o'clock both women were tired and ready to call it a day. They ordered room service for dinner, and after eating they prepared for bed.

*****

Robert received a phone call from Megan around eight the next morning, while Marie took a shower. The information from Marie was passed on and Joseph Thomas became the next name for Alan to research. The Slate Street Café was selected for their meeting and lunch later that day.

"I don't think she has any more information she can give us, Robert," Megan said. "Getting the name of the new director was pure luck. If she hadn't been there that day we wouldn't know his name at all."

"You're right, Megan. You've done well. After we meet for lunch, just enjoy the rest of the day with Marie and let her know she's welcome back anytime. We'll see you at lunch."

At twelve sharp, Robert and Julia arrived at the café near Old Town. A quiet table for four, in the dining loft, awaited them. A few minutes later the two women arrived. Formalities and introductions were made and a drink order was placed.

"Señor Robert, thank you for this trip to Albuquerque."

"You're welcome, Marie. I wanted to meet you in person before you went back to Mexico City. I know that your life has changed because I was a client six years ago."

"You have visions like I did?"

"Yes, I had an accident and hit my head. The Company discovered me and paid me lots of money to work for them. After four weeks my condition stopped. I used the money, and started my own business as an investigator."

"You are the second man I meet who have ability for numbers in future. Other person I meet in Tucson. I think his name is Ray. William Ray."

"I know him, Marie. He works with me."

"He works with you?" Marie asked. "How?"

"I'm going to tell you something important," Robert said. "I'm taking a chance giving you this information, but we are trying to stop some evil things that happened in the past. We have proof that The Company and clinic are involved in murder." Robert paused for a second to let his last statement sink in. "We think The Company killed the man you saw escorted into the clinic. His name was Mark Jones. Three other men were killed in Italy where the clinic used to be located. It's important you know what kind of people are involved in The Company. They will do anything to get what they want."

"What do they want?" Marie asked.

"Right now it's only money and the power that comes with it. They are using the money to build large plants that can change ocean water into drinking water."

"That is a good thing, no?"

"Yes and no. What we think they have planned for the future is this: Members of The Company plan to influence governments around the world. The clean drinking water supply will be greatly reduced by the present generation due to pollution."

"That is true in Mexico. Many poor people have no good water now." Marie said.

Robert continued. "Only a few countries are undergoing construction of the plants right now. It is not the plants that are the problem. It's the power these men will have over governments."

"What can we do?" Marie asked.

"We don't know yet. We were able to stop Mark Jones, but not The Company. The profits from the stock market are being used to build the plants."

"Where are they being built? Is one in Mexico?" Marie asked.

"Not in Mexico but we think there is one in South America. I don't know the location. The project is a two-edged sword. The plants are good, but the way they are obtaining the money to pay for the plants is illegal. Killing people who get in their way has to stop. Shutting down the clinic is a start." Robert paused.

"Anything I can do?" Marie's face tightened. She wanted no part in people getting killed.

"Again, I'm taking a chance telling you this, Marie. I have to trust you and Megan to keep quiet. There is nothing any of us can do for now. Your job with them is finished, right?"

"Yes. I moved out of apartment in San Miguel, and fly back to Mexico City tomorrow."

"William is not returning to the clinic because he doesn't

want to be used in any experiments. It also may be dangerous for him to visit that place right now. We just wanted to warn you about The Company."

"If I find anything else can I call you, Señor Robert?"

"Yes, you can. They won't contact you for a while because you can't be used by the clinic again for twelve months. Megan said you want to study at the university and learn about business. Go ahead and live your life. If you want to contact me, do it through Megan. I've given both of you a lot of information just now. I'm doing this for your own protection and I want you to be safe."

Both Megan and Marie sat quietly with looks of confusion on their faces. They had a lot to digest along with their meal.

Robert continued. "We need to build a network of people willing to stand up to these mad men. They're sick. Sick is one thing. Sick and rich is a dangerous combination."

Robert hoped he hadn't divulged too much. He was desperate and needed as much help as he could get to fight The Company. Joseph Thomas was a good lead to follow.

After their meal, Megan and Marie were off to revisit another store and catch the late movie matinee at the complex off the I-25. Before they left, Robert again reminded the women that the information was for their ears only. Silence would keep them safe.

After the women left, Robert looked at Julia and asked, "Do you think I told them too much?"

"Probably, but we need to take some risks if we want to create a team," Julia answered. "Murder is not what they signed up for, and they could be an asset for us down the road."

"Alan might have some information about Joseph Thomas by now. If we keep disrupting The Company they'll eventually make a mistake."

"It might work," Julia said. "I really think a government agency needs to be involved. We now have incriminating tapes. If we can get a few more member names, a domino effect might take place, and they'll come tumbling down."

Julia and Robert returned to their car, and drove home, going around the block twice to ensure they were not followed.

Alan had already downloaded the bio of Joseph Thomas by the time Robert and Julia arrived. Thomas was in the Navy and worked for their special operations division. He was not married but had a steady girlfriend who lived in Boston. His address in New York was new, and he flew back to Boston every weekend to be with his girlfriend.

Alan found the girlfriend's name using the face recognition

program. There were several photos of the two appearing in Boston social settings. The girlfriend was involved with the art world and attended the many openings held in that city. Alan found an address for her gallery. Her name was Millie Jamison and she was in her early forties, around the same age as Thomas.

The Company hired Joseph Thomas a month ago. He managed a security group in Boston before joining The Company. Thomas took the red-eye on Fridays to Boston and returned Monday mornings to New York. He was a member of the same men's club that Jason was invited to join when he worked for The Company. Thomas was a *straight arrow* compared to the lifestyle of Mark Jones.

Chapter 38

The research into Thomas continued while William and Leslie planned their two-week visit to the land of the Inca. Lima was the destination of their flight from Los Angeles. A night in Lima and a flight the next day took them to the ancient Inca capital of Cusco.

"The flight will take all night so I'm taking a sleeping pill," William told Leslie. "Be sure to pack your hiking boots as well, Sweetheart. Machu Picchu is not that far from Cusco. Also, we'll need to drink the green tea when we get to the Inca capital. It'll help us cope with the 14,000 ft. elevation. It's made from the Coco leaf."

"Does Marta know we're coming? I don't want to surprise her," Leslie said.

"Robert's agent let her know we were coming. He met with her in Italy, and according to him she sounded excited we were coming to Peru. The agent thought she might tell me more than she told him. Something about trusting me and all I did was meet her in the car that one time."

"Has her English improved?" Leslie asked.

"According to Robert's agent, she's been practicing English conversation, and taking more medical classes. She works part time to keep her nursing license current. Robert sent me the dates she'd be available to meet with us."

"Are we visiting her in a restaurant or her home?"

"We're supposed to call her when we get to Cusco. We'll find out then."

*****

The flight on LAN airlines left Los Angeles around eight in the evening with William and Leslie stretched out in first class. A movie and a late snack were all William could fit in before sleep took over.

William rose from his seat around six a.m. after a terrible night of attempted sleep. Even though they were in first class, the flight still had its bumps and shakes.

Countless black taxicabs awaited them as they exited the Lima terminal. They hired one and were soon at the Hotel Inca located in an affluent part of the city. Peru had a strong middle class, and tourism drew thousands of visitors to Machu Picchu and other sites each year.

William and Leslie arrived just in time to enjoy breakfast at their hotel. After nourishment, the need for sleep took over. Leslie purchased a book in the airport, describing the city of Cusco, and the places of interest in Peru. She stayed awake reading, while William slept.

Three hours later William woke up. Leslie was now catching up on her needed rest. During her downtime, William purchased a couple of sandwiches in the restaurant downstairs and returned just as Leslie started to stir.

"We really needed that," William said, referring to their naps.

"Yes, we did," Leslie answered. "I'd like to stick around the room for the day and read about Peru. There's not much to see in the city, and tomorrow we'll be in Cusco. That's where all the Inca history is located. There's also a jungle trip we do near the border of Bolivia. As soon as we finish our visit with Marta we're free to do some real sightseeing."

After spending the afternoon reading and relaxing, William and Leslie took a taxi to a nearby restaurant. Before entering the cab, William noticed a man he'd seen on the flight from Los Angeles. He was sitting in the lobby reading a paper. Later that evening the man was again spotted at the bar, while they were having dinner. It felt like Pisa all over again. This time, the person, who seemed to be following them, didn't have a spiked hairstyle separating him from the crowd.

William took a mental picture of the man. Robert mentioned The Company was doing surveillance on past clients while looking for a leak into their operations. William was no exception. He would have to meet Marta in a discreet location after he shook this man.

While boarding the flight to Cusco the next morning, William spotted the man sitting in the back of the plane. He kept to himself and posed no immediate threat to William or Leslie.

The travel agency, William used to book the trip, found an apartment for them located right on the main plaza in Cusco. Artists roamed the square selling their work, while tourists snapped pictures of the large Spanish church, and buildings surrounding the plaza.

A phone booth, located on the plaza, is where William made the call to Marta. A meeting location at the home of a cousin was arranged.

"Marta. Be sure you are not followed," William said after the initial greeting. "We need to keep this meeting private."

"You're right, Mr. Ray. There has been a woman watching my apartment for the last two weeks. If I'm being followed I can go out the rear entrance to my building and through the courtyard in the back. She won't see me leave."

"Good. I'll see you tomorrow," William said. "I'm looking forward to our meeting."

William put his own diversion plan into action. On the morning of the meeting with Marta, Leslie and William walked to the main plaza where the taxicabs were parked. As they entered one, William gave the driver directions in a loud voice, "Take us to the palace ruins above Cusco."

As the taxi pulled away William looked back and spotted the man who was tailing them approach one of the drivers. The driver pointed to the hill where the palace was located. By then Leslie and William's taxi was two hundred feet away and changed directions without being seen. A couple of left turns and they were back at the center of Cusco. The ruse had worked. The man, following them, had a nice ride to the palace ruins, but Leslie and William were still in Cusco.

The Rays' taxi stopped a block from the address where they were to meet Marta. William paid the driver and included an extra tip.

"If anyone asks you where you dropped us off, tell them you took us to the tourist center down the road from the main plaza," William told the driver. "Thank you for the ride."

William waited until the taxi drove away before he and Leslie walked down the quiet street to the address he'd been given. By now Leslie wondered what was going on.

"Why didn't we get dropped off at the front of the building, and why the diversion tactics?" she asked.

"We have someone following us. I wanted to make sure our

meeting place was kept secret. The Company is watching Marta as well."

"Here we go again," Leslie said. "Déjà vu. Are we in any danger?"

"Maybe. Ever since Mark Jones disappeared Robert thinks many of the past clients and employees are being followed. Marta had to come here in secret as well. After this meeting, we can travel through Peru as tourists. No connection between Marta and us can be made, and that's what I'm doing right now."

"Oh, James. You're my hero." Leslie was trying to mask her fear with a little 007 humor.

"As long as we're not connected with Marta, we'll be fine. Visiting one of the most sought after tourist destination countries in the world is not out of the ordinary."

"Let's get this over with. This better be the only time we meet with Marta. This adventure is creeping me out," Leslie added.

"Here's the apartment," William said after comparing the numbers on the door to the address on his note pad.

William knocked on the door, waited a minute, and then rang the bell. An older woman, probably in her 70's, opened the door and escorted them to the interior courtyard of the house. Marta was sitting in a chair under an umbrella. She rose and introduced herself to Leslie.

"Good to meet you, Mrs. Ray. I met your husband last year in Italy, but I'm sure he told you about that."

"Yes, he did. You live in a beautiful city, Marta. I've taken many pictures, and expect to take more before we leave. I don't know your last name so please forgive me."

"Thank you, Mrs. Ray. My last name is Ruiz, but please call me Marta."

"Call us William and Leslie. It's less formal," Leslie answered.

William shook Marta's hand and sat next to Leslie in the chairs made available to them.

"It was a strange circumstance when we last met," William began. "We left Pisa the next morning so my friend used another person to meet with you. We wanted to visit Peru so we thought we could combine our visit with a talk."

"I am honored for your visit," Marta said. "Something must have happened regarding the clinic in Mexico. This is a lot of hiding just to meet."

"Your English has really improved, Marta. The classes must be going well."

"Yes, thank you, William. I'm doing conversation every

day with an American living in Cusco. He's writing a book about the Inca civilization and hires himself out to teach English. That's why I'm developing an American accent."

"Let me catch you up with what's happened in the past year," William continued.

William proceeded to tell everything he could without divulging Robert's name or where he lived. The Mark Jones incident was also included.

The fact that The Company killed people was not news to Marta.

"I've known there were people who were harmed, and because of that I decided to quit working for them," Marta said. "I was asked to go to Mexico, but by then I had enough."

After William finished the update, Marta looked directly into his eyes. She did not have any new information for William, but she did have something to give him that would change the investigation completely.

"What I'm going to give you could help in your attempt to stop The Company and their work," Marta said. "I wanted to talk to you directly because I knew I could trust you. I can tell a pure person when I meet them. I have always had this ability. Dr. Yee was not an honest man. He did not tell you everything that happened in the clinic."

"I had a feeling he might be holding something back," William admitted.

Marta continued. "The driver named Pablo was also good. He did what he was told because the job paid well. The rest of the people working there I did not care for, except for one. I even met Mr. Jones once when he came to the clinic to talk to Dr. Yee. He had, how do you say it in English, a bad vibration?"

"Yes, he was not a nice man, Marta," William said. "He's gone now. I think most of the men in The Company are also not nice, and their intentions are evil."

Marta paused for a moment. She then pulled a lab tube of yellow liquid from her pocket and handed it to William.

"This is the final compound the research lab in Italy developed. It is probably the same formula they're using in Mexico. The reason it took so long to run the tests had to do with finding the correct dosage needed to keep the clients safe."

"This is the final product?" William was stunned as he held out his hand.

"Yes. What Dr. Yee and the doctor in Mexico did not tell you was that a small dosage could work on a person like you for a few days without any complications. They spent months testing it to get the most time from a client because of the twelve month wait period."

William sat in silence, first looking at the vial, and then at Marta.

"How'd you get this?" he asked.

"I had a close friend in the lab. We still see each other occasionally, but his home is in Europe, and I live in Peru. We like each other a lot but a relationship so far away is not possible to maintain. Anyway, here it is."

Marta sat quietly for a few seconds to let this information sink in.

"The amount is small enough that it can be hidden inside a bottle of shampoo. It won't appear on an x-ray machine at the airport. That's how I got it into Peru. You should have no trouble getting it back to your friend in the States."

"This is a complete game changer, Marta. Why are you giving this to me now?"

"I had a feeling something was happening with The Company ever since a woman started to follow me two weeks ago. Keeping this meeting secret was a good idea. No connection between us must be made. If The Company ever searches my apartment there is no longer anything that links me to them." Marta again paused. "You now have the compound. It may help you. It was insurance for me, but if it can be used to stop these men then you should have it. The strength of this compound is no longer useable. You can break down what is in the mixture and make a new batch. If you want to try it out, start with one cc of the compound. It can be injected directly into the vein in your arm. It takes only an hour to develop a small clot, which puts pressure on your brain. After that, it should last for two days before the brain absorbs the clot. Do not repeat this until a year has passed. If you try it, make sure you use the knowledge to help in the investigation."

"Marta, this will help my friend in the States immensely. This could shift the scales in our favor, and maybe shut down their clinic."

"I hope so. Even though they paid me well, killing others is not something I want to be a part of. Good luck. If you ever come back to Peru I'll be happy to show you around."

William thanked Marta for all she'd done. They could not stay long. The man, who followed them, could return, and they needed to be in town. The Rays left the apartment and walked two blocks before hailing a cab. They proceeded to the tourist section of town where their first driver told anyone, who asked, where they would be.

Leslie had a question for William but focused on gifts for the family at the moment. The variety of blankets, scarves, paintings and baby llama wool sweaters was endless. Tourism was indeed a big industry in Peru, and Leslie was supporting the economy as best she could.

After an hour of shopping William noticed a cab pull up a block away. The mystery man had arrived. William made sure he saw them before they hailed another taxi back to their apartment.

After dropping packages in their apartment, both were ready for lunch. A small Italian restaurant was just around the corner. After placing their order at Llama Pizza, Leslie asked the question she had been carrying in her head for the past hour.

"Now what? Are we going to smuggle that liquid back to Arizona?" she asked.

"I had no idea Marta was going to give us that compound," William answered. "I need to make a call to Robert this evening. He may know some way we can send it. I don't want to carry it either."

"Good. We're on the same page. We have the trip to the Rain Forest tomorrow. Let's get this taken care of right away. After the jungle visit we can go to Machu Picchu," Leslie said.

"I'm tired just thinking about all the travel. I'll call Robert this evening. He'll figure out a way to deal with this."

William hoped it was the last piece of the puzzle Robert would need to shut down the clinic in Mexico. They finished their spinach and cheese pizza and spent the afternoon walking around the town taking pictures.

*****

"Hello, Robert, guess where we are?" William was joking. He knew Robert could tell where he was because of the locating device connected with his phone service.

"Cusco, Peru. You're clowning around with me so I assume the meeting with Carla went well?"

"Better than we could possibly imagine. Now guess what I have in my hand?"

"Take a picture of it, and send it to me through your phone," Robert responded, his interest rising.

William clicked a picture of the vial and pushed send. While he waited for the photo to reach Robert he smiled.

"Got it." Robert acknowledged.

"Do you want a hint?" William asked. This was one of the few times Robert wasn't one step ahead of him.

"Maybe, but if it's what I think it is then you may have hit the mother-lode. Is that the compound the clinic developed to induce the blood clot?"

"Pretty damn good guess, Robert. How'd you do that?"

"Since Marta worked at the clinic, she might have taken

some of the compound when she left. If that's what she did then she was lucky. If she was caught I don't think she'd be in Peru today, or even alive."

"That's exactly what happened. She was having an affair with a lab tech and was given a sample as insurance. I think Marta and the tech were aware of what the Company was capable of doing and were protecting themselves."

"They rolled the dice on that one," Robert said.

"People died because of this research. The tech was trying to keep her safe in the long run," William concluded.

"How are you going to get it back to the States?" Robert asked.

"That's why I'm calling. We're not going to smuggle it back. Marta said the vial could be hidden in shampoo because she did that when she flew to Peru. It's up to you to figure out a way to get it back. No way are we going to try."

Robert thought for a moment before answering. "I know a contact in Lima," he said. "I'll call him right now. Are you there for a while?"

Of course, he knows someone in Peru, thought William. Why wouldn't he? William was amazed by Robert's wealth of contacts throughout the world.

"We'll be here until tomorrow. We're headed to the Rainforest for a few days, and then on to Machu Picchu. Can he get here in time?"

"I hope so. I'll call you right back. We don't want to trust the post office with this stuff. It's worth the expense of paying someone."

"Here is the best part of this whole scenario," William said. "Small dosages of the compound can be injected into a past client and create a clot that lasts for two or three days. What the clinic was trying to perfect was the dosage for maximum results."

Robert paused before speaking. Finally, he said, "I had no idea they could use small amounts and get short period results. Did Marta tell you how much to use?"

"Yes, she did. One cc can be injected into the arm vein, and it takes an hour to work."

"William, I need to call my contact in Lima. I'll call you right back."

Robert hung up and William told Leslie about the plan. "Robert is having someone else take it back to the States. He'll call us when he has it all setup."

"Well good for him. No way do I want to spend time in jail trying to smuggle something back to the States." She wanted a vacation, not another re-run of Italy.

William's phone rang thirty minutes later. "He'll meet you at the airport. What time did you say your flight leaves for the Rainforest?" Robert asked.

"Ten in the morning."

"He'll be on the flight from Lima that arrives at Cusco around nine. It'll be the same plane you'll take that flies to the jungle. He said the town you'll fly into is called Puerto Maldonado. He'll take the next flight back to Lima, and then on to Los Angeles tomorrow night. I'll meet him there. He knows how to smuggle small items through airport security because that's how he makes his living."

"You're not going to tell him what the compound is used for are you?"

"Hell no! This guy's a smuggler. If he knew its real purpose he could make millions. As far as he knows, it's a new mouthwash formula made from the coco leaves of Peru. I'm paying him damn good money just to get it to me with no questions asked. Telling him anything could risk losing it."

"What if he asks me what it is? What should I tell him?"

"Just what I said. It's a mixture we're going to try for a tropical mouthwash. That sounds boring enough. Remember, people like him can't be trusted."

"One more thing," William added. "We're being followed. We ditched him before we had the meeting with Marta. I don't think we want him to see me hand over a package to some guy in the airport."

"The smuggler's name is Perkins. He'll have a picture of you, William. We should use the 'pass off in the newspaper' technique."

"And what is that exactly?" William asked.

"Just sit in the waiting room and let him find you. Have the vial in a package and placed inside a newspaper. Perkins will sit next to you but don't talk to him. Get up and leave the newspaper in your seat. He'll pick it up, slip the vial into his pocket, and pretend to read the paper. Get on your flight and don't look back.

"This sound easy enough. Is that it?" William asked.

"I think so. Just make it quick. Perkins is a pro. He's paid to keep his mouth shut. If not, word will get out, and no one will use him to smuggle again. The expression 'honor among thieves' fits this situation."

"We think someone from The Company is observing Marta as well," William continued. "Neither person has seen either of us together so we should be in the clear."

"I expected The Company might be checking out previous employees. Just continue touring Peru. You're good at the tourist thing, so good luck tomorrow. By the way, great job with the Marta meeting. This could be a game changer for sure."

William closed his cell phone and lay down on the bed. He told Leslie the plan before drifting off. A busy day of travel lay ahead with a little spy work in between.

*****

Being packed and ready to leave by eight-thirty gave William time to grab a couple of bagels in a bakery near the apartment. The American diet had made its way to Peru. A taxi picked them up fifteen minutes later. Their arrival at the airport coincided with the landing of the flight from Lima. Leslie and William were seated in the terminal by the time the passengers departed from the Lima flight. The compound was securely wrapped in a package, and hidden in the U.S. News newspaper William purchased while entering the airport.

A man entered the terminal through the arrival door and passed his gaze over the passengers waiting to board the next flight. He spotted William and made a hurried walk across the waiting room towards him. The newspaper lay on the seat to the right of William, and Perkins sat one seat over. Moments later William and Leslie got up and headed towards the boarding gate. The day's version of the U.S. News was placed in Perkin's business satchel. The transfer of the vial was complete.

Leslie and William boarded the plane headed to the Rainforest. The flight was a drastic drop in elevation to the countryside below. The temperature in the Peruvian jungle during spring remained in the nineties. Upon arrival in Puerto Maldonado, shorts and tee shirts replaced warm clothing. Sandals covered the feet of the jungle population as well as the Rays. A bus ride to the departing taxi boat took about an hour. William looked for the man tailing them, but he never resurfaced. It looked like the Rainforest trip would be spy free.

*****

Perkins flew to L.A. the next day, met Robert, and was paid for his efforts. He now had the cash to visit Vegas, gamble, and lose his earnings at the tables before flying back to Peru.

Robert had his ace in the hole. How he played his trump card could be the breaking of The Company or his own downfall. He would make sure it wasn't the latter. Julia was with him so the plan would be discussed thoroughly before implementation.

The first step: get the liquid to a lab, and have its contents analyzed. Robert had a friend, working the University of New Mexico, with access to the school lab. His name was John and he'd worked with Robert on past cases. John told Robert a few days were needed to analyze the contents, and the ability to reproduce it might take a few weeks.

"What are we going to do with this stuff when we get the results?" Julia asked.

"I'm not sure," Robert answered. "We may have to involve a government agency after all. We are powerless to go after these guys on our own. Keeping out of sight is our only chance of survival. The formula might be used but right now I'm not sure how. Maybe we can call Jason and get his input. He knows The Company much better than we do. Together we may be able to come up with something."

Julia agreed. "When we get the results back from the lab, let's call a meeting. We have a small team now, and we need to get them all involved. I had to jump through a few hoops to disappear from The Company. If they find out who we are, or what we've done, the endgame will be short and swift." She touched his arm. "I want to have a family some day." Julia had a way of making her point.

Robert wanted a long life with her as well. Whatever they came up with, their identities could never be exposed.

*****

After the Rainforest, and two days of walking through the ruins of Machu Picchu, another digital chip of one camera and part of another was filled. The remaining shots would be used in the

Valley of the Gods where Leslie and William would rest for two more nights.

A week later and eight hours on LAN airlines found the Rays back in Los Angeles. They were tired but fulfilled. A vial of the compound was secured as well as hundreds of pictures documenting the Peruvian countryside and all its treasures. William delivered to Robert what he wanted, and more.

Chapter 39

Building and owning water desalination plants was a huge step towards influencing governments around the world. The Company thought they knew how the world should be managed. Making the heads of countries see it their way would solve everything, or so they thought.

Paul McClure knew he wouldn't be around to see the impact The Company would have on the world. He was 82, and old school. *Might was right.* Common people were the pawns used to protect the back row of the chessboard. The king and queen, along with their religious leaders, the bishops, were the only ones who knew how to direct the masses. The knights were the armed forces needed to make sure the king and queen were protected. It took money to keep them in power and the stock market provided that.

McClure was clearly upset. Someone had laid siege to him and The Company. Mark Jones was the first victim, but he was expendable. A tape of the Jones confession and three Company member names were revealed. Since McClure was the CEO, his job was to find where the attack came from. No one would escape the wrath of McClure. The leak had to be plugged.

The battle lines were drawn. Reports came in from the investigation team and stacked up on Paul McClure's desk. A possible lead into the private sex life of Mark Jones was still under investigation. Many women were taped going into the Jones apartment, and leaving several hours later. One of the women had disappeared from New York altogether. By the time the investigation team identified her, she was gone. Her apartment and vehicle were sold, and she'd been erased. McClure thought, how was that possible?

"Call me if you find anything out about this missing woman," McClure told his research team. "She seems to be the best lead we have."

"The neighbors in the area didn't know the two women living in the apartment where the car was traced back to," Smith, the head of security, said. "The new owner purchased it through an agent who specialized in keeping identities a secret. Even he didn't know the name of the previous owner. No surveillance cameras were in the area so a face recognition trace couldn't be made of the second woman who lived there. Both left without a forwarding address. They must have owned private mailboxes because there was no mail delivery to the apartment."

"Is that all you have?" McClure asked.

Smith continued. "The only other possible lead was a previous client named William Ray. He'd made a recent trip to Peru. One of the nurses, who previously worked in the Italian clinic, lives there. Those following Mr. Ray and the nurse failed to make any connection between the two. The Ray's were simply traveling on vacation. William is a retired teacher and not the kind of person who would make a good spy."

The families of the two men, who died in Italy, were also clean according to the report. Dr. Yee was doing his own study in Singapore, showing no signs of spying on the clinic. Suspicion led back to the mystery woman from New York. Someone with technological skills made her disappearance a reality.

McClure was stumped. Most of the previous clients had gone on to other occupations. An old client named Robert Woods, who lived in New Mexico, dropped off the grid years before. He was a recluse and couldn't be located. He was classified as someone who wanted to be left alone. Jason Burns lived in Santa Fe and was seen constantly with a woman who owned an art gallery. His new photography hobby filled his spare time, so he was written off as a person who was starting a new life.

The new clinic in Mexico was closely guarded. A woman named Marie had taken a shopping visit to Albuquerque, but could only be traced by her plane ticket. She was enrolled at the University in Mexico City, which did not allow her much time to conduct a spying ring.

McClure would continue following the previous employees as well as search for the missing woman from New York. He was determined to keep the *walls of the castle* safe. If he did not, he'd be replaced.

*****

Robert's plan was taking shape. The first step was to launch an attack on the new manager of the clinic in San Miguel.

"How do we play this, Julia? I'd like to go after Thomas but The Company is watching him closely. After Jones disappeared, they tightened their defense around the new guy. He's been observed flying to Boston accompanied by another man acting as a personal bodyguard."

"We may have to get to him through his girlfriend. What is her name, Alan?" Julia asked. "I forgot."

Alan was doing research, but his photographic memory came up with the answer immediately. "Millie Jamison. She's well known in the Boston art community. She may be a little easier to get to because The Company might not think she's a target."

The area by the pool was now cool enough to sit outside for lunch, so Carla brought out sandwiches for the three investigators.

Robert gave Alan a new assignment. "Find out Millie's routine. Include where she eats lunch, and what she does when her boyfriend's not in town. There may be a way to isolate her, and get back at The Company through Thomas."

Robert placed a call to Santa Fe. "Jason, this is Robert."

"I see you are calling me on the secure line. I bet I know why," Jason said.

"Have you noticed anyone following you or just hanging around?" Robert asked.

"Yes, about two weeks ago. A fellow ex-colleague informed me that someone else replaced Mark Jones after he disappeared. Does this have anything to do with your investigation?"

"We had nothing to do with Jones disappearing. The Company took care of that. Jones was an asshole, and the world is better off without him."

"One asshole down, but there're plenty to replace him," Jason said.

"You're right about that. We need to meet with you. The problem is, The Company is following all the past employees, and you're on that list. Is there any way we can meet without being seen together?"

"Probably, but not here. Santa Fe is too small. We may have to drive to meet you. The weather is getting cold, so Rosa and I would like a break for a few days."

"How about a private helicopter ride to Albuquerque. I can have a driver pick you two up in case there are people watching the airport. Will that work?"

"When?" Jason asked.

"Is tomorrow too soon? We want to put a plan into action right away."

"I think that'll work. Rosa will love to get away."

"I'll book a flight for you two tomorrow at ten a.m. We won't give a destination for the flight so that'll throw your 'shadow' off a bit. The driver, who picks you up, will be instructed to take you to a restaurant where we'll be waiting. How does that sound?"

"Fine with me," Jason said. "If there are problems with Rosa's schedule I'll call you back. If not, we will be at the helicopter at ten, and ready for some warmer weather."

"All right. See you tomorrow."

*****

The next day the escape from Santa Fe was pulled off without a hitch. Jason and Rosa were driven to the Church Street Cafe in Old Town and met Robert and Julia on the patio. It was Robert's favorite place to meet.

"Hello again, you two. This secret meeting is just like old times when we first met," Jason said.

"Yes, it is. The only difference, we're the ones being

followed or should I say you are."

"Doesn't The Company have someone watching you as well?" Jason asked.

"I went underground soon after I stopped working for them. My home and business are under another name. At the time I didn't know how valuable it was to have a hidden identity, but I do now."

"Is there any chance they can find you?"

"I don't think so," Robert said. "Even Julia went underground. We hid her identity after the Mark Jones incident. I think we really pissed off The Company, and now everyone is on the suspect list."

"Shall we order lunch before we discuss what you want? I know this meeting will be interesting because you always have something up your sleeve, Robert."

Lunch was ordered. The two women started chatting with each other while Robert filled Jason in on all the news since their last meeting. Having a vial of the compound was the crowning touch to their accomplishments as well as the formula to reproduce it.

"How can we help?" Jason asked. "We both want to help but I'm like William. Any sign of danger and we draw the line."

By now the women had joined the conversation, and with

their input, a plan was put together. A letter would be written to Mr. Thomas, and sent to him through his girlfriend telling about The Company and the murders.

"If Mr. Thomas continues to work for The Company after receiving the letter, then he knows about the deaths and cares little about his girlfriend's safety," Julia said.

"If we thought the Mark Jones incident upset the hornet's nest, I think this will shake them up more," Robert added.

"You're right, Robert," Jason added. "This should really rattle their cage."

"We have to be careful," Robert continued. "An angry billionaire can be dangerous to others, but also to himself. This is the time when mistakes are made, so we have to be on high alert. Paul McClure may do something while in a rage and expose The Company."

"I met McClure when I was first hired," Jason said. "When he became CEO he took himself out of the public eye. He's also in his 80's so any decisions he makes could be affected by his age."

"He's that old?" Julia asked. "I was hoping for someone younger. I know what forty-year-old men act like." She looked over at Robert and gave him a wink.

Jason continued. "The Company may be ready for a change

in leadership. McClure hasn't found the leak so this may be a turning point for him. They'll simply replace him with someone younger. He has a son who's following in his father's footsteps."

"What do you know about the son?" Julia asked. "Is he anything like his father?"

Jason thought a moment before speaking. "His name is Ian. I believe the McClure family made their millions in the bootleg whiskey business. I know a little about him because he was the boss for client managers like myself."

"Really?" Robert asked.

"He's in his late 50's so there's plenty of life left in him. We never became friends because we had little in common. He has a house in upstate New York and an apartment in the City where he spends his workweek."

"We'll investigate Ian," Robert said. "If he takes over we want to be ready."

"I'm sorry I can't be more help," Jason said. "I hope the plan works. You might need to get some government agency involved. They can use the information about the clinic and what The Company is doing. Remember one thing, the members are connected and powerful."

"You think they may somehow get off?" Julia asked.

"Yes, they will," Jason said. "Some deal will be made, and maybe a stiff penalty for being naughty. They may lose their trading license but nothing more. The government has too many interest groups and powerful people running things. The Company is no exception. They'll buy their way out of this mess."

"You're right, Jason," Robert said. "Thinking we could take The Company down was an overreach. Closing the clinic may be as far as we can take this case. We have to know what we're doing before getting government agencies involved. Right now let's get them mad. Getting the government involved could be more dangerous than we even know. If we don't get our ducks in a row, we could have agency people looking for us as well."

Robert wanted to let The Company know they were exposed. He took out a hand held recording device and composed a voice letter:

"Mr. Thomas," Robert took a breath. "This information is directed to you through your friend, Millie Jamison. The Company that you are working for is involved in murder. The activities in the Mexican clinic are also illegal. This message is not a threat to you. You have a choice. Continue working for them, and you'll be included in the list of Company members who'll answer for their crimes. Leave them, return to Boston, and your name will not be added to the list. You may or may not know anything about the murders. It doesn't matter." Robert paused.

"To clarify our position we have included the formula for the compound that recreates the brain bleed. You may show this letter to your boss, Paul McClure, and use it as a reason for leaving The Company. We'll be watching."

Robert asked, "Is there anything else we need to include in this letter?"

None of the others could think of anything.

"Getting to Thomas, through his girlfriend, is going to impact him," Julia said. "If he continues working for them she'll have someone guarding her. This will be the only time we can reach him this way. All other messages will have to be by regular mail or carrier pigeon. Nothing electronic. The possibility of being traced is always there."

Rosa added her insight. "Whoever we use to deliver the letter to Miss Jamison should visit the gallery first, and make sure she's not guarded. Also, her business will have cameras so the person needs to find their location and avoid them."

"Good point, Rosa," Robert said. I'll get our messenger to case the gallery, and see if she's protected. We can also do satellite surveillance if we need to."

"What kind of setup do you have, Robert? You sound like you have as much spy equipment as a large police department."

"We do okay. We were able to witness the termination of Mark Jones at the Mexican clinic. We have that on tape along with his drug-induced confession exposing three members of The Company. All this evidence is being kept in a safe place."

"No wonder you know so much about the Company," Jason said.

"If anything happens to us, the material gets mailed to three government agencies. Sending it to three should secure at least one package getting through," Robert added.

"You may have enough evidence to slow down McClure, but I don't think they'll pack up the clinic," Jason added. "They'll be mad and increase their hunt for the leak. If they do find you, is there a plan B?"

"Only a few people know where we live. That's why you've never been invited to our place, Jason. We're not being rude but it's for your own protection. If we can get 'truth serum' and use it on Mark Jones, the company can also use it. For now, we have to remain in the shadows."

"Understood," Jason said. "If you need us, we'll be at the Hyatt Regency on Tijeras."

Jason and Rosa called a cab to take them to their hotel in town. Robert and Julia left a few minutes later, using the time to debrief.

"What we have left is office work. Do you feel like typing up the letter while I get a hold of someone who'll deliver it to Miss Jamison? The sooner we find out how invested Joseph Thomas is with The Company, the better."

"Sure, Sweetheart. No problem," Julia answered.

Chapter 40

A week had passed since the meeting in Albuquerque. The letter was delivered to Millie Jamison by a hired currier posing as an art collector. He handed her the envelope personally. When she read the message on the front, the man looked at her with a stare that burned into her eyes, and said, "Please do what the message says. Your life could be in danger if you open the envelope." The note on the package read, *For Joseph Thomas only.*

Message received. The delivery agent turned and left the gallery before Millie could react. She thought about pushing a security button to notify the local police department but decided against it. Joseph would know what to do, and he was flying in tonight for the weekend.

*****

The Company wanted answers. McClure's position depended on his finding the leak. Killing people along the way had never been a problem before. Not knowing who the target was, put him on the edge. I'm getting too old for this crap, he thought. This would be his last operation before he handed over the reins to his son, Ian.

The Company phone rang. Only members and department heads used this line. Paul answered the phone. A feeling in his gut told him something had happened, and it was not good.

"Mr. McClure, this is Joseph Thomas. I'm calling from Boston."

"Yes, Thomas. How can I help you?"

"I've received a letter from an on ominous sender. Do you have a secure fax line I can use to send it? It's very important."

"How did you get the letter?"

"It was hand delivered to my girlfriend in Boston. The envelope said the content was for my eyes only, so no one else has read the letter."

"Is there any security footage of the person delivering the letter?" McClure asked.

"Yes, but only his back. He seemed to know where the cameras were and avoided them. He must have cased the gallery before showing up."

"988-412-3775 is the fax number. Can you send it right away?"

"Yes, I'm at the gallery, and I'll send it from here. There is a second page with the letter. I've seen the information before and can assure you it's correct. That's all I can say over the phone right now. I'm sending both papers to you as we speak."

McClure heard the fax machine start as it prepared to receive the letters. "All right Thomas. I'll call you back after I read the letter. My line is secure so we can discuss this in detail if we need to. Goodbye."

The second page was being printed out by the time Paul got to the machine. He read the message quickly and scanned the second sheet. His heart was racing. He reached for his prescription bottle and took two pills to slow his heart rate. Everything turned fuzzy as McClure sat down. He knew at that moment he would not find the leak into The Company's activities. His time on earth was over, and he fell to the floor. Ian would have to save The Company from destruction. The Paul McClure era had ended.

*****

McClure's secretary discovered the body an hour later. His son, Ian, was notified immediately and arrived thirty minutes after receiving the call. Ian knew what to do. The leadership of The Company was up for grabs, and he was in the position to receive the scepter. He loved his father, but he needed to save the business before he could grieve.

The letter, along with the formula for the compound, was handed to him upon his arrival. The persons responsible for the leaks into The Company's business were now responsible for more than information. They'd made an attack on the McClure clan. The blood pressure of Ian was on the rise, but, unlike his father, he had youth to survive the effects of his anger.

After the ambulance arrived to remove the body, Ian sent out a personal email to the other members of The Company regarding the death of his father. He then called Joseph Thomas. The fax had a sender stamp on it and said it came from Thomas three hours earlier. The phone rang twice before Thomas picked up.

"Hello. Mr. McClure. Is this you?"

"It depends upon which McClure you want to speak to," Ian said.

"This isn't Paul McClure is it?"

"No. This is Ian McClure, his son. My father is dead." Ian was still upset and blurted out the information without thinking.

"What? I was just talking to him several hours ago. I faxed him a letter I received, and he was going to call me back. What happened?"

"The ambulance people think it was his heart. The information was probably too much for his eighty-two-year-old body and he died before his heart pills could take effect. At this point, I'm taking over the investigation regarding this letter."

"Mr. McClure, I'm sorry for your loss. I also have to inform you that the note worked. I've typed up a letter and posted it thirty minutes ago. I don't know if the information about the deaths is true or not, but I've discussed it with my girlfriend, and decided to return to Boston." Thomas waited for Ian's reply.

"I'm sorry to hear that, Mr. Thomas. The letter was threatening for sure, and I understand how you feel," Ian admitted.

"We tried the distant relationship for two months, and were planning on sticking it out for a few years, but this last incident is personal. Whoever sent this letter has used my girlfriend to get to you. She knows nothing about the content of the letter, or anything I do in New York, and I plan on keeping it that way."

"From the reports I've read, you've been doing a good job working for us. I understand your concerns. This is an unsettling situation for everyone. I'm sorry your personal life was involved."

"I am as well, Mr. McClure. I'll wrap things up when I return to New York on Monday. I can stay on until you get a replacement if you like."

"I appreciate the offer, Mr. Thomas. Just a reminder regarding the non-disclosure agreement you signed when you started working for us. A lot of sensitive information has passed through your hands, and I want to make sure none of it goes any further."

"I understand. Let me know how long you want me to remain. I planned to visit the clinic in Mexico next week. I can accompany the new director, and walk them through their duties."

"That's a good idea, Mr. Thomas. I'll be sorry to see you go. The interview process will begin right away. We could have someone replace you before the Mexico trip."

"Thank you, Mr. McClure, for your understanding."

"See you next week," Ian said as he hung up.

Ian now had another duty to perform. The employee search team was notified and a list of candidates needed to be vetted. The investigation team was put on high alert due to the death of his father. Ian's mother died two years ago so it was up to him to notify family members of his father's death in the States, as well as in Ireland. The funeral would be held in Dublin where the family graveyard was located and where every McClure clan member was buried.

Chapter 41

The news of Paul McClure's death reached Jason through a friend still working for The Company. There were no details as to how Paul died, and there was a notice regarding the funeral in Ireland. A memorial service was scheduled next week in New York, where Company members and office workers could attend. Only the immediate family would be at the funeral in Dublin.

Jason called Robert to relay the news and to also warn Robert about McClure's son. "Ian is as ruthless as his father. If he takes over as head of The Company, he'll pursue his father's killer to the limit. Also, the news around The Company office is that Thomas resigned. The hiring team is busy finding a replacement for him."

The letter to Joseph worked. With Thomas leaving, Robert's team had just scored another victory. Mark Jones and Paul McClure were a good start to even the score. The body count was not Robert's goal. He wanted the clinic to shut down. It was time to plan another attack.

"Thanks for the information Jason. I'll let you know later what we do." After Jason hung up, Robert passed the news on to Julia. Her face lit up, indicating an idea had jumped a synapse.

"Jason said a memorial service would be held in New York in a few days, right?" she asked.

"Yes, he did. December 1st, at an Irish Catholic Church in The Village. What are you thinking? I can tell by your expression something is cooking."

"Yeah, but what's the main course? Who do you think will be attending the service?" Julia sat back on the couch with a smug look on her face. She was onto something.

"Probably immediate family and Company members." Just as Robert said the words, it hit him.

"You're a genius. Of course! We need to video the people entering the church and ID them. Alan can find out who they are, and separate the family members from the big guns. Man, am I glad we're doing this business together."

Julia remained silent and watched as Robert transformed into his role as hyper-detective. She was good at suggesting plans. Robert knew the right people to make the ideas work.

"I used another person in New York several times when you were busy," Robert said. "Did you ever meet Laura Scott? You two were my best contacts in New York. She still lives in the City, and can also use a camera."

"No, Robert, you didn't tell me anything about other people you hired in New York. How well did you know her?"

"I only met her at the interview and talked on the phone

twice after I hired her. Once before I met you, and once when you were working another case two years ago."

"Oh, really?" Julia said with a tone indicating her concern.

"I'll call Laura and see if she's available. She'll need a day to case out the church and see if she can get close enough to video the people coming in and out of the service.

"Give her a call, but I know someone if she's not available. My old roommate, Cathy, is good with a camera but has never worked in the spy business. She could be a backup if Laura can't do it," Julia said.

"Maybe we can use them both," Robert said. "One to film the faces going into the church, and one to video them leaving the building."

"Not a bad idea. Then we can be sure to record everyone."

"Let's call them this morning. We've only got a few days to put this plan into action."

*****

Ian was busy arranging for the memorial service and having his father's body sent to Ireland for burial. One of his cousins planned the ceremony and arranged for the Bishop from Dublin to conduct the service. Ian needed to be sure his father made it past St. Peter and into heaven.

After the memorial service in New York, and funeral in Ireland, Ian pledged to the other members that he would continue investigating the leaks. He was given a vote of confidence to take over as head of The Company. None of them wanted the job because the stress of being a billionaire was hard enough without having to look for infiltrators into their business practices.

The family priest from St. Mary's Church would conduct the memorial service in New York. Father Doug knew the McClure's well, and always had some kind words to say. A dinner buffet was arranged after the service in the Hilton Hotel, only a block away from the church. Those attending the service could walk there afterward.

*****

Robert and Julia were in luck because both Cathy and Laura were available for the job. Arrangements were made for them to visit the church together. Finding the best locations to video those attending the service was important.

The next day a report came back to Robert. The office building across the street gave Cathy the best angle to film those leaving the church. Laura's location was from the apartment building next door to the church. The angle was a little awkward but 90 percent of the faces would be visible. Alan assured Robert that anything over 80 percent was enough for the facial recognition program to work.

Cathy made the call to Julia to report their progress. She also asked about Alan and wanted to know how he was doing. "Tell Alan I'm doing well with my computer classes, and learned a few systems. When this investigation is over, and everyone is in a safe place, I would love to come to New Mexico and meet Alan."

"Alan is really quiet, Cathy," Julia said. "He's nothing like you at all. A little nerdy but really a sweetheart. Right now, he's starting an Internet dating service for computer people and calls it *Geek Mingle* or something like that. He's really smart and could be the next millionaire in the computer world."

"Now you really have me interested, Julia. How old is he?"

"I think around 22 or 23. He started attending the university after working for Best Buy for a few years. He realized he knew more about computers than anyone in the store, so he saved his money, and started taking classes two years ago. The professor recognized Alan's genius with computers and told Robert about him. Robert hires all his assistants through the University and gives them a good salary to help pay for their education."

"He's only a few years younger than me, Julia," Cathy said.

"Try five years, Cathy. I know how old you are."

"Just let him know I'm interested in meeting him. I won't ruffle his feathers much. I really do love the quiet, smart ones."

"We'll see. I'll tell him you called. I don't want to get him too excited," Julia said.

"Fair enough. Thanks for thinking of me for this job, Julia. We'll get back to you right after the memorial service."

"Bye, Cathy, and stay safe. The new head of The Company is not a nice man so be careful."

"We will."

Julia hung up and said a little prayer for Cathy and Laura.

"What do you think about sending a letter directly to Ian?" Julia asked. "Just think how pissed he'll be when he gets a note from us."

"How much information should we include?" Robert asked. "I want to keep the bastard off balance as much as possible. Too much information could put our own people in jeopardy."

"Let him know that we have the tapes from Jones, and we wrote the letter to Thomas. Give Ian a choice. Shut down the clinic or names will be given to the proper authorities. Connecting the clinic in Pisa with the deaths of the three men would start a full investigation. Does Ian want that? I'll bet he doesn't."

"No, I'm sure he won't," Robert said. "At the same time, he's desperate. Killing the 'Golden Goose' would put a damper on their operation. They still have the ability to use the formula on clients at a later date. Maybe we should mention we would not tell government agencies about them if the clinic closes. We could leave it at that."

"That might work," Julia said. "That could be our bluff card. I wonder if Jason knows anyone who is willing to flip on The Company and work for us?"

"He has a friend who's still working there. He told Jason about the death of Paul McClure and the memorial service. We could have another talk with Jason, and see if this is even possible," Robert added.

"It's worth a try. The memorial service is tomorrow. We should wait on the letter, see how many people Alan can identify from the videos, and then add them to the letter."

"Good idea, Julia. I'll start the letter. This might be the note that breaks The Company's back. We can only hope."

*****

The last minute details were completed and the family priest arranged the activities inside the church. The body of Ian's father arrived in Ireland the day before and was placed into a solid oak casket with an engraving of the McClure Crest on the cover. $100,000 for a fancy box that would rot in the ground for the next ten years was pocket change to Ian.

Ian sent a car to pick up his son who had flown in from Notre Dame. He was a senior and had to fly right back after the ceremony. Only Ian and his wife would attend the burial in Ireland due to school finals.

The memorial service was scheduled for one o'clock. Ian arrived around noon to make sure everything was in place. The police were in the position of directing traffic, re-routing cars, and only allowing vehicles to drop off their passengers.

Cathy was in position with the rooftop location on the office building across the street. The office elevator took her to the roof. The angle was good for the video because the structure was only five stories tall. Laura had secured a second story apartment window after arranging to rent the space from a student occupant for $200. She told him she worked for the local paper and she was filming the memorial ceremony that was taking place next door. She had the apartment to herself for two hours while the young man was studying at a local Starbucks, using their Wi-Fi. Coffee, extra cash, and the Internet were always a good combination.

The first cars arrived soon after twelve. Ian and his son stood at the door to greet each of them. Ian's wife was already inside the church. By five minutes to one, all the guests had been dropped off and were seated in the designated area for the ceremony.

Laura had good video footage of those men getting out of

their cars. Her job was done. She called Cathy to let her know. "Cathy, I think they're all inside. I got some good face angles. I'll see you back at the restaurant." She left the apartment and made her way out the side entrance.

Cathy had to wait for the service to end. She had a good angle of all attendees leaving the church. Her digital video camera was wrapped in cloth to reduce the reflections from the sun starting to sink in the west. None of the security men, working the street, bothered to look up at the surrounding buildings, because their focus was on the foot traffic.

Most of those leaving the service walked to the buffet. The older company members were picked up by car and left around two.

At two-thirty, Cathy felt it was safe to leave the office roof. She sent a text to Laura. "I'm on my way. See you in twenty minutes."

Laura was seated at a table with her computer when Cathy arrived. She had already sent her own digital clip to Alan showing the guests entering St. Mary's Cathedral.

"How did it go for you, Cathy? Any hitches?"

"Not bad. I had to be sure all the guests had left before I could vacate the office roof."

"I've sent my video on to Alan. Give me your camera chip and I'll send that to him now. After that, we're done. Not a bad afternoon's work considering what Robert paid us." Laura loaded the video and sent it to Alan.

"This is the first time I've worked for Robert. I used to be the roommate of his girlfriend who got me the gig. Have you done a lot of work for him in the past?"

"This is the third time he's used me. He pays well, and the danger is usually minimal. I don't even know where he lives. He interviewed me a few years back, but after that, he only calls me for jobs. Do you know much about him?"

"Not really. I don't know where he lives either." Cathy made sure Julia's name wasn't mentioned, or where she moved to when she left New York. Julia's safety was important and silence was the best way to ensure that.

"Well, I hope he uses us again. We make a good team. Do you want to get together some time and have a drink?"

"Sure, I'd like that." Cathy still had her defensive radar up, but decided a social get together with Laura would be fine.

"Here is my number. I usually go to a bar called Leggs near my apartment. It's a watering hole for professional women who want to meet other ladies with IQs higher than 85. In other words, it is a place where women can go to have a conversation with each other without being hit on by the mental midgets of New York."

"Oh, I like it already. I've had my fill of idiots in my lifetime."

"Some Lesbians go there as well, but they understand and respect everyone's space, and don't bother the straight crowd. They only hook up with other gay women. The heavy duty Dykes don't go there at all, so it's a mellow place to have a drink and talk."

"I'm available tomorrow night. I have a gig at the Biltmore but should be done by six. Half past six sound okay?" Cathy asked.

"I can be there by seven. They serve food as well so we can have dinner. Do you know where it is?"

"I'll Google it. I'll have a drink while I'm waiting. This has been a great afternoon, Laura. I'll see you then."

"It's been really great working with you. If anyone hits on you at Leggs, just tell them you're straight, and they'll let their other Lesbian friends know. You'd be amazed who the gay women in New York are. Some are models and many are professional women. I'm fine with them. The way I look at it, there is less competition for the good men in New York. Believe me, that number is getting smaller all the time."

"I know what you mean, Laura. I may have to go out of state and start looking if nothing shows up soon. I'm almost 30 and thinking about settling down with one guy. Playing the field is tiring and the typical drinking crowd is just that. Typical. I would like to meet an interesting man and the bar scene has not produced one of those in my experience."

"I hear you, Cathy. Well, I have to go. See you tomorrow."

Laura caught a cab. Cathy decided to walk for a while before heading home. She'd just made $5,000 for a four-hour job and the desire to buy something took over. A nice woman's clothing boutique was two blocks away from the restaurant where she met Laura. She had the money to treat herself with a gift. This lifestyle suited her, and she hoped Julia would think of her again when Robert needed help.

Chapter 42

Alan downloaded the videos sent to his computer and ran each image through the facial recognition program. The software identified eighteen men as company members. Background information was a more difficult to obtain, but Alan had the skill to get through most security walls. By five that evening, he'd printed out everything he had. The information, plus the pictures obtained by Laura and Cathy, was enough for Robert to put a real scare into the operations of The Company.

"I've got them all, Robert." Alan handed Robert the stack of personal bios along with their pictures.

Robert sat on the couch in the office and grabbed the first file from the pile. Julia entered the office and picked up a bio as well. Silence prevailed in the room for an hour. By the time the two had finished, Alan had gone home, and Carla let them know dinner was almost ready.

"Can you believe how many of these members earned their money?" Robert asked. "Only a few of them inherited it. Most were engaged in illegal activities." He tapped the picture of a thin-faced man. "This one actually started out as a cocaine smuggler in the 70's but never was convicted. He had 'fall' men take the rap. He took his millions and started investing in start-up companies in the late 80's. Now he's worth 2.6 billion."

Julia put down the file she was reading. Her face was flushed. "This guy, named George Marlin, got his start in Vegas. He owned a few cathouses and also ran drugs. He took his wealth and turned it into millions when he bought into one of the new casinos. The stock market came later and he's now worth 1.5 billion. This is a group made up of men who started out in illegal enterprises and are now respected NYSE investors. What's this country coming to? Crooks and thieves are controlling the financial world! We really need to keep our identity safe, Robert. Killing us would not faze any of them."

"I need to get that letter to Ian written today," Robert said. "Let me write it first and then I'll have you proofread it."

Julia agreed and went out to the pool. The house was now empty except for her and Robert. Carla left after placing dinner in the oven. The pool was heated by the solar panels that lined the border of the property, and the water remained at 85 degrees. Julia slipped out of her clothes and entered the warm, clear water. She liked to swim in the nude, but could only do it when Carla and Alan were gone. First, she swam a few laps to help relieve the stress of the day and then climbed onto the floating water lounge.

Robert appeared by the pool, carrying his laptop, just as Julia was dozing off. "I finished the letter. Shall I read it to you? You look pretty relaxed."

"Go ahead. After that, you need to join me in the pool. We

have it all to ourselves."

Robert knew what Julia really meant. Pool sex was his favorite. He did his best not to sound rushed, but the expectations of what was to come increased his reading pace a bit.

"To Ian McClure;" Robert paused.

"This is a time of mourning for you, and for that I'm sorry. You are probably feeling much like the two wives when their husbands died because of your clinic in Italy." Robert cleared his throat.

"This is our message to you. Shut the Mexican clinic down like you did in Italy. The only difference is that you won't move it to another location. By now, you must realize your actions cannot be hidden. We have eyes on you." Robert took a second before continuing.

"Included with this demand are the names and pictures of most of the members of your investment business known as The Company. We have also obtained the compound that you used with previous clients. This practice will stop. If we find out you are continuing to use people to predict stock market closings, we will send our information to the authorities who will make your life miserable." Robert again paused.

"Nothing will be done for now. Go ahead and bury your father, but you must also bury your illegal activities. This is not a threat but a promise. Stop trying to find the leak into your business. If anything happens to any member of our team, the information will be sent automatically to the proper authorities. This is your last warning."

"Have a pleasant trip to Ireland. I understand your son graduates from Notre Dame this year. May his future be bright and may he find an honest way of making a living."

Julia remained silent. She slipped off the floating lounge chair and swam up to the pool's edge. "I think you got your point across." She said. "There doesn't appear to be any wiggle room for Ian. Are you going to send that letter before he leaves for Ireland?"

"I need to get it to him right away. He may be feeling grief for his father, but people like him have little regard for other humans. We may succeed in putting The Company out of business, but only time will tell. Crooks like him don't quit, so we may have to send a few packages to different agencies. An investigation into The Company's stock market activities should tie them up for a while. We'll have to play the game called, 'wait and see'."

"I think the letter is fine just the way it is," Julia said. "Put the computer back in the office and come join me. We haven't had any pool fun for a while, and I think we're ready to relax a bit."

Robert turned towards the office and calmly walked to the door. He felt like running but he was now practicing self-control.

He loved having sex with Julia, but he did not want to appear excited. He even took his time undressing before entering the pool. By now, Julia was the one who was more than ready to engage in lovemaking.

The early November sun was starting to set, and the pool waters started to churn. Not much foreplay. The body heat of the two lovers raised the pool temperature another degree. Dinner would wait.

*****

Ian was just leaving the office when the special delivery letter arrived. He and his wife were flying to Ireland the next day. There was no return address on the letter. He sat down before opening the envelope.

Five minutes passed after reading the letter. Ian's thoughts were racing. How did this happen? Who were these people? They had the names of everyone in The Company except the two who were not at the memorial service. That was it, he thought. Someone was at the service and identified everyone there. How in the hell did they do that?

Ian had to make a decision, but not right now. He needed to bury his father first. A meeting of all The Company members was a must. His son was also mentioned in the letter. This group seemed to know everything about him and his family.

Before he left the office, Ian gave instructions for his secretary to set up a general meeting. The member having knee replacement needed to attend as well, even if he was in a wheelchair. The other missing member would be back from Chile by then. Attendance was mandatory. Ian knew these men did not like to be told what to do, but this was different. The life of The Company depended on the outcome of this meeting.

*****

Ian and his wife stayed at the estate of his cousin, Sean. The large 10,000 square foot home, about thirty minutes from Dublin, was purchased during prohibition in America when his father made millions. Sean's income was much smaller than when his father ran the whiskey business but it still enabled him to buy whatever he needed to live well.

The funeral, scheduled for two in the afternoon, happened on time. It was now ten in the morning. Sean observed his cousin who seemed distracted and had a lot on his mind. Ian could barely function doing the routine duties involved with the funeral. All Ian needed to do was make a speech, while Sean and his brothers took care of the other arrangements. Burying a McClure was a huge undertaking.

"Can I help you with anything, Ian?" Sean asked.

"Sorry, Sean. I'm a little preoccupied. It's moments like this that makes me wish my father stayed in the whiskey business. We've hit a few bumps."

"The McClure family sticks together no matter where they live or what they do, Ian. I have people that work for me in case any tough jobs need to be taken care of. You just say the word and we'll handle whatever needs to be done."

"It's not that easy, Sean. There's a leak into The Company, which threatens the way we do business. If we change our practices we would see a big drop in our incomes. I have to find out from the other members how they want me to deal with the situation. We have a meeting scheduled when I get back, and it's weighing on my mind."

"You call me if you want any Irish help. We know how to take care of problems the old fashion way. We don't use the court system. Troublemakers just disappear." Sean had a look that told Ian he was serious.

"I have men that can handle things in the same manner. My first problem is to find out who's behind the leak. I've only a few days before the meeting to try and find out. Putting the decision to a vote is what I'll have to do if nothing turns up."

Sean smiled. "Well, if you find out who it is, and need backup, I'll send help."

"Thanks, Sean. I appreciate all you've done with the

funeral. This is a difficult time. These people caused dad's death. He received a troubling letter from them and had a heart attack before his pills could take effect. Finding them and taking them out is my vendetta, and I plan to do so, no matter what The Company decides."

"It sounds personal. Anyway, you know how to reach me."

The funeral commenced without any difficulties. The Bishop gave his blessings and prayers to ease the loss of Paul McClure. A fleet of black limos drove the twenty-five miles back to the estate of Sean McClure where the buffet was prepared.

*****

Ian and his wife left the next day on a flight to New York. His secretary scheduled The Company meeting in two days. He was at a loss as to what he could do. Was this the end? He saw no way out.

The day of the meeting arrived and took place at the private home of Paul McClure just outside New York City. All members were present including the three identified in the Mark Jones tape. Ian needed to come clean with everything that he and The Company faced. He felt his blood pressure rise as he stood in front of the members to address them.

"Gentlemen I have some troubling news. I've called this meeting because we all need to know what has recently transpired.

Ever since the Mark Jones incident, we realized our security was breached. Someone is getting information about who we are, and what we're doing. For the past month, old clients and employees were followed, but so far nothing has turned up other than vague descriptions of three different women. This is what we know so far. All the information is in a folder in front of each one of you. We have to vote whether or not to continue our way of doing business."

Several Company members stood to pose a question. Ian said he'd answer any questions after his speech.

"The second breach came when a mystery man presented a letter to the girlfriend of Joseph Thomas, hired to take over for Mark Jones. Thomas sent the letter to my father. The letter said Thomas needed to stop working for us or face the consequences. Included was the formula for the compound we developed in Italy. The letter said The Company needed to shut down the clinic in Mexico and stop any further trading using client information. In other words, it was a 'Cease to Exist' letter. I also believe that this message is what killed my father. He died of a heart attack after reading it."

A moan came from several of the older members of The Company. Ian waited before he continued, to make sure none of these men collapsed, and joined his father.

"The last letter came to me the day before I traveled to

Ireland for my father's funeral. Included were the same demands. The pictures of each company member who attended the memorial service, including your personal information, appeared in the letter. We have all been identified." Another member tried to stand up to comment, but Ian again asked him to wait until the end.

"My team has made every effort to discover who these people are but so far we only have sketches with no facial matches. The man who delivered the letter to Thomas's girlfriend in Boston was able to avoid the security cameras. A professional team is conducting this attack, and we have to make a decision today. The letter tells us what they know. It also states if we comply with their demands none of the information will be handed over to the authorities. The clinic must close, and not reopen again. Basically, we would be on our own in the investment world."

From the looks of the member's faces turning pale, Ian knew shock was just setting in. Several members reached for their heart pills.

"How much time do we have?" The question was thrown out by a member in the back row.

"The letter said they'd give me time to bury my father. After that, we had to make a decision. We are faced with the option of continuing what we are doing and deal with possible investigations. If we close down all of this goes away."

"What about the treatment plants? Where is the money going to come from to keep that project going?" a member from the front row asked.

"Nothing was mentioned about the plants," Ian answered. "Future funding will have to come out of our own pockets. If we choose to shut down, we can continue to invest, but face the same risks the rest of the world faces. Nothing is a sure thing."

"I have a house being built in the Canary Islands," a Company member said from the back. "You mean I'll have to spend my own savings to finish the 50 million dollar project. I was counting on clinic information to pay for that house. Doesn't keeping people employed count for anything?"

A few more member comments focused on how much they might lose without receiving the investing number. Some expressed their fears of no longer remaining billionaires. They might have to fly first class after selling their private jets.

"Gentlemen, we have to make a decision today. Shut the clinic, and return to the old way of making money, or face investigations, and possible criminal charges. Each of you received a pen and a ballot. A 'yes' vote means closure of the clinic. A 'no' vote means continuing. If we continue, this group will send in all our names to authorities, including those who voted 'yes'. The only two members not on the list are James Roll and Thomas Cook." Ian looked at both men. "You two were not at the memorial service so your pictures weren't taken."

Another member stood up and almost shouted at Ian. "Can we have more discussion on this topic? This is really unsettling. How do we know our names won't be turned in even if we vote to shut down the operation?"

Ian thought for a minute and replied in a calculated voice. "We don't. But here is my take on this situation. If the clinic is no longer in operation, there is no evidence that we are involved with inside trading. What can an investigation turn up? If we wipe the slate clean there is nothing to investigate."

The same member continued his questioning. "If we vote to close down, are we still going to go find out who did this to us. I'm willing to pay as much as it takes to find these assholes. If we wipe them off the map we can re-open the clinic and continue our operation."

"The letter stated that if we attempt to go after them, or even harm any of their team, the information will be sent to the authorities at once. The letter did not state which branches would be involved, but I can imagine they know who to send the information to. If we vote to shut down, we have to pledge that none of us will attempt to go after them on our own. All of our lives are subject to harm. I for one do not plan to test their knowledge. My father died because of this group, and now I have to protect my son and wife. These people know about my personal life and each of us is subject to the same scrutiny."

A silence fell over the crowd. The mood was serious. Many of the Company members needed to change their lifestyles. Owning eight or nine homes was not uncommon for people at their economic level. Having to cut back to five homes would be a challenge. Reducing down to one yacht and selling off other investments meant a total life change for many of them.

None of the men wanted to be hindered by lawsuits. The run on the stock market was over. The final vote tally was unanimous. The clinic and the operations of The Company had come to an end.

When Ian read the vote results, each member nodded his head in approval. They'd all made hundreds of millions of dollars. They were now on their own. The older members decided to live out their lives on the assets they had accumulated. The younger men in the group, who had social contact with each other, planned to continue investing, and share information. The only topic that was not included in the conversation had to do with the desalination plants.

Ian made one last comment before closing the meeting. "Some of us need to meet again. This is the question: What do we do about the water project? I know there are members who didn't invest in this venture, so you're off the hook. Those who are interested in continuing, please raise your hand."

Ten members raised their hands and agreed to another meeting at Ian's home on Martha's Vineyard.

Ian took on the job of letting The Company employees go and writing severance paychecks to hold them over until they could find work. The new director of the clinic, Jack Wear, was directed to travel to Mexico and oversee the closing of the clinic. After paying the staff and doctors for three months, he'd sell the clinic, collect all the files, and return them to Ian. Mr. Wear would stay in Mexico until everyone was gone.

The Company was finished. They had no choice. It had to be done. Involving government agencies, that watched the activities on the NYSE, was the turning point for all the members.

The McClure family was worth three billion. The remaining ten men, investing in the water plants, were also in that financial range. A little over a million dollars a month was projected for each remaining investor to keep the water project going. The 'Golden Goose' may be dead, but Ian and the other members made sure they could influence government decisions based on controlling clean drinking water.

*****

The news of The Company shut-down reached Robert through Jason. Jason's friend in The Company received three months' severance pay. He and the other employees hired headhunters to help find employment in the financial sector.

Alan continued to monitor the clinic in Mexico by satellite. "I think you pulled it off, Robert. They seem to be packing everything up."

"I can hardly believe it. Jason called yesterday and said it's happening. David hit Goliath right smack in the forehead, and the giant is reeling in his tracks. This nightmare may be finally over."

"Where do we go from here?" Julia asked. "It feels like all the air has just been sucked out of the room and I can hardly breathe. Do you really think Ian has called it quits?"

Robert thought for a moment and finally answered. "Right now we can chalk it up as a win. This is what we hoped for, and I don't think we should expect much more. We'll keep an eye on Ian for a while longer because I don't believe he can walk away from his father's death like this. He's still dangerous, and we can't let our defenses down."

"We also need to let our team know the situation," Julia said. "William played a big part in this along with Leslie. I know they want to live a peaceful life in Tucson. With The Company closing shop, they may not have to look over their shoulders any longer."

"You're right, Julia. Without William, we could still be looking for a way to close the clinic. Cathy and Laura played a big part too. All in all, our little team pulled off a pretty big stunt by shutting down a bunch of crooks. We were lucky to get out with our lives."

"Are we in one of those 'wait and see' situations, Robert? If so I would like to do something fun. This has been a stressful situation for sure."

"I think we can do something fun, but we still need to keep our guard up. We may have dodged a bullet and were lucky in a few instances but the gun is still loaded. Ian can pull the trigger at any time, and we wouldn't know what hit us. Right now we've accomplished what we wanted to do. The Company is no longer in existence and the financial world is safer than before."

*****

The sun started to set in the west. Another day was ending. William and Leslie were safe in their home in Tucson. Robert and Julia had wrapped up their biggest case so far and were looking for some downtime together. Jason and Maria were starting a new life as a couple in Santa Fe, while Alan had placed the groundwork for his new 'on-line' dating service for geeks.

A time for rest and reflection had arrived for some.

Deep in the depths of New York, Ian McClure brooded over all that had transpired. He hadn't thrown in the towel just yet. Licking his wounds was one thing, but he was not finished. He was Irish and the Irish do not turn and run. Revenge was on his mind, and he'd return when the time was right. Nobody, including himself, knew when that was but he'd be back. Count on it.

www.ingramcontent.com/pod-product-compliance
Lightning Source LLC
Chambersburg PA
CBHW060139260626
47160CB00001B/36

* 9 7 8 0 9 8 5 2 2 3 2 9 8 *